"Mallory ... what are you doing?"

"You have a silky complexion," he said, a finger moving to explore the contour of her chin and to run the graceful arch of her neck.

"Mallory," she whispered.

"Matt," he corrected, his exploring fingertip playing havoc with the rim of her ear.

She swallowed. "Matt ... stop." For the past week she had longed for him to call, prayed that he hadn't lost interest in her. Now that he was proving that he hadn't, she was afraid.

"Why?" he asked distractedly. His fingers were combing her hair, causing a ripple of feeling along her scalp and down her spine.

"Because ... it won't work."

"What?"

"Us."

"Hmm." His voice was thoughtful. "I feel it working already. Come here...."

ABOUT THE AUTHOR

Muriel Jensen started writing in the sixth grade and has never stopped. Writing full-time has led to this, her third romance novel. Along with her husband and three children—and her collection of cats, both live and porcelain—Muriel makes her home on the Oregon coast.

Books by Muriel Jensen

HARLEQUIN AMERICAN ROMANCE
73–WINTER'S BOUNTY
119–LOVERS NEVER LOSE

The Mallory Touch
Muriel Jensen

Harlequin Books

TORONTO • NEW YORK • LONDON
AMSTERDAM • PARIS • SYDNEY • HAMBURG
STOCKHOLM • ATHENS • TOKYO • MILAN

To Ron, who could always sell me anything.

Published November 1986

First printing September 1986

ISBN 0-373-16176-X

Chapter One

"Eldon," Randy Stanton said patiently, "the Russells were Bob's customers. He called them in, showed the car, found a buyer for their trade-in when we couldn't pay the price they wanted and finally closed the deal. The commission is his."

Eldon Phillips was a tall, thin man in his late forties who dressed as if he worked on Madison Avenue, and he was voraciously greedy. He was cunningly ruthless in skating customers from Bob McGraw, Randy's other salesman. In the two years that Randy had owned the dealership, most of her wit and energy had been expended in arbitrating the two salesmen's arguments. And, she sometimes felt, in keeping them from killing each other.

"I did the two hours of paperwork because Bob had to take his daughter to the doctor. We should split the commission."

"He offered to split it with you," Randy reminded.

Phillips sneered. "Twenty percent is not a split."

"He did eighty percent of the work, Eldon!" Impatience was beginning to register in Randy's voice, and she drew a steadying breath.

"When the old man was here—" Phillips's eyes went scornfully over Randy's vanilla silk blouse, visible to him over the top of her desk "—anyone who did the paperwork split the commission fifty-fifty."

Randy got to her feet and walked around her desk to where Phillips stood just inside her office. She folded her arms and knew her eyes showed him the same contempt he felt for her.

"The old man isn't here anymore, Eldon. I am. He had a lot of policies that weren't fair, and I've changed them. If you'd be happier elsewhere, there are three other dealerships in this town. I'm sure any one of them would be pleased to have you."

That wasn't true, of course, and both Randy and Phillips knew it. Before Randy bought the dealership, Phillips had done the rounds of the other three, failing to get along any better with them than he did with her.

"Does that mean I'm fired?" he asked defensively.

Silently wishing that she had the internal fortitude and the financial freedom to shout, "Yes, you're fired!" Randy just shook her head, because Eldon was a good salesman and brought in many repeat customers.

"No," she replied quietly. "It means that you get twenty percent of the commission here when you do somebody else's paperwork. Not fifty. Twenty."

He looked at her for another scornful moment, then shrugged carelessly.

"So it's twenty," he said, and turning on his heel, stormed across the showroom to go out the door.

As Randy watched him go with a good-riddance feeling she was not entirely ashamed of, she noticed a customer pacing around the new Flambeau on the showroom floor. Bob, she knew, was out to lunch, and

Eldon had apparently gone to walk off his anger. That left her.

Almost hoping that the man was simply a tire kicker so that she could dispense with him and get back to her paperwork, Randy squared her shoulders and walked out onto the floor.

"GOOD AFTERNOON," Matt Mallory said as a salesman came toward him. "I'd like..." He paused in midsentence to watch the man storm blindly past him and out the door. Irritated, he looked at his watch. As much as he liked this Flambeau, if someone wasn't out here to help him in twenty seconds, he was taking his business elsewhere.

Matt pulled the driver's side door open on the light green sedan and slipped in behind the steering wheel. He was checking out the controls when he found himself distracted by a pair of female legs.

His head snapped up from the dashboard to watch the legs, visible to him beneath the hem of a black skirt, move down the brief four steps that separated a series of offices from the showroom floor. They had long, slim calves, silky in black stockings, and he felt his heartbeat accelerate as they seemed to be making their way toward him. He got out of the car and slammed the door, leaning against it to await the arrival of the owner of the legs.

Ordinarily, he would have straightened and watched the woman's approach with the gentlemanly respect that he was taught by his Italian mother, while mentally forming the seductive approach learned from his Scottish brigand of a father and refined by his own inimitable style. But something in the woman's eyes put him instantly on the defensive and made him deny her the attention he felt sure she usually commanded.

His eyes had impatiently surveyed the austere skirt and jacket and the bland silk shirt and come to rest on a face that was startlingly handsome. Not pretty or cute or simply attractive but handsome.

He felt the jolt of contact as he looked into green eyes the color of sage. She looked at him directly with an open expression that he was surprised to find himself resenting. He had never thought of himself as a chauvinist, though he did prefer his women in ruffles and just a little less sure of themselves. But something about the take-me-as-I-am confidence she exuded challenged him with surgical precision right where he felt most vulnerable. He could handle a woman being his equal, but he'd be damned if he'd know what to do about one who thought she was stronger or smarter than he was.

He straightened, more to assume a defensive posture than to show deference to her approach, and studied the only feature about her that implied vanity rather than a strong character: a luxurious fall of red hair that was tucked behind a pearl-studded ear on the left side of her face and hugged a deliciously creamy cheek on the other.

He saw a perfect nose and a shimmery pink mouth ready to smile at him. He fought back a flinch, almost afraid of what the smile would do to him.

A corner of his mind not totally occupied with her presence was wondering who the hell this woman was and what she was doing in an automobile showroom in this charming but small and fairly remote backwater town.

So, Randy thought dryly, looking into the puzzled face of the man leaning against her favorite Flambeau, the heir to the Mallory millions was shopping for an economy car. They hadn't been introduced. But the *Scannon Cove Journal* had made sure that his handsome face was familiar to its readers in the year that it had taken to build the local Mallory Inn and the brief two weeks since Matthew Mallory had arrived in the small Columbia River town to take up his position as manager. The *Journal* had devoted a lot of space to the young man whose job it was to open the new hotels for his family's company and then, in a year or so, when the job was done, move on to the next project. His much-publicized Midas touch brought news to an otherwise predictable front page.

Another reliable source of news was Vivian Payne, Randy's bookkeeper and girl Friday. Viv had stood behind Mallory in line at the bank one lunch hour and had talked of nothing but him for several days.

"He's about six foot seven with the most gorgeous blue eyes and a smile that... Well, he had Mrs. Magruder eating out of his hand!" The dragon of a loan officer had destroyed many sales for Stanton Motors by withholding financing. Her intimidating, mirthless expression was well-known.

Viv had a tendency to exaggerate, Randy considered as she looked over her customer while he continued to study her. She'd put him at about six feet two. His eyes were an unusually dark shade of blue, with a sort of translucence, like the twilight of a clear day. But she found nothing about his smile to pine over. In fact, she saw nothing of his smile at all. He was still frowning at her in a sort of annoyed puzzlement.

"What do you think of our Flambeau?" Randy asked, gesturing with a sweep of her hand, hoping to distract his eyes from her.

That clear, blue gaze went over Randy quickly once more; then he replied coolly, "Good-looking. And if it's all National Motors' advertising says it is, it may be what I'm looking for." He glanced at his watch. "Look, I'm on duty in twenty minutes, and I've been waiting here for at least fifteen. I'd like to see whoever's in charge.''

Randy fought down her annoyance at his remark. She couldn't decide in her own mind if it resulted from his preemptory attitude or because the interest she had noted before in his eyes as she was walking toward him was suddenly gone.

''I'm in charge,'' she assured him.

''The manager,'' he said, betraying a loss of patience.

''I'm the manager,'' she told him.

He looked over her head at the glass walls of the empty offices and shook his head. ''I'll come back after lunch.''

Randy folded her arms. ''I'll still be the manager at two o'clock.''

She saw irritation and surprise war in his eyes. He simply smiled and started to move away. ''I want to see Randy Stanton. *Him*self. I'll be back.''

As he turned to leave, Randy halted him with a hand on his arm, trying hard not to betray her own annoyance. As a woman in a male-dominated field, she came up against men who wanted to father her or to be a big brother to her and many who simply wanted to put her down. But those who treated her as though she were a pretty child at play in a man's world made her the angriest.

There were a lot of things on the tip of her tongue, the last of which was a friendly introduction, but she could use the sale of a new Flambeau. It had been a slow month.

Composed, she extended her hand. ''Miranda Stanton,'' she said, adding crisply, ''*Her*self.''

He looked properly surprised. He took her hand, and Randy thought, fighting back a wince, that Viv had been right in describing him as athletic.

"And I presume it's not your father's agency." Something quirked at his lip.

"Or my brother's or my husband's."

"My mistake," he apologized with an inclination of his head. "You can understand my confusion."

"Of course. Are you interested in the Flambeau?"

He looked warily at the car, then at her.

"Or," she asked impatiently, "would you rather go to one of the other dealerships where a *man* can sell you an overpriced luxury car or a death trap of a foreign import?"

Mallory arched an eyebrow, then reached into the open window of the car and pulled the hood release. The wedge of the hood snapped up, and he raised it farther with a long arm, indicating the mass of wire and metal.

"Tell me about your Flambeau, Miranda Stanton."

It was a strange world, Randy philosophized as she moved to stand beside him, looking down at the neat three-liter V-6 engine. Women were now in operating rooms, in courtrooms, on Wall Street, on telephone poles and in space. But a man, this one in particular, felt his manhood challenged if a woman understood what went on under the hood of a car.

Randy glanced up at Mallory and found that he was looking at her hair.

"Pay attention, Mr. Mallory," she said stiffly, turning back to the car before noting the answering lift of his eyebrow. "This car deserves your respect. This is a three-liter V-6 gasoline engine with fuel injection and electronic ignition. To you that means a responsive power plant plus a high degree of fuel economy." She indicated the dipstick. "The components are easy to get at for service, and you have a no-service battery that doesn't need water. The fluid containers—" she tapped the large plastic jugs fitted one on each side and at the back "—are transparent so that you can check on fluid levels without having to open them.

"There's an electronic control module, a minicomputer, mounted behind the fire wall. There's also an oxygen sensor in the exhaust manifold that measures the amount of oxygen in the exhaust gases. This tells how rich or lean the mixture is in the carburetor. It sends this information to the computer, which then adjusts the electromechanical carburetor."

Randy was leaning over the engine now, engrossed in her explanation. She glanced sideways to find Mallory leaning in beside her, looking at her and not the engine. Flushing, she looked back at the shiny components.

"That's simply a standard carburetor with an electronically controlled metering rod. The computer fine-tunes the position of the metering rod ten times per second to make sure the proper amount of fuel mixes with the air passing through the carburetor. This, of course, assures you optimum performance and fuel economy while still meeting the federal pollution standards." She slipped out from under the hood and held it up, allowing him to retreat also. "This is only one of three engines available. There are also an economical four-cylinder gasoline engine and the most economical 4.6 diesel."

Randy slammed the hood down and looked into his now reluctantly respectful eyes.

"Technical enough for you?" she asked sweetly. "Or do I have to put on my coveralls and rebuild an engine before your very eyes?"

Mallory shook his head at her, a grin forming. "You are defensive, Miss Stanton."

"You're right, Mr. Mallory," she replied quietly, her eyes making very loud accusations. "I wouldn't presume that you're an inadequate hotel manager because you look like you belong on a basketball court. You shouldn't presume that I don't know what I'm doing because I'm a woman working with automobiles."

He frowned. "How do you know what I do?"

"This is a small town. Word gets around."

"True," he agreed. "The word I heard was that I'd get a fair deal here. But I'm not sure I like your attitude."

Randy folded her arms and met his judicious look. "You don't have to like my attitude, Mr. Mallory, only my car."

"My goodness, Miss Stanton. You do seem to be all combustible fuel and exploding cylinders. Perhaps you've been in this man's world you're so proud of too long. You need a hiatus at a flower shop or a perfumery."

Without knowing why, Randy was stung by his retort.

Mallory saw the hurt in her eyes and was pleased to have scored one against her, but at the same time he felt sorry for his harsh tone. The sage in her eyes seemed to bleed, and at that moment he would have done anything to call the words back. They were interrupted by a distraught young man in greasy coveralls who was being dragged across the showroom toward them by a short older man in a felt hat.

"I didn't see it!" the boy was pleading. "I—"

"You never see anything!" the older man shouted. "You race around here like it's Le Mans!"

Then, as they reached Randy, the man shoved the boy toward her and raved on.

"I told you you shouldn't have hired a kid, even for a job like washing and moving cars. But no! You wouldn't listen."

"What happened?" Randy asked calmly.

"I didn't see it!" the boy insisted.

"Didn't see what, Jake?"

The boy shrugged his bony shoulders and said almost in a whisper while he wrung his hands, "It shouldn't have been parked there."

"That's a parking...lot!" Gordie Walsh, Randy's office manager, roared, separating the words for emphasis. "You don't race through a parking lot!"

"You don't park cars in the driveway," Jake shouted back, "of a parking lot!"

"Oh, God," Mallory said in a strangely fatalistic tone of voice. "How many pieces is it in?"

"One," Jake replied with a wince. "It's just...a slightly different shape than when you left it in the driveway," he added with a judicious glance.

"Oh, God," Randy repeated Mallory's words, closing her eyes. When she opened them, it was to see Mallory's formidable back headed toward the parking lot.

"WE DO THE BEST bodywork for a hundred miles," Randy said thinly as Mallory ran his hand along the now concave driver's side door of his glistening blue Camaro Berlinetta. The car looked a little as though it had placed last in a destruction derby.

"There's never anything parked in the driveway," Jake was explaining to the man. "I was moving Mr. Morrison's truck off the rack and was going to pull it out onto the street, only—"

Mallory sighed. "Only I was in the driveway."

To Randy's complete astonishment, he clapped the boy on the shoulder.

"I shouldn't have been there. I was just running in to take a quick look at the Flambeau I saw through the window. I was distracted," he said significantly into Randy's eyes, astonishing her again, "by a pair of pretty legs."

He looked into her flushed face. "How long will it take to fix it, and do you have a car that I can rent in the meantime?"

"A couple of days," she said, knowing a busy man like Mallory would hate being without his own car that long. "I'm sorry, but with a small crew and previous commitments, that's the best I can do. I'll check the used-car lot to see if there's something we can loan you."

"There isn't," Walsh said, his words halting her as she would have turned away to do just that. "Until we get the Impala off the rack. That'll be sometime this afternoon."

Randy sighed defeatedly, waiting for her customer to explode. Instead, he suggested mildly, "At which time someone from this dealership will drive the Impala to the hotel parking lot and leave me the keys?"

His attitude rankled Randy, but she nodded. "Of course."

He glanced at his watch again. "In the meantime, I'm already ten minutes late for work."

"Isn't that the prerogative of the heir to the Mallory Inns?" She couldn't resist gibing.

"Are you ever late for work, Miss Stanton?" he countered.

She had to smile, however reluctantly. Though poles apart in career channels, she suspected that they approached their work in much the same way.

"She has come to work with the flu, on crutches and with a hangover," Walsh provided with a fond smile. "Always the first one here and the last to leave."

Mallory looked at her in surprise. "With a hangover? You don't look the type."

"I'm not," she admitted. "One glass of Chablis and I'm under the table. But we had sold a fleet of limousines to the mortuary the day before. That doesn't happen every day."

Mallory smiled, and Randy was again astonished as she saw fleetingly what might have softened tough-as-nails Mrs. Magruder. Her heart fluttered, and her eyes reacted. She saw Mallory note that, and she turned briskly to Gordie Walsh.

"Take Mr. Mallory to the hotel, Gordie. I'll—"

"You take him," Walsh said. "The Morrisons are due any minute to pick up their truck. I'll have to explain to them why it now has a dent it didn't have when they left it with us."

Randy groaned.

"Go ahead," he urged, turning a relieved-looking Jake toward the shop. "I'll hold down the fort while you're gone." And he and the boy disappeared into the darkened garage.

Randy stared after them, reluctant to face the fact that she now had to drive this irritating man to work. Then she glanced at his wounded Camaro and the hanging bumper on the Morrisons' pickup and decided it might be the lesser of two evils.

"Cheer up," Mallory said, putting a fraternal arm around her shoulders. "My day isn't going well, either. Where's your car?"

"Parked in front. I suppose you're going to want to drive." She glanced up at him dryly as he led her in the direction she indicated, his arm a warm, pleasantly heavy burden on her shoulders.

"No." He grinned down at her wickedly, noting her discomfort. "I'll just stare at you while you drive."

It doesn't bother me that he's turned in his seat, staring at me, she told herself firmly, trying to appear relaxed as she proceeded along Concomolly Boulevard. The busy downtown thoroughfare-cum-interstate highway was thick with lunch-hour activity. Randy had often sworn that every man, woman and child in this town of only ten thousand owned a car and drove it between noon and two o'clock, Monday through Saturday.

"Am I making you nervous?" Mallory had the audacity to ask as Randy watched the road ahead, betraying her dismay by the subtlest moistening of her lips.

"Very," she admitted quietly.

He allowed a moment of silence, then observed, "I like that."

"Making me nervous?" she asked.

"No, the fact that you'll admit you are."

She shrugged. "That's simple honesty, Mr. Mallory."

"I know. Rare in a beautiful, ambitious woman."

Even in profile her frown was apparent. "I'm not ambitious."

"If you weren't ambitious, you'd work for an auto agency, you wouldn't own one." He put a hand out to brace himself against the dashboard as the traffic light they approached warned caution. She pulled to a neat stop as the light turned red.

"I'll get you there in one piece, Mr. Mallory, I promise." Then, as though watching herself perform the action and unable to stop herself, she gently grasped his forearm that was braced against the padded dash and brought it down beside him, feeling his muscle react under her hand. "But if we do hit anything, you'll break that arm." She slanted him a taunting glance. "I own the agency because old Bert Cummings, who had the dealership before me, was a friend of my foster father's and gave me a job when I graduated from Oregon State. I spent time working on the grease rack, in the parts department and in the office. Then he taught me sales. When he decided to retire, I pleaded with him to give me an opportunity to buy him out. By then my foster parents had been killed in a plane crash on a flight to Portland. I used my inheritance money from them and a large insurance settlement for a down payment and paid the balance with a buy-in plan where I could manage the agency and pay for the rest of the franchise out of the profits. National Motors approved, bless them."

"That's not a very common occupation for a woman," he remarked, and before she could reply, he added thoughtfully, "But then, you're not an average woman, are you?"

Randy smiled at the road and accelerated as the light turned green. "I'm not sure how you mean that, but no, I'm not average when compared to most women, and not just in my profession."

"How's that?"

"I'm not at all domestic. In fact, I'd be the stereotypical liberated woman except that I'd love to have children and I'd love to be devoted to them."

"With or without their father in the picture?" he asked.

She shot him a glance and grinned. "I'm not that different."

"Society no longer frowns on single mothers."

"It doesn't," she agreed, her grip tightening perceptibly on the steering wheel. "But I do. My single mother finally abandoned me when I was nine years old. Foster homes are a port in the storm, but they're not home.''

Mallory was silent for a moment, and Randy spent the long seconds wondering what had ever made her tell him that. She wasn't abnormally secretive about her past, but that wasn't the sort of thing you told someone of such short acquaintance, and a customer at that.

"I can't even imagine how that must have been for you," he admitted quietly. "I'm the product of an effusive Italian and a clannish Scotsman who thought that their two sons were veritable miracles of nature."

She glanced at him again, saying with genuine sincerity, "That's terrific."

He nodded, frowning. "It was. Even now their caring is something I lean on and draw from often. I'm sorry you don't have that."

Randy forced a light tone to her voice, feeling suddenly vulnerable in the face of his empathy. "Actually, I have some nice memories. There were times when I thought I would die of the loneliness and the uncertainty. Then, when I was in high school, I came here to live in Scannon Cove with a couple named Al and Donna Curtis. Al piloted a small plane between here and Portland and loved to tinker with engines. Donna was small and round and did all the things I loathe—baked, canned and sewed—but she didn't demand that of me. For the first time in my life, someone let me be me. And—'' she turned into the parking lot of the Scannon Cove Mallory Inn and pulled up effortlessly to the front entrance ''—unfortunately what that is is the proverbial grease monkey.''

He studied her gravely. "I don't think it's unfortunate that you're a grease monkey."

His steady blue gaze unsettled her, as did the smile that formed when he realized she was ruffled.

"Come now, Mr. Mallory," she teased. "Let's not lie to each other. At least not until we're negotiating the sale of your new Flambeau."

His smile broadened, and her heart somersaulted.

"You do think I'm unfortunate as a woman. Don't deny it," she added quickly. "I can read it in your eyes."

"No," he insisted. He flicked a disparaging finger at the collar of her vanilla shirt. "That blouse is unfortunate. You, on the other hand, are an experience."

They stared at each other for a moment, a kind of dynamism at work that appeared to puzzle him as much as it puzzled her.

"I'll bring the loaner car by as soon as I can," Randy said briskly. "I'll leave the keys at the front desk."

"No, bring them to my office," he countered. "The desk is busy, and they have enough to worry about without being responsible for the boss's personal details."

"All right."

Mallory stepped out of the car, and holding the door open, leaned back in to smile at her again. "Thank you, Miss Stanton."

She nodded back with the same formality. "My pleasure, Mr. Mallory."

He studied her another long moment, then, adding quietly, "Until later," straightened and closed the door. Randy sped away without a backward glance.

There would be no later, she told herself as she returned to the dealership through the now thinning traffic. She would send Jake—no, she would send Gordie—with the keys and be sure that he delivered them to Mr. Mallory's office and not the front desk.

Miranda Stanton was going nowhere near the Mallory Inn again. Mallory was gorgeous; Viv was right. But Randy suspected that for her Matt Mallory would be trouble. She wasn't sure where the notion sprang from or why she, who dealt in fact and never played a hunch, could be so certain of a suspicion. But she was.

Chapter Two

Randy stood alone in the middle of the garage at the dealership, where she had expected to find her office manager. Gordie certainly had been right when he said she was always the last to leave, she thought resignedly. The lights were out, and everything was still. There were several automobiles in various stages of repair standing about in the dark, cavernous room like petrified metal beasts, one gaping jawed and one—Matt Mallory's Camaro—with the evidence of a disabling body blow.

Now there was no one around to deliver the Impala to Mr. Mallory at the inn. Gordie had been so busy all afternoon placating the Morrisons that she'd had little chance to speak to him. At this point she would have even sent Jake on the errand, but he had baseball practice and had left early.

Philosophically tossing the keys to the Impala, Randy locked the garage door, then gathered her purse and jacket from the office and slipped into the car.

It had been a long time since this particular Impala could have been called a cream puff; Randy would be the first to admit it. It had been serviced by her shop several times before it was taken as a trade-in. But even with every conceivable part repaired or replaced, it seemed to have a mind of its own.

Randy turned the key and prayed for ignition. The motor came to life, even if a little consumptive in sound, and she hoped that it would continue to function for Matthew Mallory.

After parking the car at the Mallory Inn, Randy confidently approached the plush sixth-floor administrative offices of the hotel, relieved to see a slim, gray-haired woman at a reception desk. Certainly the keys could be left with her.

"Certainly not!" the receptionist informed Randy. "Mr. Mallory would like the keys delivered to him personally. He's in the dining room."

"But—"

"Or maybe the kitchen."

Randy didn't argue. Efficient older women were one of the few species who intimidated her. Turning away, she got back on the elevator and rode it down to the main floor.

Admiring the exotic lighting fixtures, which looked like enormous cylinders suspended from a five-story central prism, Randy wound her way among the hotel's guests and down a soft lavender-carpeted lobby. The wide corridor was decorated with artwork by some of the Oregon coast's finest artists. She found the dining room but no Mr. Mallory. With an irritated sigh, she then entered the kitchen. It was large, filled with white and stainless-steel mysteries that never found their way into the ordinary kitchen. White-garbed men and women were hurrying back and forth, and the din of pots and pans and laughter was loud enough that one would have to shout to be heard. The aroma of different foods cooking was debilitating.

Randy was about to approach a young man who was making daisies out of carrots when a familiar voice called, "Randy! Over here!"

She turned to see Matthew Mallory in a dark suit and pale blue shirt. He was leaning against a stainless-steel counter where a tall, paunchy man wearing a chef's hat was putting the finishing touches on a beautiful baked salmon.

Unwilling to proceed farther into the room, she dangled the keys, hoping Mallory would come for them. But he waved for her to come in, then turned back to the chef.

Again, irritated, Randy walked across the room to deliver the keys. But as she opened her mouth to speak, he put a forkful of the salmon into her mouth.

The flavor was enough to quell her indignation. She closed her eyes to savor all the subtle spices and the delicious meat itself.

"Meet David McIntyre," Mallory said when she opened her eyes. "Head chef at the Cove Mallory."

The man was a giant, his girth a hearty recommendation of his culinary skills. He wiped an enormous, scrupulously clean hand on the front of his apron and offered it to Randy. His smile was as broad as his middle.

Randy shook his hand, then looked down hopefully at the plate of salmon. "Could I have one more bite?"

Mallory laughed, dipping the fork into the fish once more. "You don't like to cook, but you like to eat, right?"

"You've got my number," she admitted.

"Now that you've eaten half my dinner—" he grinned, watching her chew "—will you join me?"

She glanced from the plate to his face and swallowed. "Was that yours?"

"I wouldn't feed you from a guest's plate."

"Of course not," she said, feeling suddenly uncomfortable with the entire conversation and the speculative look she was getting from the chef. She waved the keys at Mallory again. "I've just come to deliver these and then be on my way. It was nice to meet you, Mr. McIntyre."

The keys still dangled between them, waiting for Mallory to claim them. Instead, he picked up the plate, and another that looked identical, and headed out the door.

"I asked you to deliver them to me personally," he said. "I'm going to be in the dining room."

He disappeared through the swinging doors. With a forbearing look at the chef, who still studied her with that strange expression, Randy followed.

She found Mallory at a small table for two in a far corner of the room. She approached the table with her best take-it-or-leave-it expression and dropped the keys on the table.

"Thank you for the invitation, Mr. Mallory, but I have plans for the evening."

He pulled a chair out for her. "I thought we weren't going to lie to each other until I buy that Flambeau," he reminded.

She turned to look at him, shocked that he would point out that she wasn't telling the truth.

He shrugged apologetically. "I'm sorry. I wouldn't be surprised if you had plans, but..." He studied her thoughtfully. "You haven't, have you?"

"No," she admitted, "I haven't. But it's rude of you to make a point of it."

"The only point that I'm trying to make," he insisted, "is that I'd like your company for dinner tonight."

The slightest pressure of his hand on her shoulder pushed her into the chair, and he eased it to the table. He called a waiter, ordered a bottle of Chenin Blanc and spread his napkin on his lap.

Now resigned to having dinner in his company, Randy grudgingly did the same with her napkin.

"The only reason that I'm staying is because it's Mr. McIntyre's salmon." She felt she needed to explain her capitulation.

Mallory inclined his head in agreement. "Reason enough. David and I went to the Culinary Institute of America together. He's as warm and giving as he looks. And a genius in the kitchen."

Randy picked up her fork and looked at him in surprise. "You went to chef's school?"

"A good restaurant is the heart of a good house," he explained. "My father thought I should know what goes into one even if my talents lie in another direction."

"Where do your talents lie?" she asked. A forkful of salmon was halfway to her mouth before she realized what a leading question that was. A glance at his face told her that he chose to interpret it in just the wrong way. For the first time in years she blushed.

"No innuendo intended," she said, taking the bite, hoping to distract him by assuming the initiative herself.

"Pity," he replied, his eyes laughing. "I was just about to boast of my prowess."

"Boast away," she encouraged, busily eating. "I work in a man's world, remember? I hear it all the time."

"Are you comfortable in such an environment?" he asked, as though he genuinely wanted to know.

She thought about that a moment, glad that the previous subject had been diverted. "Usually. Most of the time it isn't easy to be involved in something that isn't feminine. Other women think you're strange, and men are afraid of you."

She looked him straight in the eye, daring him to deny that her statement was true. Instead, to her surprise, he nodded in agreement.

"It is threatening to a man to see a beautiful woman." His eyes grew thoughtful again as they went over her face. "Especially one he would like to have, and then to also see the sparkle of wit and intelligence in her eyes."

Randy frowned in perplexity. "Why don't you find the prospect of a relationship with an intelligent woman exciting instead of frightening?"

"It depends on the circumstances," he said, considering a parsleyed potato with the tip of his fork. Then he looked up at her, his bright blue eyes filled with honesty. "If a woman's profession is something different from what I do, then there's no problem. But if she might be better than I am at what I do, I don't think I could handle that."

She asked candidly, "Ego?"

"I suppose at rock bottom it's ego. But at gut level it's simple pride in wanting to be someone your woman can look up to, someone she can run to for solace or protection or just lean against."

"But one can be smart and not be strong," Randy suggested.

Mallory shook his head. "A man can, but not a woman. I know enough about today's world to know that a woman who makes it professionally makes it because she's as strong as she is smart. Like yourself, for example."

Randy shrugged. "I made it because I wanted it."

"That's the point. To get what you want, you have to be strong—man or woman." He stabbed at the potato. "What are your plans for the future?"

The question so surprised Randy that she looked across the table at him and blinked. His gaze remained interested and steady.

"To expand the dealership," she said after a moment. "To offer a broader selection of lines. To become truly competitive, with the same deals a big-city store can offer."

He nodded, smiling. "I might have figured. But those are business plans. I was talking about personal plans."

"Those are my personal plans, as well."

Mallory looked pained. "To excel in business is your plan for a personal future?"

She faced him defensively from across their wineglasses. "Is there something wrong with that?"

"Not if you've got a three-liter V-6 engine for a heart," he said, shaking his head in response to her challenging question. "But you look very flesh and blood to me. And are you going to curl up with the Dun and Bradstreet report or the N.A.D.A. Official Used Car Guide at night?"

"I don't plan to curl up with anyone!" she said a little too emphatically. As heads turned in the dining room, she joined her hands in her lap and then stared down at them.

"I should have left the keys with your dragon of a secretary!" she spat quietly.

"She's not a dragon," he defended. "She's more of a mother hen. She likes to help me get what I want. Tonight I wanted to have dinner with you."

Glancing around to find that her interested audience had gone back to their dinners, Randy glared at her host. "So how do you like it now that you've got it?"

His blue eyes ran over her face in thoughtful perusal, then settled on her smoky eyes. He grinned. "I find that

I have a touch of the masochist in me. You're the kind of pain that promises pleasure.''

Randy rolled her eyes heavenward. ''To think I could be home washing my hair.''

''After dinner,'' he suggested while continuing with his meal, ''I'll wash it for you.''

''Mr. Mallory—'' she began.

''If we're going to get as intimate as hair washing,'' he said with a bland expression, ''call me Matt.''

''All right, Matt,'' Randy said, the candlelight in her eyes sparking like fireworks. A flaring temper gave her complexion a rosy patina, and her hair seemed to blaze because of it also. Her entire demeanor took on a touching dignity of which she was totally unaware. ''I am smart and I am strong. And though I try never to be, I can be tough. You're dealing with a salesperson, remember, so don't try to sell me on a night in your suite. My mother was the victim of a charming flirtation, but I'm the one who paid the consequences. Please keep your seductive wit to yourself. I'm not amused.''

For a long moment he studied her as though he hadn't even heard her statement and was concentrating on something else entirely—something only he was aware of. Then he refocused on her flushed cheeks and inclined his head in apology.

''Sorry. I thought we were just having a little harmless battle of the sexes.''

That was all it was, of course, Randy realized. But her own fears and insecurity had blown the little interchange all out of proportion.

''But just out of curiosity,'' he continued, leaning toward her on his folded arms, ''what do you do at night when everyone else goes home to a wife, girlfriend, husband or lover?''

Randy sighed, suddenly very tired. It had been a long day all in all.

"I want only two things out of life, Matt," she said, enumerating the first one on her little finger. "I want financial security so that I am never again dependent on the goodwill of others for a roof over my head." Then, on her next finger, she continued, "And I never want to move again—ever. I'm tired of new beginnings. I want this one in Scannon Cove to take. I don't ever want to pack another bag or look into another pair of eyes that is wondering whether or not I'll fit in."

"You have to move ahead or you'll fall behind," he said gravely. "It's a law of nature."

"I have to be secure," she said. "It's a law of Miranda Stanton. In Scannon Cove, with my dealership, I'm secure."

"But doesn't it concern you that you're alone in your security?"

"No. Because most likely a husband would be transferred or want to move away."

He frowned at her. "Randy, it sounds as though in your bid for security you're building yourself a prison."

"Perhaps to you it's a prison. To me it's the secure base I've never had. For the first time in my life I have charge of my own destiny."

For a moment she thought that the conversation was over. Then he looked at her consideringly and asked, "Despite the fact that you claim to be smart and strong and even tough, are you afraid that if push comes to shove you'll be no stronger in the clinch than she was?"

She looked puzzled. "Who?"

"Your mother."

Mallory saw that his remark hit home, and again he felt instantly sorry. For a moment she looked so hurt.

Then her eyes turned to ice, and with an angry toss of her flaming red hair, she was on her feet, ready to leave.

"Randy—" He caught her hand, trying to prevent her escape. But she yanked it away with a strength that surprised him.

"Goodbye, Mr. Mallory."

"You haven't got a car," he reminded her as he stood.

She paused a moment to give him a lethal look. "I'm sure the front desk will call me a cab."

And before he could say any more she was gone.

Matt sat down again and studied the seat that she had vacated, waiting for the solution to this dilemma to come to him. But it didn't. This was no managerial problem that could be solved with his innate cleverness and considerable experience. This was a woman, and a complex one at that.

He had experienced the magic of sexual chemistry with a woman before, but this was more than that. He wanted Miranda Stanton, and not simply in body. He wanted to hold her, to make her his, until the fears he saw imprisoned in her eyes were banished forever.

He finally picked up his fork and stabbed it into the flaky salmon, wondering idly if Randy's presence in his life was a divine answer to his mother's constant prayers for a daughter-in-law.

NOT USUALLY A VICTIM of her moods, Randy was unpleasantly surprised to find herself irritable and short-tempered for the balance of the week. She knew that the root of her mood was anger at herself for allowing Matt Mallory to put her in the position where he could make such a suggestion about her or—closer to the point—see so clearly what she tried hard to hide from herself. As recently as last weekend she had been feeling positive about the niche she was establishing for herself and her business in this little river town. Now, since that evening with Mallory, she felt strangely out of sorts, confused, uncertain. She didn't like that. It was too much like the old days when she was growing up.

By Friday afternoon, with everyone but Eldon Phillips and Bob McGraw gone, Randy slipped on her coveralls over her blue slacks and blouse. Then she tucked her hair into Jake's cap and went to work under the hood of her demonstrator. The engine had been missing lately, and she preferred to service her own vehicles. She trusted her crew, but she always found time spent under the hood therapeutic when she was troubled.

She hung the droplight on the hood-lock mechanism and went to work.

A half hour later, scrutinizing a fouled spark plug, she thought she had the problem localized. Then another problem surfaced from an entirely different direction.

It began with a nudge on her backside from a strong but rounded object, probably a knee.

"Where's your boss, Jake?" the voice that belonged to the knee asked.

Recognizing the voice immediately, and instantly indignant over the nudge to her bottom, Randy jackknifed to an upright position, forgetting to watch her head.

She collided with the droplight once, then again, as it swung like a crazy pendulum. Mallory caught it, saving Randy from yet a third thump, then pulled her toward him as she tried to back away with both hands to her head.

For a moment she had trouble deciding whether the spinning sensation she felt was because of the blows or from contact with Matt, who swept off her cap and ran both his hands in her tumbling hair, checking for any injury.

"I'm all right!" she declared aggressively, her hands yanking on his forearms with little effect.

His hands tightened on her scalp like a vise, not hurting but making it impossible for her to draw away.

"Be still," he ordered quietly, "and let's be sure."

Unable to do anything but comply, Randy stood limply while Mallory's strong fingers covered her scalp from her forehead to the nape of her neck. The sensation was insidiously delicious, and she felt a ripple of feeling from the base of her skull to her tailbone. Then she flinched when he touched the area right on the crown of her head.

"I don't think the skin is broken," he said, "but I'll bet you end up with a good bump and a headache." He put both his hands in the pockets of a short leather jacket. He wore corduroy slacks and rubber-soled oxfords. His expression was resigned.

"That didn't score me any points, did it?" he asked.

Thinking that the casual attire lent him a relaxed air that was almost more appealing than the formal elegance of his dinner clothes, Randy forced a casual tone to her voice as she turned the light off and unhooked it from the hood of the car.

"No one's keeping a scorecard on you, Mr. Mallory." She rubbed absently at the sore spot on her head.

"Mr. Mallory again," he said, brushing her hand aside as he pulled the hood down. "That tells me what the tally is. Even the other night, when you were angry with me, you called me Matt."

Randy gave him a glaring glance as she replaced the light in a toolbox. "Maybe we were both a little too personal the other night."

"I'm sorry," he said. "It was simply an observation. I didn't mean to hurt your feelings."

"Simply an observation!" she shouted, turning on him. She would have been a comic picture in the large coveralls had she not been so formidable in her anger. "You implied that I was weak and selfish and irresponsible!" She would have shot past him toward the corridor that connected the garage with the showroom, but he caught her arm.

"You misunderstood me," he said, firming his grip as she tried to pull away. "I was suggesting that you might be vulnerable to feelings and emotions, not that you would abandon a responsibility. Even the strongest of us is weak in the face of passion, particularly if it's coupled with love."

"I," she said firmly, "am not."

Mallory folded his arms and considered her with an expression she mistrusted. "Have you ever been in that position?"

She thought of lying, and she considered telling him it was none of his business. But the truth was that she had never known passion, because she'd been afraid to let any man become that important in her life. In the time that it took her to think about a reply, Mallory read the answer in her face.

"I thought so," he said. In a gesture so unexpected it drew a startled gasp from her, he took the collar of her coveralls in one hand and swept the front zipper down with the other. "Get out of those," he directed, "and let's see how well you know yourself."

He turned her around and yanked on the sleeves until they came off, allowing the garment to slip down to her knees. Then he turned her back and held her hand while she stepped out of the coveralls, her heart rocketing.

"I don't like you, Matt Mallory," she said candidly as he stood purposefully in front of her.

He tapped a long finger lightly on her sternum. "If there's a woman still alive in there, it shouldn't matter."

The urge to run was almost overpowering, but Randy's pride held her in place and even lifted her chin upward as Mallory framed her face in his hands. She felt strength in his fingers and almost panicked again, but now it was too late. His mouth was coming down to hers.

The kiss was swift and gentle. Wary, Randy looked into his eyes as he drew away slightly to study her face. Then, smiling, he kissed her eyelids as they closed, and Randy went blindly into the next encounter, her pulses beginning to clamor.

Warm and dry, his lips became subtly more demanding, moving on hers, drawing from her the response she had feared was there all along.

A hand between her shoulder blades pressed her pliant body against his chest, and then a reaction flared in her. Feeling the shudder that ran through her body, Mallory pressed his advantage, and Randy, who put all her stock in security, felt the world drop away from under her feet.

She had a vague recollection of something he had said about a prison, and she wondered idly if it crossed her mind because she felt suddenly so free. His arms around her were shackling, one at her shoulders the other at her hips, and her feet were clear of the ground. She could neither move nor run. Yet it felt as though little corners of her being that had never known the light of day were bathing in a stream of sunshine. Her breath was trapped in his mouth, and when he freed her lips to chase kisses down her neck and shoulder, she gasped as though she could not dispel the air fast enough.

Then he took her mouth again, and the paradox seemed suddenly acceptable, because logic and reason had fled. She became all shuddery limbs, with a wildly beating heart, insatiable lips and hands that clung to him as a lifeline.

It was a moment before she realized that he had set her on her feet and that he couldn't straighten himself because she was clinging to his leather jacket.

She released him and stepped back, looking at him as though he were Jack the Ripper.

"She's alive in there, Randy," Mallory said, his long arm bridging the distance she had tried to put between them as the tip of his finger again touched her sternum. "We can still save her."

She was angry now. Paradoxes were all right while she was in his arms, but she had to keep her grip on reality. And in real life she didn't like riddles; she liked security. And this man's sole purpose seemed to be to destroy it for her.

"We?" she asked coolly.

"It's hard to do that by yourself."

"I don't like you," she said again.

He smiled. "The woman hiding inside you does."

"Frankly, I don't like her, either," she said, snatching the coveralls off the floor. "All of us have an alter ego living inside who'd like to live only for pleasure and excitement."

"Pleasure and excitement aren't evil," he said forcefully. "I think you're confused, Randy, about which one of you is good and which is bad."

"Mallory, I don't want to get involved with you!" she shouted. She started to walk away from him, and he pulled her back.

"Have you ever considered," he asked, angry now himself, "that a relationship could end in love and marriage instead of abandonment and single parenthood?"

She shook her head. "That wouldn't matter."

"Why not?" he demanded.

She sighed. "Because he'd get transferred or want to move from Scannon Cove."

"God!" he groaned. "That's too idiotic to even comment on."

She smiled. "Then you're free to go, aren't you? Good night, Mr. Mallory."

Randy walked swiftly down the corridor that led to the showroom, anxious to get to her office before she collapsed. She felt exhausted, as though she'd been in physical combat. She could not imagine feeling worse.

Randy entered the showroom to the sound of raised voices. Eldon Phillips and Bob McGraw, her two salesmen, were squared off between a station wagon and the Flambeau Mallory had admired.

"What's the problem?" she asked from across the room, hoping she could still make it in a straight line to her office.

But neither of them heard her.

"You skate one more of my deals and I'll lay you out!" Bob shouted.

Eldon bunched his fists. "Maybe you'd like to do it now!"

Randy had worked around men long enough to distinguish the prelude to a real fight from a simple quarrel. She didn't like the way this looked and started toward them.

"Stop that!" she shouted above their hot words, hoping to distract them, but Phillips spat an obscenity at McGraw, who then drew his fist back.

"I said stop it!" she shouted again, stepping between them and throwing her arms out to push them apart. She felt taut anger against the palms of both her hands and looked from one to the other with an expression that would have stopped Atilla the Hun.

"If you carry this any further," she warned quietly, "or if it ever happens again in my showroom, you're both fired. You're not warring adolescents; you're professional salesmen. I will not have brawling in my store."

"He—!" Phillips began, and she silenced him with a raised hand.

"If you have a complaint, I expect you to settle it between yourselves without violence." She frowned darkly at McGraw. "If that's impossible, we have staff meetings once a week for airing any grievances. If it can't wait, you know I'm available anytime."

"Then I'll be in your office at eight o'clock tomorrow morning," McGraw said with a murderous look at Phillips.

"Fine," Randy returned calmly. "I'll expect you. Now, I'm sure both your families are wondering where you are. Good night, gentlemen."

After a moment of angry silence, McGraw stalked to his office, and Phillips left, banging his way through the heavy double-glass doors.

With her head throbbing, Randy went to her office and closed the door. She fell into her chair and leaned her head back, closing her eyes as the tension began to dissipate.

"I thought so," a voice said from her doorway.

Randy sat forward, startled. Matt Mallory moved into her office and came to sit in the chair facing her desk.

"You're right; you can be tough." His clear blue eyes studied her troubled green ones. "But it's a pose, isn't it?"

"In that instance it was," she admitted, sinking back into the depths of the chair. She had no energy left to resist him. "Violence makes me want to run in the other direction, but I couldn't very well let them duke it out on my showroom floor, could I?"

"No, you couldn't. I expected to have to step in, but you did very well. You have the kind of presence that would do a street cop proud. I'll bet you could use a drink."

"I have a bottle of Bloody Mary mix at home," she said, pulling her purse out of a bottom drawer.

"I'm partial to Bloody Marys myself," Mallory said.

She smiled at him. "Then you should buy yourself a bottle of mix."

"Couldn't we share yours?" he persisted.

"It's late."

He looked at his watch, then skeptically at her face. "I know this isn't Bourbon Street, but it's only seven forty-five."

"I'm usually in my jammies by now," she said, getting to her feet, "watching M*A*S*H reruns."

"I like M*A*S*H reruns." His grin broadened. "And I'd like to see you in your jammies."

Randy smiled, wondering what he would think of her pajamas if he could see them. "They're flannel, and they have feet."

He shook his head despairingly. "What are we going to do about you? Here I am, new to the community, trying my best to become acquainted with my fellow tradespeople, and what do I get from you? Rejection at every turn."

The sore spot on her scalp was now throbbing, and she rubbed it gingerly.

"I've got it." He stood and leaned across the desk toward her, his eyes gently teasing, his voice quiet. "I'll take you home, mix you a Bloody Mary, help you into your jammies and leave."

Randy rolled her eyes and found that it hurt. A ride home was suddenly appealing. "I'll get into my own jammies."

He sighed exaggeratedly. "Have it your way. Let's go."

He led her out to the Impala she'd brought to the hotel the other night and helped her into it. She found herself grateful for his gentle attentions as her headache worsened. A knot of tension had formed at the base of her skull and was warring with the bump on the top of her head for supremacy. She leaned her head against the seat and closed her eyes, opening them just long enough to direct him to her small cottage on the outskirts of town. He pulled into her driveway and turned off the motor. Then he put on the car's interior light and shifted in his seat to study her face. Her brow was furrowed with the persistent pulse of the headache.

"Let me help you inside," he suggested gently, his earlier teasing replaced by genuine concern. "I'll mix you a drink while you put yourself to bed."

She looked at him doubtfully.

"Would I dare do anything disreputable before we come to terms on the Flambeau?" he asked, the lazy humor back in his eyes.

She smiled tentatively. "You won't tell anyone about my sleepers? They're red-and-white striped."

He shook his head. "I doubt that anyone would believe that, anyway. Sit still and I'll help you out."

At the door Randy handed him her key. Once inside, she pointed him to the kitchen and shuffled off to her bedroom, calling instructions over her shoulder. "The mix is in the fridge; the vodka's right there on the countertop."

Within five minutes her clothes were draped over the chair. She wasn't usually so careless with her clothing, but she was taking no chances that he would appear with the drink before she had put on her pajamas.

She was pulling the blankets up over her body when he rapped lightly on the door.

"Come in," she said, propping herself up against a pillow.

Matt's eyes ran over the rounded softness of her bosom in the red-and-white striped top of her pajamas as he came around the bed to hand her the Bloody Mary. "You look like a most delectable candy cane," he said, then sat on the edge of the bed and leaned sideways, placing a hand on the bed on each side of her knees.

Randy's throat constricted, and the sip of drink that she tried to swallow made her choke.

"Too strong?" Matt asked.

She shook her head. "Wrong pipe," she gasped, her eyes filling with tears as she choked again. If only she had followed her first inclination and insisted on leaving him at her door. She was beginning to wonder if that bump on the head had affected her brain.

"You're so tense you can't even swallow," Matt said with a frown, moving to sit beside her, pushing her pillow aside. His gentle hand to her back pushed her slightly forward. He reached under her hair to run his fingertips along her vertebrae to the base of her skull. Gooseflesh tingled where he touched.

"What are you doing?" she asked breathlessly.

"Trying to see if we can loosen you up," he said absently, his fingers searching for the spot of tightness but wreaking havoc all along her nervous system. "I think that little episode in your office with the salesmen, on top of that bang on the head, was more than you needed. You should let Walsh handle that kind of thing."

"I was there," she reminded him. "He wasn't."

"Hostility should never reach that point."

She sighed as his fingers began to work at her hairline. "There's more to Bob and Eldon's problem than appears to the casual observer."

"Maybe," he conceded, now plying both hands along her shoulders, his thumbs massaging a rhythmic pattern. "But I wouldn't make a habit of leaping into the middle of two men squaring off. If McGraw had let fly with that fist, I'd be looking at your pretty little nose back here somewhere."

"Oh, Mallory," Randy groaned, his warning forgotten as a feeling of bonelessness overtook her. "That feels so good." Her head lolled forward as his fingers moved up into her hair.

"Wouldn't it be worth it," he asked, "to be with a man who could do this for you even if he did ask you to move away with him?"

Randy's back stiffened instantly, and she pulled away, her soft mood dissolving. He dropped his hand from her.

"No," she said simply.

Mallory stood and pulled her pillow back in place, his hands on her shoulders easing her back to lean against it. "Have you considered," he asked, "that emotional security is as important as physical and financial security?"

"I learned early that there's no such thing." She pulled the blanket up under her arms and held it there, her fingers absently working on the satin binding. "I learned to rely on what I know will be there. People change their minds. They move. Buildings usually remain—businesses, too, if they're sensibly operated."

He sat on the edge of the bed again, studying her with a frown between his eyebrows. "So you're rooting your future in concrete and profit-and-loss statements."

She shrugged, smoothing the blankets. "We all need different things out of life."

He indicated the empty side of the bed. "Don't tell me you're never awakened in the night and wished there was a man on the other side whom you could cuddle up against, awaken, maybe, and rouse to lovemaking."

She looked at him levelly, struggling to remain impassive against the image his words painted in her mind. Somehow she could see his face on the imaginary man.

"Yes," she said candidly. "Often. But having him wouldn't be worth it to me if he made me leave here."

He looked down at her, then noticed the forgotten drink in her hand and urged it to her lips. "Finish that," he said, getting briskly to his feet, "and get a good night's sleep. I'll pick you up in the morning."

"That won't be necessary."

"You left your car at work, and you might feel a little unsteady in the morning." He began to tuck the blankets in at her feet, then stopped to pull the blankets out from under the mattress. He lifted the edge of the blanket and peered underneath.

"Red-and-white feet!" he exclaimed in amazement. "You weren't kidding."

"I told you!" she said, drawing up the objects under discussion. "My feet are always cold."

He tucked the blankets in again. "If you had a man on that side of the bed—"

"Good night, Mr. Mallory," Randy interrupted, sliding down and readjusting her pillow.

"Good night, Randy." He paused at the doorway. "I have to go to Portland on Monday. Do you have any objection to my taking the car that far?"

"No, of course not," she assured him, silently hoping it would make it the hundred miles on the tortuous road to civilization. "Stop at the shop and we'll gas it up for you."

"Fair enough. Anything you need before I leave you?"

"Nothing, thanks. Good night."

Matt Mallory winked and turned out the light.

Chapter Three

"He took you home?" Vivian was perched on the edge of Randy's desk, oblivious to the Monday afternoon hubbub going on around her. Her dark eyes were wide with interest. "What happened?"

"Nothing," Randy replied, "I was in pain and not very...lively."

"I'd have thought that he could make a corpse come alive." The bookkeeper rolled her eyes dreamily. "Are you seeing him again?"

Randy shrugged. "I suppose I'll run into him when he picks up his car."

Vivian grimaced in mute despair over the other woman's inability to make the most of a promising situation. "You're hopeless!" Then she handed Randy a telephone memo. "Kurt Daniels called to remind you about the Downtown Committee meeting next week."

Randy nodded, reaching over her employee to answer the shrill ring of the phone. "It's on my calendar. Hello."

"Randy!" a familiar male voice barked. "About this car you loaned me."

The telephone line had the subtle hollow sound of long distance, and Randy guessed what had happened even before Matt Mallory spoke the words.

"It broke down on the Interstate Freeway. I'm going to have to leave it here for repair."

"Rent a car, Mr. Mallory." Randy tried to sound in control despite the fact that Vivian was straining to hear the conversation. "We'll pick up the tab, of course."

"Don't 'Mr. Mallory' me!" he said firmly. "There is not a car to be rented in this town, and the bus doesn't leave until tomorrow morning. I have an eight a.m. meeting in Scannon Cove."

"Not a car to be rented in all of Portland?" she asked skeptically.

"You have heard of the Rose Festival?" he asked impatiently.

She groaned. Was it that time already? Week-long Rose Festival activities in early June brought eager participants and visiting dignitaries to Portland from all over the country.

"Where are you?" Randy asked.

"In the Red Lion coffee shop at Jantzen Beach."

"I'll send someone for you."

"You gave me this consumptive piece of junk!" he accused. "You come for me."

"I have a business to run," she said coolly.

"So do I," he returned. "And thanks to you I'm stranded out here a hundred miles from it."

"Have lunch, Mr. Mallory." Randy's voice remained even. "Someone will be there for you in two hours."

That someone, she realized grimly fifteen minutes later, would be herself, and she would be late.

Gordie was with a customer, Jake had a baseball game, Bob and Eldon couldn't be spared from the sales floor, and Vivian was entirely too willing to go. While Mallory might have enjoyed the woman's flirtatious nonsense at some other time, Randy had a feeling that uppermost in his mind at the moment was getting home.

"We do have a dealer trade that has to be delivered to Rose City Motors." Gordie excused himself long enough to tell her. "Bob worked on it this morning. It's the new Flambeau four-door. Take it. I'll get Viv to prepare the check for you and call to tell them you're on your way so they won't close till you get there."

It was twenty minutes before Randy had the check in her hand and was heading east on Highway 30 to Portland. She would pick Mallory up at Jantzen Beach, then head downtown to Rose City Motors, where she would trade the Flambeau sedan for a station wagon for the return trip home. She would send someone to pick up Mallory's loaner car the following week.

She realized later how foolish she had been to think it would be so simple.

As she maneuvered her way through the Red Lion's parking lot in Jantzen Beach, she spotted Mallory in a brown three-piece suit, leaning against a pillar supporting the marquee in front of the motel. He looked like a clothing ad in *Gentleman's Quarterly*.

She pulled up beside him. He moved slowly, stopping to toss his briefcase into the back seat of the car before climbing in beside her.

"Hello, Randy," he said with a significant glance at his watch. "Two hours?"

"Sorry," she said, pulling away. "I know it's been three. But no one else was free to come for you, and I discovered that we had to make a dealer trade in Portland, anyway. So I waited for the paperwork. It's also rush hour."

"I noticed," he said conversationally. "You should see rush hour in Boston. I think it's the only place in the world worse than Rome."

"I don't want to."

"What?"

"See Boston."

She felt him glance her way for a pensive moment, then look back to the road. "You're right," he said. "The important thing now is to get back to Scannon Cove."

"First we have to deliver this car to downtown Portland. We'll be driving a station wagon back home." She was trying hard to make easy small talk, trying hard not to betray her sudden shortness of breath.

Mallory was turned slightly as he spoke to her, his arm flung along the back of the bench seat, his fingertips brushing the ends of her hair every time she turned or looked up into the rearview mirror. Unaware that the proximity of his long, graceful body caused hers to act unpredictably, Mallory stared ahead. Randy smiled, having found that most men watched the road a little more anxiously when riding with a woman driver.

"Any more brawling in your showroom?" he asked.

She signaled to change lanes. "No. I held a staff meeting this morning and repeated that if anything like that ever happened again, I'd sack them both." She pulled onto the freeway, and Mallory remained silent until she had eased into the traffic.

"Did you find out what the fight was all about?"

"I know what it was about," she said, the resignation in her voice telling him that it was an old problem. "Eldon Phillips has been a salesman since he was eighteen. He's been through the boom years in automobile sales. He's used to hefty commissions—lots of them."

She gave her passenger a dry glance. "You know what's happened to the automotive industry over the past five years. With the decline in sales, we're bargaining down lower with the customers, so commissions are considerably less for the salesmen. A man can still make a decent living at it, but Eldon's used to big bucks, and he doesn't mind snatching some of Bob's customers to raise his sales."

"McGraw seems like a nice enough guy."

She smiled at the road. "Bob's a good man. He had a marine-supply store that went out of business when the government began regulating fishermen so heavily. With so few boats making fewer and fewer runs, he finally had to give up the business. Every time Eldon skates one of Bob's deals, Bob feels he's taking food off his family's table. Bob lost a lot when the business failed, and he's got three kids and a wife to support. They're barely making ends meet. I guess Eldon and Bob both have lost the life-style that they're used to. And each in his own way is trying to make it in a business that's no longer lucrative in Scannon Cove. Maybe it'll change one day, but for now a lot of us are hanging on by our fingernails."

The hand behind Randy's head played with the curling end of a tendril at her ear.

"I don't suppose you've considered selling the dealership?"

"I thought I was going to have to in January," she said, slapping his hand away. "Do you mind? I'm trying to concentrate on the traffic."

"Sorry."

"But the dealer who wants to buy me out is Lester Boyle, across the river in Fairview, Washington."

"And?" Mallory asked.

She glanced at him again, her green eyes snapping. "He called me 'Toots' and told me that a gorgeous little thing like me doesn't belong in a man's world. Then he offered me thirty thousand dollars less than my rock-bottom price. So I held on. And I'm still here."

Mallory laughed and rubbed her shoulder. "Good for you."

"Funny," she said, trying to think about the road instead of his hand. "I'd have thought you'd agree with him."

"A week ago I might have," he admitted, then added sharply, "Watch the truck!" as a pickup pulled in front of her with little warning and no signal.

"I am watching!" she shouted at him, braking immediately. "And if you'd keep your hands home, I could pay attention to the road!"

He drew his hand away but continued to study her as they crossed the bridge into downtown Portland.

"Does it upset you when I touch you?" he asked.

"It . . . distracts me," she said.

"Well." He straightened in his seat and looked at the scenery with interest. "That's a beginning."

Portland in the waning sun was a beautiful sight, with its tall buildings bordering both sides of the Willamette River and the U.S. Bank Corporation building a tower of pink in the dying sunset. The green hills were a soft backdrop to the portrait of a busy, healthy metropolis.

Randy pulled into Rose City Motors at five minutes to six, driving around to the service department, where she was confident that the station wagon would be waiting for her.

It was. She got out of the car, her spirits buoyed as a salesman came toward her with the paperwork for the car she was to pick up. She had traded with this dealership several times in the past but had always dealt with the manager.

The tall young man walked past her to Mallory, who had wandered over to the wagon.

"Here you are," he said, offering the packet of papers.

Mallory glanced at Randy with an amused grin. "You want to speak to the lady," he explained. "I'm just along for the ride."

"Oops," the young man said, turning to Randy with a sheepish look. She dismissed his mistake with a glare at Mallory.

"Give me a minute to check it out," she said, going over the required extras in her mind as she opened the door on the driver's side. She spotted the AM/FM radio instantly, and her heart sank. She straightened and leaned disconsolately against the open door.

"It's supposed to have an optional stereo with a cassette deck and visual equalizer."

"It is?" The salesman rifled through the papers and apologetically shrugged his shoulders. "It is. Sorry. Can you have one of your own men install it and we'll deduct the amount and give you another check? I'll have to mail it to you, though. There's nobody left in the office but me."

Randy closed her eyes and fought to control her frustration. "I have one man who can do that, and he's on two weeks' vacation. You were told specifically—"

"I see that," the salesman said, apparently as frustrated as she was. "I'm sorry. We have the stereo in stock, but the best I can do is to have somebody install it first thing in the morning."

"Meanwhile we're stranded here without transportation. This gentleman—" she indicated Mallory with a nervous swipe of her hand "—has a meeting a hundred miles away at eight o'clock tomorrow morning."

"Randy, it's all right," Mallory said, coming up behind her.

"No, it's not all right. We—"

"I said it's all right. If there's nothing we can do about it now, there's no point in fighting about it." Then he looked at the salesman. "But you'll see that it's taken care of first thing in the morning."

He extended his hand. "That's a promise."

Mallory shook it. "All right. We'll be back at eleven o'clock in the morning. Where's a good place for dinner?"

"The Benson Hotel, which is just two blocks in that direction." The young man pointed north, and Mallory went back to the Flambeau for his briefcase.

Randy still stood in the middle of the parking lot, staring at the station wagon and its simple standard radio.

"Come on," Mallory said, trying to draw her away. "You'll feel better after a glass of wine and a steak."

She turned on him, her eyes and her hair spewing flame. "Don't tell me I'll feel better! I'll feel better when people start doing what they're supposed to do!"

"You," he said, pulling her firmly along with him, "are tired."

"Yes, I am!" she said, trying to pull her arm away to no avail. "I had already had a long day when you insisted I come and get you! I've driven all afternoon through heavy traffic, and now here we are, stuck in Portland until tomorrow morning. And why are you being so cheerful? This morning you insisted that someone pick you up to bring you home tonight!"

"This morning that was a choice I had," he pointed out reasonably. "Tonight I no longer have it. You don't fight circumstances that you can't do anything about. Haven't you learned that yet?"

"Don't get philosophical with me!" she snapped, yanking free of him to start walking.

Matt caught up with her and pulled her to a stop, calmly tucking her arm in his. "Look," he said reasonably. "I know you're tired; I know you're angry. I can't do anything about the reason—all I can do is deal with the result. We're stuck here in Portland. We have to eat and find a place to stay tonight. I see no other choice."

"You also see no other cash." She made a Spartan effort to calm down and patted her purse. "I have exactly six dollars and sixty-two cents and not one credit card."

"We'll put it on my charge card," he said, drawing her with him toward the Benson, "and square up later. It's no problem."

Randy couldn't equate her behavior with anything she knew about herself. In all her twenty-seven years she had seldom panicked or failed to handle a problem in a logical way. Then what on earth accounted for this sudden angry display, this uncharacteristic whining in the face of a situation she could not change?

It was Mallory, she thought peevishly. Matthew Mallory was making her crazy.

The Westin Benson Hotel was located on a block of early-century elegance in a run-down area of commercial Portland. Having attended several meetings there, Randy understood Matt's reaction to what he saw and waited silently as he looked about. He was unabashedly impressed by the Circassian walnut panels, the elegant red carpet, the velvet drapes and a chandelier reflecting light in the mirrored wall behind the desk. Potted palms and small antique tables dotted a lounge area at the far end of the lobby.

"What a treasure!" Matt breathed, taking Randy's arm as he led her to the desk. "We'd like two rooms, please," Matt told the clerk, reaching into his breast pocket for his billfold.

The clerk appeared doubtful as he studied a chart of rooms. Randy gave Matt a grim look, images of the two of them spending the night on a park bench floating across her imagination. She was sure that with Rose Festival activities scheduled for this week, vacancies were sparse. As she was about to despair, the clerk's face lightened.

"We have adjoining rooms on the third floor. Numbers 312 and 314."

"Perfect," Matt said, and handed him a card.

After a moment the clerk gave Matt his receipt and two room keys, then lifted his hand to signal for a bellman.

"Ah...thank you," Matt said. "We won't need him."

The clerk peered down at their feet, and seeing no luggage, gave their faces a quick and knowing glance, then went back to his work with studied casualness. "Of course. Enjoy your stay at the Westin Benson."

Randy, who still harbored a few small-town sensitivities about this type of thing, couldn't stop the blush she felt rising. Matt's twitching bottom lip and barely repressed grin didn't help. Alone in the ancient elevator, they dissolved into laughter, and her earlier irritation was forgotten.

"I think we've just played the classic scene," Randy said. "Registering in a hotel without luggage. What odds would you take that he'd believe why we're really here?"

Matt mimicked the clerk's air of distant disinterest. "'Of course. Enjoy your stay at the Westin Benson.'

What style! Have you ever seen such complete detachment? That only comes from long experience and dedication to the trysting couples of the world." He fought a fresh bout of laughter. "I hope he never finds out why we're really here. It'd probably destroy his faith in human nature." The doors parted, and Matt held them open for her, handing Randy her key.

"How long do you need to freshen up?" he asked, watching room numbers as the two of them moved soundlessly down the hall. He paused at 312, pointing it out to Randy as he moved on to 314.

"Fifteen minutes will be plenty of time," she said dryly, "considering I have nothing to change into."

"Okay." He unlocked his door and pushed it open. "Knock on the adjoining door when you're ready."

The Victorian charm of the room arrested Randy's attention as she closed the door behind her. Instead of the usual nicely appointed but Xerox-copy look of most hotel rooms, she found a brass double bed, a Queen Anne chair beside it, highly polished hardwood floors and burgundy velvet draperies. A small bedside table held a hand-painted oil lamp. There was no television.

Randy headed for the bathroom and turned on the light to discover that it was modern and equipped with shampoo and conditioner. If only she had her blow dryer, she thought glumly, looking in the mirror at her disheveled hair and wrinkled suit.

After washing her face and applying fresh makeup, she brushed her hair into order, then rapped on the connecting door, resolving to make it through dinner without quarreling with her companion.

MALLORY STUDIED RANDY as she sat across the table from him, working daintily on a piece of Boston cheesecake. She looked distracted, a small frown between her unfocused eyes.

He picked up his coffee cup, wondering if she was thinking about him, even if she did seem to have forgotten about his physical presence. She seemed nervous about having to spend the night in Portland, and he found himself oddly pleased about that.

Difficult woman. The night she'd stepped between her two quarreling salesmen he'd learned something interesting about himself. He enjoyed women, all types, but for this one he seemed to have a special set of sensors. She confounded him, frightened him, annoyed him and was beginning to drive him to fits of adolescent longing. He could feel the tension in her without touching her, the fear and the loneliness.

Yet she was strong, determined, dedicated—but, he suspected, not as self-sufficient as she liked to think. When he thought about how she'd grown up, his heart ached for her.

She reminded him of some exotic candle, one of those intricately crafted, beautifully shaped pieces that was never meant to be touched with a match. She was all classic lines, elegantly limbed and with beautiful posture, and a face in which every feature was now beautiful to him. Her hair was the color of a flame in the night.

As Randy's eyes finally focused on him, reflecting that wariness he found so often in her gaze, he promised himself that one day she would look at him with love.

Matt dropped his credit card on top of the check on the silver tray and smiled at her. "How about a movie?"

She blinked. "A movie?"

"A movie," he confirmed. "How long has it been since you necked in the balcony while sharing a box of popcorn and a cola with someone?"

She shook her head. "I never did that."

He frowned. "You're more deprived than you realize. How come?"

She gave him a small smile. "When you can fix a guy's car for him, you're his buddy, but he doesn't take you to the movies."

"Well, thank heaven for the enlightened contemporary male." Matt indicated himself with a modest inclination of his blond head.

"What's playing?" she asked.

"I checked with the desk when you were freshening up. A horror double feature or a Neil Simon movie with a spy thriller."

"Oh?" She made a soft sound of acceptance and picked up her purse. "I love Neil Simon. But I want my own box of popcorn."

"You're a very demanding woman," Mallory said, handing Randy her own box of popcorn as he led her toward the dark theater entrance.

"We're not going to neck, either," she said over her shoulder.

"Now, wait a minute..." he teased, pretending to back off.

She took his arm and pulled him along with her. "Stop that!" she whispered harshly. "There are people behind us."

"Then let's give them something to look at," he whispered back as they started down the aisle.

"Do you never let up?" She found two seats on the aisle and led the way in.

The Neil Simon movie made them laugh, then made Randy cry. Unprepared for tears, she accepted Mallory's handkerchief and did not object when he put a comforting arm around her shoulders.

The second feature was a little too complicated for her weary state. She found the arm around her a firm pillow against which she leaned contentedly.

When Randy awoke, the theater lights were on, and people were moving toward the exits. She looked up at her grinning companion with an embarrassed smile. "I'm a dull date, aren't I?"

"Actually, the quiet was a nice change from when you're awake," he sidestepped artfully. She grimaced at him.

"A drink before we go back to the hotel?" he suggested.

She shook her head. "No, thanks. I could use a good night's sleep."

She wondered if he knew that she was bluffing. She would probably not sleep a wink tonight. There was nothing remotely suggestive about spending the night in different rooms in the same hotel, yet she could feel her body being seduced by the very idea. He could slip quietly into her room under the cloak of darkness, or she could slip into his, the moonlight outlining her round form in its transparent negligee. She shook her head to clear it as they stepped out of the theater into the mildly chilly air filled with the big city smells of exhaust and asphalt. She felt a sudden stabbing of homesickness for Scannon Cove and a shattering of her romantic mood. In truth, there was no moonlight and no negligee. And in another year Matthew Mallory would be moving on.

Matt took Randy's key, unlocked the door to her room and pushed it open. She turned in the doorway to smile sleepily at him. With a hard swallow, he jammed his hands in his pockets.

"I enjoyed the movie," she said softly.

He leaned against the wall. "We'll have to do it again sometime at home."

She nodded. "Sure." Then she shrugged her shoulders awkwardly. "Well..."

"Have you got everything you need?"

"I don't have anything," she said. "But I guess I'll manage. Although I do wish I had my toothbrush."

"They've got them in the gift shop." He straightened, looking almost relieved to leave her. "I'll get one for you and some toothpaste. Anything else?"

She looked at him hopefully. "If the coffee shop is still open, do you think you could get me a cup of tea? I always have one before I go to bed."

He laughed. "I thought you had a Bloody Mary before going to bed."

"Only on days when I'm suicidal. Are you sure it's not too much trouble?"

He took the point of her chin and pinched very gently. "For you? Of course not. Be right back."

When Randy took her clothes off in the bathroom, her hands were shaking. *You are twenty-seven years old,* she told herself firmly. *All he did was pinch your chin. Lighten up, for heaven's sake.*

She wound her hair up in a knot and stepped into the shower. She let the water beat for long moments on her back, the hot, sharp needles massaging away the tension.

Wrapped in a towel, Randy went into the bedroom and found a small travel toothbrush and trial-size tube of toothpaste on the dresser. Somehow the fact that Matt had been back while she was in the shower was further unsettling.

Brushing her teeth almost restored her equanimity until she realized that he would be back in a few minutes.

She would either have to get completely dressed again or get in bed with the covers pulled up to her chin. Neither idea appealed to her. After the shower she was too wide awake for sleep, but the idea of donning her gray wool suit again made her look for a third alternative. She found it by putting on her slip and blouse and sitting up in bed, leaning against her propped-up pillows.

Fifteen minutes later Mallory came through the door that connected their rooms, balancing a tray that held a teapot, two matching bone-china cups with saucers and a plate of cookies.

"How did you do that?" Randy asked in amazement. Her watch read just after eleven o'clock.

He put the tray down on the lamp table by the bed. "I found the coffee shop closed, so I paid a visit to the night manager, and we got to swapping stories about the hotel business. As it turns out, he was just going to the kitchen to get his own snack. Making two pots of tea and filling two plates of cookies was just as easy as making one. I think for my valiant efforts on your behalf you should let me join you."

"Of course," she said, maintaining a firm hold on the blanket as she wriggled to sit up straighter.

"Good," he said. "You pour. I'm going to get rid of this jacket and tie." He disappeared through the connecting door and was back in a moment, rolling up the sleeves of his white shirt.

He looked less fresh than his *GQ* ad appearance of earlier this afternoon, but somehow he seemed more dangerous now. His blond hair was a little mussed, his eyes a bit more lazy, and his body moved with languorous grace rather than the taut energy that always controlled it. He settled in the Queen Anne chair near the head of the bed as she held out the china cup for him.

"Do you like tea?" she asked in surprise.

He shook his head, studying the cookie plate carefully before making a selection. "Not particularly. But I like being with you." He bit down on the cookie, chewed and swallowed. He nodded approvingly. "And the cookies aren't bad, either."

Randy found the tea hot and bracing, and she was able to look at Mallory and ignore the carefully banked flame of desire in his eyes. She could see that he was determined to play the gentleman about this situation, but she knew that if he changed his mind, there would be little she could do about it physically—and little she would want to do about it emotionally.

"So what'll we talk about?" he asked, carefully tasting the steaming brew.

"Tell me about your family," she said. "According to all the news stories, everything that's important in your corporation is done by the Mallorys. Are there really that many of you?"

He laughed, reaching for another cookie. "No, but my father and my brother cause enough commotion for ten men."

"You work together and you all get along?"

"Usually. When we don't, it's very dramatic. Lots of yelling and an occasional disowning. My father's like a load of nitro on a bumpy ride."

Randy laughed at his simile, taking another sip of her tea.

"Anyway," he went on, "fortunately we're usually far enough apart that those things don't happen too often. Dad's at home in Connecticut, planning and buying property. Will comes in with his crew to build the hotels; then I take over to get the house on its feet. Hopefully."

"And your mother?"

"She runs around checking on everybody. She's due here anytime. I haven't seen her since Boston."

"Boston?"

"That's where I was before I came here."

Boston, she thought. Three thousand miles away. Aloud she asked casually, "So you really do move around a lot?"

He replied as casually. "A lot. I spent almost two years in Seattle. That's the longest I've ever been anywhere since I joined the business."

"How do you stand it?"

He gave a shrug that said it wasn't difficult. "It's what I do. I move in, hire staff, get everybody whipped into shape and try to establish the house as part of the community. Then it's time to move on."

"I would hate that," Randy said with feeling.

"You've never done it," he pointed out. And as she began to protest that she had, he qualified his statement. "I know. You were shoved around a lot as a child, but that's not the same as going where you're welcome with an entourage of friends, watching a hotel come alive under your direction and making new friends along the way. It's very exciting."

"Entourage of friends?"

"David comes with me to start a new kitchen, Katie Kaufman to establish an efficient desk, Bob Harper to set up our books. The four of us have done three other hotels together—Dallas, Seattle and Boston."

"What about their families? Don't they mind the separations?"

"David's wife and two sons are with him now in their own suite, Katie's married to a pilot who says he doesn't care where she goes as long as he can find her when he comes in, and Bob's single." He grinned. "He loves being able to cover the country with his charm."

Though she was interested in his gypsy life, it held no appeal for her personally. Randy poured more tea for herself. "What about when you're not building a hotel? Where do you live then?"

"We have an estate in Connecticut."

"And you all live there?"

"In shifts. Will and I are there with Mom when Dad's out buying new sites. Then Will meets Dad, and they begin the project together. Dad comes home, Will and I manage the details; and when it's built, I take over, and Will goes home. We're usually together for Christmas and birthdays."

Christmas. Christmas was always hard for Randy. And she couldn't recall the last time she'd had a birthday cake.

"My uncle and two of my cousins are also involved in the administration of the corporation." He offered her the plate of cookies, and when she would have taken a spritz, he pulled the plate out of her reach. She looked up at him in surprise, and he grinned. "That's the last one, and I like those."

Mercilessly, Randy snatched it up. But instead of popping it into her mouth, she balanced her cup carefully on her knees and broke the cookie in half. She held half out to Mallory.

"A Solomon-like solution," he applauded. "And that about covers my family history. Want to tell me about yours?"

He spoke the question easily, too easily, Randy thought. He seemed to sense that she rarely discussed her background.

"My what?" she evaded.

"Your family."

She shrugged, staring into her cup. She lowered her knees and took a slow sip. "I told you about all there is to tell."

"What was your mother like?" he asked.

She sighed, leaning her head back against the pillows, trying to think. She had put the woman out of her mind long ago, and dredging up a mental image was difficult.

"She was tall," Randy said, closing her eyes, trying to get the memory of her mother in focus. "And blond and kind of pretty. She was a waitress."

"How did she treat you?" Mallory asked quietly.

"Oh..." Randy had to think about that, too. That had hurt at the time, and it was something else she had put out of her mind. "Not badly. Sort of like...a friend." Then her voice hardened, and she put her cup of tea aside. "Actually... more like a casual acquaintance. I wasn't ignored or abused, just kept at a clinical distance. And when she found a man who wanted her but didn't want me—" she looked at Matt with a hard expression that was intended to tell him that it didn't matter but told him something else entirely "—she...just walked away."

He returned her look levelly, making no judgments. "How old were you?"

"Nine years old." She continued to talk, now plagued by the memory. "I remember her taking me to a big office." As she heard herself speak the words, she was suddenly back in time, standing in the middle of that office. She closed her eyes as emotion welled up in her. She had not cried that day all those years ago, and she hadn't cried over her mother since. But suddenly the hurt and the terrible anxiety she had felt came back to her as though it were all happening now. She could see the back of her mother's blond hair, with its long, shiny waves, and the belted back of her red vinyl jacket and blue jeans.

"A woman came out of a closed office and took my hand," Randy said, her voice strained, "and my mother just walked away. I stared at her while she walked all the way across that long office, and she never turned around once to look at me. No sad smile, no parting wave, no...nothing."

Randy looked up at Matt, and for the first time he saw—really saw—what it must have been like for her.

"There was nothing," she said as though the surprise were fresh, "to indicate that she was sorry."

Matt moved to the side of the bed, his eyes filled with sympathy and anger. He put gentle hands on her forearms.

"You've got to put that behind you, Randy," he said quietly.

She shook her head in puzzlement, surprised by her own anguish. "I thought I had."

He framed her face in his hands and looked into her brimming eyes. "I think you've pushed it down, but you haven't pushed it away."

Her voice rose in impatience and distress. "What am I supposed to do?" she demanded. "It happened to me. It's part of me."

"I know," he said gently, his hands stroking up and down her arms, cold now in the light silk blouse. "Let the experience be a part of you—you can't change that. But let the anger go. Look at it, Randy. Remember the picture you just told me about. Remember her walking away from you."

She made a gesture of denial, drawing away from him. But he was stronger and shook her lightly.

"Randy, please," he said quietly. "Look at that picture in your mind."

It came back to her, though Randy willed it not to. She watched her mother walk away while typewriters tapped and telephones rang and people in the office talked and laughed together. She recalled the anguish she felt, the utter terror, and the dignity that controlled her even then and wouldn't let her cry.

"She was a weak and selfish woman, and she walked out of your life." Matt's voice pierced the nightmare she relived. "She's gone, Randy. You are all that remains of that ugly scene, and you're intelligent and successful and beautiful. All that remains of that awful day is you." He shook her again, and she opened her eyes to look into his. They seemed to be grieving for her, yet somehow applauding her at the same time. "That must put you right up there with diamonds as one of the most enduring substances known to man. You're someone very special, Randy."

"Then how," she asked, as she had asked herself a million times, "could she have done that?"

"I can't even hazard a guess," he admitted, an undercurrent of anger in his quiet words. "But it was a flaw in her, not in you."

She drew a deep, steadying breath, trying to hold back the tears that were gathering in her throat. She didn't understand what was happening to her. Over the years she had dispassionately thought about her abandonment a hundred times. Perhaps the difference was that she had never brought her mother into focus before, never mentally confronted her with the unspeakable cruelty of what she had done.

Tears began to spill, and she looked at Matt in surprise, lifting a helpless shoulder as though to say, "I can't explain what's happening to me."

He pulled her into his arms and rocked her gently back and forth.

Tears were streaming down her face now in a grief too deep for sobs. "I wanted her to turn around and look at me!" she wept.

"I know. I know." He rubbed her back and continued to rock her, encouraging her to cry and let out her anger.

Randy had never wept in anyone's arms. Al and Donna Curtis, her foster parents, had loved her, and she had laughed in their arms, but she had never cried. A part of her was vaguely surprised by that realization. And, strangely, safely held against Matt's shoulder, she did not feel embarrassed, only comforted and understood.

She finally drew in a ragged breath and pulled away. Matt handed her a handkerchief. "What happened after that?"

Randy felt drained and calm and able to relate the awful years that followed without emotion. "There were a dozen houses in a dozen towns that never became home because I wasn't there long enough. There were as many schools with loud, happy kids, but I was never part of them, because I came to town in a state of Oregon car." She smiled thinly. "I was different, and kids don't like that. And I was skinny and had this hair. They weren't really cruel to me, just . . . just wary. And I was quiet and scared, so that didn't help much. Then pretty soon it was into another car and off to another house, another school. . . ." She shook her head, remembering that it had always seemed to be raining during those rides, the landscape grim to match her mood and her prospects.

"When did you come to the Curtises?"

"I was fourteen years old." She smiled, not so thinly this time. "Al came to the front door with a wrench and a greasy rag in his hand. Donna came up behind him, wiping her hands on her apron. Something clicked between us. I don't know what it was. Maybe because they didn't have any other kids and for the first time in my life someone concentrated on me. They liked me. Suddenly my life established a pattern all the other kids' lives followed. I made friends. There were other kids who wanted to do things with me. We'd go fishing or to the movies or to the pier to watch the boats. I found my niche in Scannon Cove." She paused, then added feelingly, "I think I'd die if I ever left there." Then she yawned, unaware of the look in the eyes of the man who watched her.

Matt eased her back onto her pillow and brushed the hair out of her eyes, smiling. "Sleepy?"

She felt unutterably weary. "Very." Her brow furrowed, and she sighed. "I talked too much, didn't I?"

"No," Matt said firmly. "You talked enough. Feel any better?"

She closed her eyes and analyzed the question. No, she concluded, she did not feel better. But she didn't feel worse, either. She just felt tired.

"No, I just feel sort of . . . empty."

"You need a good night's sleep." Matt pulled the blankets up to her chin. "I'll leave the connecting door open between us. If you need anything, just call me." He turned the light out, then moved the tea tray to the dresser.

"Matt?" Randy called.

He came back to the bed and leaned down to her. Even as close as he was, she couldn't discern his features in the dark, with the only light coming from behind him through the open door to his room. She put a hand up and connected with his solid upper arm. She squeezed it gently.

"I'm not sure what to say," she whispered.

His teeth flashed in a smile. "Good night seems appropriate."

She swatted that strong forearm. "You know what I mean."

"Yes, I do." He leaned down to kiss her forehead. "There's nothing that has to be said. Except good night."

She sighed, surprised to discover that the empty feeling in her had been replaced by contentment. "Good night, Matthew."

"Good night, Miranda."

Chapter Four

Under the shower the following morning, Randy tried to decide whether she had dreamed that discussion with Matt Mallory last night about her mother or it had really happened. But she felt emotionally bruised this morning, a little withdrawn and wary. It had happened.

The confounding thing was that a host of trained caseworkers had tried to force the past out of her. Half of the foster mothers she had lived with had tried to make her talk about her natural mother. And Al Curtis had told her once, while she'd helped him service his airplane, that hate was a canker that would eat you from the inside out. But only Mallory had been able to bring the past out of her over a pot of tea in a strange hotel room. Panic rose in her, quickening her heartbeat. What was happening to her?

While drying herself off and brushing her wild hair with the small folding comb/brush in her purse, Randy wondered how Matt would behave this morning. Would he wear a knowing look that presumed he knew all about her because she had divulged a painful part of her past? Or would he be embarrassed because she had shared more than he wanted to hear?

She had her answer fifteen minutes later when he knocked on the partially open door that joined their rooms. Her suit looked relatively fresh considering the long day it had put in yesterday, and her blouse was primly buttoned to the neck. With fresh makeup and her hair brushed to a fine burnish, she pulled the door open, her expression daring him to bring up last night's events.

But his eyes went over her with a flirtatious warmth and the irrepressible good humor that was so typical of him. Her aggression melted.

"If you came with a pat of butter, a pitcher of syrup and a side of sausage," he said, taking her hand and pulling her toward the outer door, "I'd stop and nibble on your ear. But you're empty-handed. So nothing is going to stop me from eating the biggest stack of pancakes this side of the Rockies."

"You know," he said an hour later as the waitress cleared away their dishes and poured more coffee, "we should get you something to commemorate our stay in Portland."

Her sage-green eyes were uncertain. "Why?"

He leaned toward her conspiratorially. "Because you've been away from Scannon Cove for almost twenty-four hours. Considering your attitude about the place, that's probably a record and maybe even a turning point in your life."

"Really?" she asked skeptically.

He nodded. "I think it's a step toward your emotional maturity as a woman. Now you can see that you don't have to cling to places, people or buildings to make them yours." He glanced at his watch. "We've got an hour and a half before we have to pick up the car. I think we should buy you a dress."

"A dress!" she said in horror. "Mallory..."

"A dress," he insisted. "And since I'm the giver of the gift, I get to pick it out for you."

"Mallory—" she began again, shaking her head.

"And," he interrupted, "call me Matt. You say 'Mallory' as if you're one of the guys, but when you call me 'Matt' in that husky voice of yours, delicious fantasies race through my mind."

Randy swallowed, unconsciously fanning her blush with her napkin. "The only fantasy I have is to separate you from a large chunk of your yearly income and put you on the road in my Flambeau."

He shook his head in resignation. "You're going to separate me from my sanity. Let's go."

AFTER FINDING the downtown Frederick and Nelson Department Store, Matt led her through the cosmetics and handbags to the lush racks of women's clothes. He waved a disparaging hand at a display of tailored silk blouses, saying grimly, "You've got enough of those."

They passed slacks, shirts, blazers and sweaters until he found the wall rack of dresses.

"May I help you?" A gorgeous blonde who looked like a *Cosmopolitan* magazine cover appeared at Matt's shoulder.

He turned to her and gave her a warm smile. "Yes, please. We'd like a dress for the lady." He reached back and drew a reluctant Randy forward.

The young woman, whose badge said she was Rayanne, looked up and down at Randy's gray suit and gestured back toward the tailored blouses. "Perhaps—" she began.

"No!" Matt said firmly. "A dress. Something feminine."

Rayanne looked at Randy doubtfully, and Randy gave her the look that she reserved for customers who offered her three thousand dollars less than the automobile of their dreams was worth.

Rayanne turned back to Matt. "Color?"

He turned to look at Randy consideringly. "I don't know. That's supposed to be a problem for redheads, isn't it?"

"No," the clerk said authoritatively. "Not anymore. She'd probably look dynamite in lavender."

"Lavender!" To Randy, who always wore brown, blue or black, the very thought of that color gave her chills. And extending the mental image to lavender ruffles almost sent her into a swoon.

"Matt," she argued reasonably, "please don't waste money on something that I'll never wear. I..."

But he was looking through the rack with Rayanne, neither of them listening to Randy. Then Rayanne pulled out a dress the color of heather. It was shapeless on the hanger, and it appeared to Randy that it would not cover her adequately above the waist. A deep ruffle ran diagonally from the left shoulder to the right side of the waist. Across from the ruffle was nothing. "What do you think?"

"You're not buying me a dress that isn't all there," she said.

He grimaced at her. "You're the only thing that isn't all there. Try it on."

"Matt—" She was interrupted by his frown of disapproval.

"Please," he said, holding the hanger out to her. "Humor me."

Sagging defeatedly, sure that she would hate it, Randy took the garment into the dressing room. Rayanne helped her shrug the ruffle into place, pulling the dress down when Randy tried to cover the swell of a breast with the delicate fabric.

"You haven't got enough to worry about," the clerk said. Then, glancing up into Randy's wounded expression, she added with a smile, "I didn't mean it that way. I meant that it's a perfect fit; you're supposed to expose just a little. I'm sure he'll like it."

The dress was all there, Randy realized, looking in the full-length mirror. And it had a curious way of pointing out that she was all there, too. Her ivory shoulder presented an interesting angle in contrast to the soft drama of the ruffle running diagonally across her chest. The softly draped skirt halted at her knees and made her trim legs look fragile.

Rayanne fluffed out Randy's hair and pushed her toward the counter where they had left Matt. "Go show him."

Randy was surprised to find herself nervous, wanting Matt to like her in the dress.

He was lounging against a rack of jackets when Randy emerged. She was suddenly reminded of the day she had first met him, when she walked toward him across the showroom floor at her dealership.

Stopping several feet away from him, she spread graceful arms out and did a balletic turn. "What do you think of our lavender model?" she asked, mimicking the first words she had ever spoken to him.

"Good-looking," he replied with a grin, obviously recalling the same encounter. "Might be just what I was looking for."

Randy lowered her eyes from his penetrating look.

"You don't think it's too..." A wave of her hand at the top of the dress brought a smile from him and an instant shake of his head.

"Not at all." Then he said to Rayanne, "We'll take it."

Randy returned to the dressing room, wriggled out of the filmy lavender garment and handed it to Rayanne. Then she slipped into her conservative skirt and blouse. Her hands were shaking. Matthew Mallory was getting too close. In the past eighteen years, Randy had steered carefully clear of situations in which she would find herself vulnerable. Yet here she was, liking this man more than she cared to, reacting to him both emotionally and physically and wanting him to react to her.

She recalled how his eyes had slipped over her body only a moment ago when she had done a turn before him in the dress. Something from their clear blue depths had touched her, finding the woman she guarded inside herself. It was with the same gentle ease with which he had located the bruised little girl within her last night.

Matthew Mallory knew the real Miranda Stanton, and that was scary.

Matt noticed the shadow that had slipped over Randy's mood as they walked to Rose City Motors at 10:45 a.m. There was panic in her eyes and a little suspicion when she looked at him. She needed distance, he guessed, before she could understand what was happening between them. Patience, he thought dryly, was going to be the story of their relationship.

The manager apologized profusely and offered to pay their hotel bill.

"I've taken care of it," Matt insisted.

"But it was all our fault that you had to stay over."

"Perhaps," he agreed with the most suggestive glance at Randy. "But we made the most of it, anyway."

Horrified, Randy looked from Matt to the older man, who was smiling.

"Glad to hear it," the manager said. "Take care."

With a flushed face, Randy got into the car and slammed the door. Matt slid into the passenger side and observed her crimson cheeks with a bland expression. *Keep your distance,* he told himself, resisting the impulse to pull her to him and kiss away her indignation.

"Why did you do that?" she demanded angrily.

"What?"

"Let him think we had . . . made the most of it."

"Didn't we?" he asked innocently. "The movie was fun. We had a nice talk—"

"But he thought . . ." Randy turned away from him in irritation and started the motor. "Never mind."

As Randy pulled out onto the busy street, Matt leaned back against the headrest and closed his eyes.

He had been pleased to note that there had been a flush of excitement behind the indignant color in her cheeks and a little bit of a thrill in her angry glare, as though she hadn't really minded being thought of as his, even if she did feel obliged to protest.

Halfway to Scannon Cove, Randy pulled over in front of a coffee shop. She was tired, and every muscle in her body ached from tension.

"Mind if we stop for coffee?" she asked Matt. He had thrown his suitcoat into the back of the wagon and rolled his sleeves up. Wind that came through the open window had tossed his hair, and he smoothed it with his fingers.

"Of course not."

It was early afternoon now, and a young summer breeze perfumed the air. A random collection of old and new houses dotted the hilly south side of the main street on which they had parked. The commercial side of the street bordered the river, and a small fishing boat slid past them as they walked across the parking lot. Matt stopped to admire it.

"Pretty sight," he said when all that remained in view was the lacy wake.

"Oregon's a beautiful place."

He put an arm around her shoulders and led her toward the restaurant. "The world is full of beautiful places," he said.

"I like this one," Randy insisted.

He squeezed her shoulder. "I know."

Feeling somewhat restored by the hot coffee, Randy followed Matt back across the parking lot to the car and was surprised when he opened the passenger-side door and gestured her inside.

"I'll drive the rest of the way home," he said. "You look tired."

When Randy hesitated, he grinned reassuringly. "Don't worry. I won't wreck the wagon for you."

Before he had driven a mile, Randy was asleep.

When she awoke, she was being carried across the living room of her cottage. "What—?" she began to protest.

"The day's almost over, and you were fast asleep. I thought that I might as well bring you straight home. I know you didn't sleep well last night."

They had reached the bedroom, and he deposited her on top of her green-and-white bedspread.

"I should have gone to the shop," she complained.

"We did," he said. "I handed the papers for the car out to Gordie and told him that I was taking you home and would be back later with the wagon."

Great, she thought despondently. *We must have made a terrific picture returning home twenty-four hours late, with Matt behaving in his take-charge manner and me sound asleep in the front seat.*

"Thank you." Her gratitude was a little stiff. "I'll call you when your car is ready."

"Thanks. I'll be sticking close to the hotel, with my loaner still at the garage in Portland."

"I'm sorry. I just don't have anything else that's insured to let you use."

"It's all right. Do you think that it'll be more than a week before my car is ready?"

"No, we'll get on it as soon as the door arrives."

He nodded. "See you, Randy."

She waved halfheartedly as he headed for the living room and the front door. Sitting in the middle of her bed as the sound of the station wagon's motor died away, Randy wondered why she was angry at Matt. Was it because he had brought her home instead of taking her to the shop or because he hadn't mentioned last night's conversation except to say they'd had a nice talk? Of course, even though she did share her most private feelings with him, she saw no future in their relationship. So it didn't matter if his attitude seemed suddenly a little casual, a little cavalier? Did it?

IT WAS EARLY MORNING in the middle of the following week, and Randy was trying to double-check the figures on a payment schedule Eldon had prepared. She was impeded by the presence of Vivian, who had perched on the edge of her desk.

"Well, what did you do?" the woman demanded outright after ten minutes of circuitous questions hadn't produced any answers.

"We traded a sedan for a wagon," Randy replied, putting figures into her calculator.

"I mean," Vivian clarified impatiently, "what did you do...at night?"

Randy smiled at the calculator, her attention drifting. "Went to a movie."

"And?"

"Had popcorn and a cola."

"And?"

"We spent the night at the Benson."

Vivian was beside herself with excitement. "That romantic place? Then what happened?"

"Then..." Randy came back to the present, giving Vivian a wry look. "We got naked and sprayed each other with whipped cream. Viv, I have work to do."

The bookkeeper closed her eyes and shook her head. "Randy, Randy, Randy," she said as though enumerating three of the four Horsemen of the Apocalypse. "Do you realize that you're pushing thirty and you've never had a serious relationship?"

"I'm twenty-seven!" Randy corrected.

"Before you know it, you'll be forty with nothing to show for it."

"Viv..."

"You're gorgeous, and you're a fairly successful businesswoman, but you're an embarrassment to our sex!"

"Because I haven't begun an affair with a man who's going to be gone in a year?" Randy threw her pencil down, her green eyes snapping at her friend.

"Because you won't let a man into your life to care about you. You, Randy Stanton," Vivian said, poking her shoulder with a pearlescent fingernail, "are an engine without spark plugs!"

Randy fell back into her chair and closed her eyes, trying to blot out the normal workday confusion going on around her. But the thought that struck her in the brief moment in which she was able to concentrate was that an engine without spark plugs is a dead engine.

Then the telephone rang, and knowing that Vivian couldn't have reached her office yet, Randy picked it up. "Stanton Motors."

"Hello, Randy."

The masculine voice that had haunted her thoughts and lived in her memories now brought her upright in her chair.

"Hello, Mallory," she said, forcing a note of coolness to her voice, annoyed at him for being so important to her.

"Matt," he corrected.

"Hello, Matt."

She waited tensely for him to state his business. Was he about to invite her to dinner? Had he found some excuse for them to meet?

"Is my car ready?" he asked.

Randy fought to keep her irritation from crossing the telephone line to him. She pretended to cough to disguise the disappointment that replaced her little flight of hope.

"The door hasn't arrived yet," she said without the regret she should have expressed to an unhappy customer.

"You said it wouldn't be a week. Tomorrow it'll be a week."

"I don't control the factory. I didn't think that it would take this long, but apparently it will."

"Meanwhile I'm without transportation," he said with a calmness that held an undercurrent of impatience.

"I can put you in a new Flambeau for a very low down payment," she said with exaggerated sweetness.

"Is the loaner back from Portland yet?" he asked, ignoring her sales pitch.

"Yes."

"Can I have it?"

"Sure. You can pick it up anytime."

There was a pause during which she could almost hear him counting to ten. "I'd appreciate it if someone from your dealership would bring it out to the hotel."

"I can't spare anyone today," she said lightly. "Sorry."

Another pause. "Couldn't you bring it?"

"No."

A sigh. "Very well," he said. "I'll be by for it tomorrow morning."

"I'll be out, but Gordie will see that it's ready for you." Randy slammed the receiver down into its cradle. She hated herself for thinking he had called about something personal and for feeling excited at that possibility.

Across town in Scannon Cove, in the administrative office of the Cove Mallory, Matt leaned back in his leather chair and smiled over his orange juice. She had sounded very irritated. Could it be that he was getting to her, that his plan to give her distance was beginning to have an effect? He could only hope that eight days without seeing or hearing from him was making her as edgy as it was making him. He saw her in his mind's eye day and night and hoped that one day soon this nonrelationship they shared would take a positive turn.

Matt downed his orange juice and went back to his paperwork.

Chapter Five

Kurt Daniels, chairman of the Scannon Cove Downtown Development Committee, called Randy Thursday morning.

"We've got a new member joining us tonight," he said. Daniels was a mortician, and Randy always thought that he fit the role as though Hollywood had cast him in it. He was gaunt and pale and had a voice like Peter Lorre's.

"That's good news," Randy enthused. "I hope he's one for our side and not Mr. Grissom's."

Sam Grissom owned a men's clothing store and wanted nothing to change in Scannon Cove. With a well-established clientele of local professional people, he hadn't experienced the ups and downs faced by most of the local merchants who depended on a waning consumer market. With logging and fishing practically halted by legislation, canneries and lumber mills, once the backbone of the coastal and riverfront towns in Oregon, had all closed down or moved away.

The other half of the committee, spearheaded by Daniels and strongly supported by Randy, was trying hard to encourage the redevelopment of an old block by the riverfront that was owned by the city. The vision was that of an exclusive little mall that would attract local shoppers and those from the large metropolitan area across the river in Washington.

Grissom envisioned a multilevel parking structure instead.

"It's a little hard to tell," Daniels said. "He's very much his own man. But he's got a good reputation both personally and professionally. If we can get him working on our side, it's said that he has the Midas touch in everything he does."

"Who...is it?" Randy felt a little stab of alarm.

"Matt Mallory," Daniels replied predictably, "Manager of the new hotel. By the way, could you pick him up for the meeting, Randy? His car is in the shop, and he said he'd take a cab, but that wouldn't be very hospitable of us."

"Sure," Randy agreed halfheartedly.

"If it's a problem..." Daniels began, obviously catching her tone.

"Not at all," she said more firmly. "I'll be glad to pick him up."

"Good. Perhaps you'd better call him."

Randy suppressed a sigh. "Perhaps I'd better. See you tonight."

Apparently busy, Matt was courteous but abrupt on the telephone.

"I'll be by to pick you up for the Downtown Committee meeting," Randy said, her own tone brisk.

"What time?"

"Seven-fifteen?"

"I'll be ready."

A very disappointing conversation, Randy thought with a frown as she hung up the phone, though she couldn't imagine why she had hoped for more or why she missed the bantering that had marked their meetings in the past.

Working late to close a deal for Phillips, she had a bare fifteen minutes to change clothes. Randy shuffled through her blouses and finally decided on simply changing the one she wore for a pale yellow one that Vivian had given her for Christmas. It had an embroidered neckline and cuffs, and Randy had found little opportunity to wear it.

She shrugged into it quickly now and was surprised to find herself pleased with the way it looked. The fit was perfect. It did make her hair appear more carroty, she thought, but donning her black jacket would soften that. Vaguely wondering why she was taking such pains with her appearance, she ran a brush through her hair, then raced out to her car.

She pulled up in front of the hotel's large double-glass doors to find Matt standing outside, laughing with a bellman. When Matt saw her, he clapped the other man on the shoulder and sprinted across to her.

"Nice of you to pick me up," he said, slamming his door as she pulled away.

"Kurt Daniels asked me to," she felt obliged to tell him, her voice a little breathless.

"And I thought it was all your idea," he said, grinning wickedly. "Pretty blouse."

Why she blushed so profusely she couldn't understand. Except that she felt as though he'd seen right through her and guessed that she'd chosen it because she'd be seeing him.

She pulled up at a stoplight, and he took the opportunity to cup her head in one large hand and turn her face toward him. Her eyes were wide and wary as he looked into them.

"That color puts a sparkle in your eyes," he said, suddenly sober. "And in your hair. You look like you're trapped in a moonbeam."

Would being trapped in a moonbeam make one breathless? she wondered. She sensed the light change to green and accelerated. But she was still looking into Matt's face—into the warm silver in his eyes and the unusual seriousness there.

Then his smile flashed, and he grabbed the steering wheel to correct her course. Horrified that she had been staring at him instead of the road ahead, Randy brushed his hand aside and resumed control—of the steering wheel, at least.

The meeting went pretty much as Randy had expected it would. She sat back in her seat in quiet frustration as Grissom summed up the arguments that had been waged for the parking structure during the past hour and a half.

"City, county and hospital personnel take up most of the downtown area parking. We merchants and our customers have to park blocks away from the shopping area. As hilly as Scannon Cove is, that's a serious—in some cases even unhealthy—inconvenience for the older members of our community. And with the city determined to make the bulk of its revenue from parking meters, the problem is compounded. If you do find a parking place downtown and don't plug the meter, you get a ticket. If you find a convenient spot and plug it all day, you still get a ticket for overparking. I move that we make a decision tonight in favor of asking the city council to put up a parking structure at Scannon Square."

His piece spoken, the tall, slender man in the three-piece suit sat down. A few "here, here's" echoed in the room throughout the twenty or so members in attendance.

Randy rolled her eyes at Daniels, then turned to Matt, who sat at the far end of their long table, and found him watching her. Although it was difficult to tell how he felt, she admired him for keeping a low profile the first time he met with this warring group.

She, however, had no intention of remaining silent.

"Mr. Chairman." Randy stood to face Kurt Daniels. "Instead of solving our parking problems, which are difficult, though not impossible to deal with, I think we should do something to stimulate revenue in the area. With a parking structure, the builder is the only one who prospers. If we save the block and put in a mall filled with shops and a restaurant with a view of the river, we'll not only renew interest in shopping locally among our own residents, but also draw people from across the river in Fairview, Washington."

Grissom leaned back in his chair, dismissing her argument with a wave of his hand. "Fairview has everything they need."

"But Oregon has no sales tax. And nobody minds traveling a little farther to find something special, something that he or she doesn't have to pay tax on."

"And where," he asked arrogantly, "will all these shoppers park?"

"It's right across from the fairgrounds," Randy replied, her voice calm and polite.

"What happens when the fairgrounds are in use?"

"During the summer for one week it's filled to capacity. Then there's an occasional one-day flea market. Otherwise it's empty. I think that problem can be dismissed."

"We're looking at an expensive proposition," one of the other members offered.

"True," Randy agreed. "But no more expensive than having the block torn down and putting up a parking structure. And it'll generate revenue and interest. I'll bet I could line up six tenants for it tonight."

"And who would renovate it?"

"Bill Berger is interested," she lied. He was interested but admitted to Randy that he hadn't enough capital to begin such a venture. But she would find someone.

"Bill Berger is broke!" Grissom said with a careless laugh. The rude remark was typical of his self-absorption.

"You know what it can do to your cash flow when customers don't pay their bills on time," Randy said casually and with a sweet but meaningful glance his way.

It was common knowledge that Berger had remodeled Grissom's store. Everyone who dealt with Grissom knew he paid his bills slowly despite apparent affluence.

He blustered some reply, and Kurt Daniels stood.

"I'd like to see us consider commercial growth instead of expanding parking. Not only would the mall that Randy's proposing be more eye appealing than a parking structure; it would preserve an important part of Scannon Cove history."

"God!" Grissom grumbled. "We've got a maritime museum, a historic house and a city and courthouse that date back to 1873. What more do we need?"

"A little history right downtown might bring people here." Randy sighed and pleadingly looked around the table. "That block has been an eyesore since I came here as a teenager, and probably long before that. We're all agreed that something should be done about the area. Wouldn't it be better to use that beautiful river frontage for a place people could use and enjoy rather than a place that they would walk away from after parking their cars?''

Silence. Members looked at each other; some appeared to consider her suggestion, while others looked at Grissom, waiting for him to express an opinion.

''I think it's foolish to even consider it when we need parking so badly,'' he said, his self-important manner evident as he looked over the members at the table.

''If we don't do something to revitalize the downtown area,'' Randy argued, ''there won't be any cars to park anywhere. People staying at Mr. Mallory's hotel will go shopping in Fairview, Washington, instead of their residents coming here to shop.''

The meeting ended in a stalemate, but Kurt Daniels considered that a victory.

''We've still got a chance,'' he said, patting Randy's sagging shoulders as they walked out to the parking lot. ''Let's try to line up a builder on speculation and see if we can get at least a verbal commitment from some merchants.''

''Bill Berger *is* broke,'' she admitted quietly.

''I know,'' Daniels said. ''But there must be a builder out there with enough financial backing to want to work with us.''

''Okay.'' Randy forced a smile. ''I'll see if I can line up some shopkeepers. Can you work on the builder?''

''Sure.'' He reached out for Matt's handshake. ''Good to meet you, Mallory. Hope that you'll join our fight for the square.''

''I'll see if I can get Miss Stanton to fill me in on some background information.''

''Good idea.''

Daniels waved, and Randy and Matt continued across the parking lot to her car.

On the way back to the hotel, Randy stared pensively at the road.

"Could you really line up six merchants tonight?" Matt asked, moving into his usual sideways staring position. But tonight she didn't care.

"Easily" was her absent reply.

"What'll you do for a builder?"

She shrugged. "Kurt will think of something."

"What if Grissom tries to bulldoze his parking structure through in the meantime."

"He still has to have half of the votes on his side."

"I was watching the field tonight," he said. "Some of your team members are a little shaky, and all of Grissom's people are afraid of him."

"I know." She sighed heavily and turned into the driveway of the hotel. "I just keep hoping I'll hit a sensitive nerve in somebody; it'll only take one person to turn the vote around. Well, here you are. Thanks for taking an interest."

He made no move to leave the car. "Would you join me for a drink?"

She shook her head, glancing at her watch, suddenly nervous. "Thanks, but I have to be up early in the morning."

"It's only ten o'clock," he coaxed. "And I'd like to hear more about that notorious block."

Randy looked at him suspiciously. "Why?"

"As a new member of the committee, I have to make an intelligent decision when it finally comes up for a vote."

"I'm afraid I'll present a very biased side."

"I assumed that." He smiled, and Randy kept a firm hold of the steering wheel. "I noticed you've laid some interesting groundwork to get me to vote on your side already.''

Perplexed by his remark, Randy frowned at him. ''What do you mean?''

''Thanks to Stanton Motors,'' he said dryly, ''I have nothing to park.''

Randy's laughter rang out in the dark confines of the car, and Matt watched her with a contemplative smile. Behind them a driver honked his horn impatiently.

''You're blocking the driveway,'' Matt pointed out. ''Pull into that space and let's have a drink.''

Randy did as he asked, trying to ignore the gentle grip of his fingers on her elbow as they walked up the hotel steps.

In the lobby Matt led her toward the elevators instead of the lounge.

''Where are we going?'' she asked.

''My suite,'' he replied.

Randy's heartbeat accelerated as she passed him to step through the parting elevator doors, and she was having difficulty breathing again.

Matt Mallory's suite was everything one would expect of the room occupied by the manager of one of the country's largest hotel chains.

Here was not the Spartan simplicity often found in a single man's surroundings but a lot of soft green and gold colors, touches of red and muted browns. There were plants, polished oak tables, bookcases and a coach lantern hanging on a swag chain.

''You're a romantic,'' Randy said in surprise, looking around the suite herself.

He frowned at her quizzically as he picked up the telephone.

"You hadn't guessed that already? Sit down. Hi, John. Would you send up..." He paused, looking at Randy in question.

"Gin and tonic," she supplied.

"A gin and tonic," Matt repeated into the phone. "And a Scotch. And would you check with the kitchen and see if there's any of that cheesecake left that I saw David working on this afternoon? Thanks."

As Matt pulled off his jacket, he crossed the room to turn on the stereo and adjust the lighting to a low but warm glow. Then, throwing his jacket on a chair, he joined Randy on the sofa. She smiled at him, her hands folded quietly in her lap. Inside, her heart was beating like a trip-hammer.

Matt sat facing her, seeing apprehension in her eyes and trying not to notice. Warmth spread to his limbs as he studied those wary cat's eyes. The vibrating thud of his heart and her torch of silken hair made him tell himself firmly to slow down. He had time.

"So fill me in on this project of yours. I don't remember noticing anything special along the riverfront," he said, striking a casual attitude, letting his arm rest on the back of the sofa between her and himself.

"It wouldn't stop your eye like Victorian spindles and fretwork, although it's from the same period. It's one enormous brick building that has been vacated for forty years. About ten years ago the city bought it to save it for its historical value but has never gotten around to doing anything with it. Anyway, what's happened there is fascinating." Randy shifted to adjust her jacket, suddenly feeling warm.

"Let me hang that up for you," Matt said, standing to help her out of it.

"I'm fine, really."

"Your cheeks are flushed."

Rather than let him suspect that her color was high because she was nervous, she stood to let him slip the jacket from her shoulders.

Then a knock sounded on the door.

"Come in!" Matt shouted as he disappeared into a corridor off the living room.

A young man in kitchen garb walked in with a tray bearing their drinks and two slices of cheesecake.

Randy groaned as Matt came back to the living room.

"Thanks, John," he said as the young man turned to the door. Then he smiled at Randy. "Don't look like that. Two million calories won't hurt you."

She gave him a teasing grimace. "You've got a bigger frame on which to hang all those calories."

Randy picked up a fork and dipped into the cake. The taste was indescribable. She rolled the bite on her tongue, trying to analyze the flavor.

"Orange and...?"

"Cappuccino," he said, sitting down again. "Shall I leave mine in case you want seconds?"

"That might be wise. Thank you," she said as she accepted her drink from him.

"So what's happened on the old block is fascinating." He prompted her to continue with her story.

She nodded. "It was built by a wealthy merchant at the turn of the century and was filled with all kinds of neat shops: a tobacconist, a corset shop..." She grinned at that, and captivated by her smile, Matt grinned back. He tried not to let her see the picture that was forming in his mind of Randy in just such a lacy confection. "It also had a stationer, a bakery, a chocolate shop, a bookstore...."

She stopped, realizing there was no point in continuing through the list. "Anyway, there was a fire in the thirties that destroyed a lot of the waterfront because there was no equipment then to fight the flames from the river side. The fire chief was dynamiting buildings to try to stop the fire from spreading. But the owner of the square and his sons stood on all four corners of their building with shotguns, refusing to let anyone near it. The fire was finally stopped about a block short of Scannon Square."

"Scannon," Matt said consideringly. "Was that the name of the merchant?"

Her smile flashed again, and Matt decided that he could become addicted to it.

"Scannon was Meriwether Lewis's dog."

He arched an eyebrow. "Dog," he repeated. "This town was named after a dog?"

"Scannon was a beautiful Newfoundland and was a real favorite with the Indians who fished and hunted here. They called this area Scannon's Place. So when Lewis and Clark marked their maps, the cove became Scannon's Cove because the expedition's mascot was so popular here."

He was smiling at her enthusiasm, and she lowered her lashes, striving for a less intimate mood between them.

"I had an engineer friend of mine look over the square, and he thought it was pretty sound structurally. It would need a lot of cosmetic work, of course, but that Italianate architecture is sturdy as well as interesting. I can just see it filled with bright shops, a restaurant, offices on the third level. With the colors that they used in the nineteenth century and bright awnings, I think it could be so appealing."

"If the city owns Scannon Square," Matt said, "what you're proposing would be too commercial a venture, wouldn't it?"

Randy shook her head. "I checked it out with the council. If we restore the outside, it will maintain its designation as a historic building, so we've saved a little history. The city can lease the building to a manager and use the proceeds for other city projects. Then we've made it pay its way. If I can just get our committee to agree, I'm sure we can get the city council to move on it."

Matt nodded thoughtfully. "I'll have to go take a look at the building for myself."

"Dress casually if you go. It's pretty messy inside."

"Speaking of dress," he said, resting his now empty plate on the coffee table, "I like your blouse. It's so feminine."

"It isn't functional," she said calmly, putting her cheesecake and drink aside because she could no longer breathe and eat at the same time.

"But it's so flattering," he said, his hand reaching out to tug at the ends of her hair. "It makes you look like a candle flame."

Randy looked back at Matt, unable to speak. No one had ever said anything that romantic to her before. Her face beamed as though there were truth to his comparison.

He smiled, and his hand moved from her hair to rest against her cheek. A corner of her mind not occupied with panic at his touch noted that it was pleasantly cool against her blushing face, soft yet full of a tensile energy that was strangely exciting.

"Mallory," she breathed, afraid to move. "What are you doing?"

"You have a silky complexion," he said, a finger moving to explore the contour of her chin and run the graceful arch of her neck.

"Mallory," she whispered.

"Matt," he corrected, that exploring fingertip playing havoc with the rim of her ear.

She swallowed. "Matt...stop." For the past week she had longed for him to call, prayed that he hadn't lost interest in her. Now that he was proving he hadn't, she was afraid.

"Why?" he asked distractedly. His fingers were combing into her hair again, causing a ripple of feeling along her scalp and down her spine.

"Because...it won't work."

"What?"

"Us."

"Hmm." His voice was thoughtful. "I feel it working already. Come here."

She wasn't sure whether she moved or his voyaging hand had scooped her over to him, but she found herself trapped against his chest by a pair of confining arms. Their pressure was gentle, but she was still unable to move.

Matt leaned back into the corner of the sofa and pulled her with him so that she lay along his body, her softness indented by his muscle.

"Why won't it work?" he asked absently.

"Because..." She found it hard to concentrate on the question. "You'll be...leaving."

"Sometimes," he said quietly, following the line of her eyebrow with his lips, "something that won't work in the long run will work for a shorter period of time."

Unable to make sense of that remark as his lips moved to her mouth, she concentrated on his kiss, its touching tenderness and its thrilling ardor.

When he drew away, she asked breathlessly, "For a . . . shorter time?"

"Mmm," he replied, suddenly fascinated by an eyelid. "Until I leave."

"You mean," Randy suggested, leaning her head back to look into his eyes, "a short affair?"

His blue eyes were watchful, waiting, as he pulled slightly away. "Yes."

She pulled her arms up between them and pushed against his chest. She was disappointed, and though she knew that made no sense, she couldn't help it.

"What's the point?" she asked grimly.

"The point is," he explained patiently, "that for the time we've got we can make each other very happy."

She gave him a sad smile that dissolved his light, teasing mood and made him wonder if this added ploy to give her distance wasn't going to give him more distance than he wanted.

"Thanks, Mallory," she said, pushing against him until he let her go. She slipped into the shoes she had kicked off when he drew her into his arms. "My life has been a long series of short affairs. I had an all too brief relationship with my mother, remember, and with a whole series of foster families. I'm tired of relationships that end before I'm ready." She stood and tucked in the tail of her yellow blouse.

Matt unfolded to his feet. "I can't offer you anything permanent when I'm moving on in a year or so. You've made that clear."

"I know." She turned away to the corridor down which he had disappeared with her jacket. Randy halted at a half-open door, and finding a bathroom, continued down the hall until she found a large bedroom at the end of it. She went straight to the closet and slid one door aside.

"Are you planning to leave the hotel in disguise?" Matt asked from the doorway as she faced a rack that was filled with men's shirts, pants and jackets.

She spun around, her anger mounting, ready to explode at any minute. "Where is my jacket?"

He pointed behind her as he moved toward her. "On the valet."

Randy turned and found her jacket hanging neatly on the hanger back of his dressing bench. She snatched it off, shrugged into it and started for the door, her blood now running like a swollen river.

Matt stood at the foot of the bed, obstructing her exit.

"Feel better," he asked, his expression unreadable but still unsettling to her as he ran a finger along her lapel, "now that you've got your armor on again?"

She moved as though she would knock him down, and he caught her forearms. "Don't get physical or you'll hurt someone, Randy."

"Then move out of my way," she ordered quietly.

"Calm down, Miranda. You're going to self-destruct in a minute. This fight isn't my fault, you know."

"Then whose is it?" she demanded, her hands in fists at her sides. "Why couldn't you be a plumber or a city employee or a fisherman? No, you've got to be some high roller from across the country who moves from place to place like some damned circus!"

He folded his arms and frowned at her. "I wish I had my lion tamer with me."

"Don't you dare be clever!" she shouted.

"You were going to tell me about Scannon Square," he reminded her, standing firm.

"Yes, I was." She angled her chin and drew a steadying breath. "And you took the opportunity to invite me into an affair. I'm sure ninety-nine percent of the world's women would be flattered to be offered a place in Matthew Mallory's bed, but this one will have to pass."

"And yet," he said, his lazy eyes wandering from her wildly disheveled hair to her beautiful legs, "you're the one standing at the foot of it."

"I also have found that life is filled with paradoxes when in your company. May I leave?"

He shifted his weight. "No. So, a relationship won't work for a long term, but what's wrong with a short one?"

She stabbed at his chest with her index finger. "I told you I didn't want to get involved with you, but you wouldn't listen, and now here we are..." She shrugged helplessly, and he nodded.

"Involved," he said. "So what have we got to lose?"

"Everything!" she screamed at him. "Take it from me. I won't fall in love with you just to have you leave me!"

"Then you'll have to build a long-term relationship with a man you can chain to the Scannon Cove city-limits sign!" he shouted back.

Randy started to cry, and Matt threw his head back in exasperation. She took that moment to race past him to the living room. She snatched her purse from the coffee table and ran to the door, yanking it open. She stopped abruptly, finding herself face-to-face with a short, plump, middle-aged woman. She had salt-and-pepper hair swept back in an elegant chignon, and she wore a full-length white mink. Her face was beautiful and curiously familiar.

From over Randy's shoulder, Matt said in surprise, "Hi, Mom." He pulled Randy back inside, then reached for his mother, pulling her in, too, as he closed the door.

"Mom, this is Miranda Stanton. Randy—my mother, Julia Mallory."

The woman was looking shrewdly from the angry snap in her son's eyes to the tears in Randy's. "Did I interrupt something?"

"No," Matt said lightly. "We were just screaming at each other."

"Oh." Julia nodded, looking Randy over and nodding again. "How can one trust mother nature," she asked conversationally, "when she gives you such a lovely face and body? And such hair!" She swung her small leather clutch at her son's midsection. "She's much too pretty for you to yell at."

Matt gasped dramatically. "She started it."

Julia Mallory turned to Randy. "Did you?"

Randy sighed. "I suppose so. Your son is a little hard to take sometimes, Mrs. Mallory. If you'll excuse me, I was just leaving."

"But I hope you're not leaving on my account," Julia said. "I can make myself scarce."

Matt looked down at his mother with a dry smile. "Don't fib, Mother. When you're around, it's like living in a blender."

"I really was leaving," Randy insisted, enjoying the way the small woman glared up at her son. "It was nice to meet you. It appears that all your son's personality problems must be your husband's fault and not yours."

Julia smiled. "I've always maintained that myself."

"Good night."

"Good night, Miranda."

Matt grinned at his mother as he pulled the door open. "Put the coffee on, would you, Mom. I'm going to walk Randy down to the parking lot."

"I can get down to the parking lot by myself," Randy said, feeling the rapid escape of her breath.

"I know. I just want to get you in an empty elevator." She turned to him in annoyance. "Matt . . ."

"Relax," he said. "I was kidding." In the hall he stabbed at the elevator button and leaned back against the wall to wait. "Will my car be ready tomorrow?"

A little surprised by his sudden change to a business-like attitude, Randy leaned against the wall on the opposite side of the hall. "Yes," she replied. "Late morning."

"Good." The elevator doors parted, and Matt held them open as Randy stepped inside. "Maybe you could give Jake tomorrow off?" he suggested with a grin.

She fought a smile. "I'll lock him in my office."

"I'd be eternally grateful."

The doors closed, and they stood several inches apart, leaning against the chrome handrail at the back of the car. If only things were different, she thought. There was such kindness in his face, such good humor.

He turned, feeling her gaze, and she saw wit and energy alive in his eyes. He was everything she wanted in a man, everything she could love, but his work required that he be mobile, and she never wanted to move from Scannon Cove. How thoughtless fate was to have placed them in each other's path.

"What is it?" he asked quietly.

In answer she moved closer. Placing one hand at the back of his head, she applied the barest pressure and reached up to meet his lips. She kissed him with the warmth she had felt upstairs in the apartment and the sadness she felt now at the realization that there could never be anything between them but this frustrating attraction.

When she pulled away, he gripped her arms, holding her in place.

"Am I permitted to comment on that?" he asked.

"Of course," she conceded, unsure whether or not to brace herself for another approach about a short affair.

But his reply was nonverbal. He put a hand out to depress the Close Door button and pulled her to him with the other one twined in her hair.

There was none of the hesitant manner or subtlety in his touch that she had shown him. He was passionate and thorough. Then, finally, he pulled away, looking at her for another long moment before bestowing one final, punctuating kiss and straightening to release the elevator button.

The doors parted, and Matt led Randy across the lobby with an arm around her shoulders. They walked slowly across the parking lot without speaking, the balmy, scented night dark and quiet.

Matt drew a deep breath. "This place smells like Eden," he finally said.

"I know," she agreed. "It's my theory that passing freighters on the river are still bringing perfume from the Orient."

There was a smile in his voice. "You've a touch of the romantic yourself."

"In an automobile salesperson?" she scoffed.

"Must be that little lady inside." He squeezed her shoulder gently as they reached her car. "I caught a glimpse of her in the elevator."

"No," she said solemnly. "That was me."

"Oh?" He took her keys from her and opened the car door. "What happened to the spitfire of ten minutes ago?"

She frowned. "That's me, too."

"You're a complex little package, Miss Stanton."

"You're not very easy to understand yourself, Mr. Mallory," she countered. "I think each of us is too much of a puzzle for a brief relationship. We'd spend all of our time trying to figure out where to start with each other."

"We seem to have little trouble starting."

"Not starting to kiss or starting to touch," she corrected gravely, "but starting to understand each other. Neither of us does that very well."

He shook his head, holding the door aside as she slipped behind the wheel. "I think I understand what you want," he said, leaning down to look at her. "I just don't know how to relate it to what I want—and what my job requires of me."

"The old battle of the sexes was so much simpler. All a woman had to do was win her man and then follow him."

"Would you have followed anyone?" he asked quietly. "Even then?"

She smiled. "Not away from Scannon Cove. I belong here."

He grinned. "Would you have tried to win me?"

"You're the one with the Midas touch," she said with a laugh. "It would have been easier for you to win me."

He rolled his eyes. "That's gossip-column propaganda. The Midas touch is nothing more than being willing to work twenty-four hours a day if you have to, to achieve whatever it is you want. I do that, so things happen for me. But there's nothing magic about it. You know that."

"Yes, I suppose I do. Well, good night, Matt." She pulled her skirt in, and he leaned down to tell her to drive carefully before pushing her door closed.

He returned her casual wave as she pulled out of the driveway, and she caught an image of him in her rear-view mirror, hands in the pockets of his slacks, watching her drive away.

She felt a strange sense of separation as she drove home, as though she had left something vital to her survival behind.

Chapter Six

Matt wandered slowly back to his suite, pushing thoughtfully through the door, leaning against it with a frown.

"I was beginning to think I'd never see the day," Julia said from the kitchen. "You're in a tailspin, Matthew."

"Tell me about it." He grimaced wryly. "I may even go down in flames."

"Her hair does inspire that analogy," she concurred as she beckoned him to the bar where the coffee was.

"Her whole being is like flame to me." He perched on a stool while watching Julia pour the coffee. "The warmth in her draws me, but it also keeps me at a distance."

"Afraid of getting burned?" Julia came around the bar to sit beside him.

"I could take being burned. I just don't want to be destroyed."

Julia frowned. "I saw her for such a short time, she doesn't seem like a user to me. You can sense that about someone."

"No, it isn't that." He explained about Randy's abandonment, her long succession of foster homes and her unwillingness to leave Scannon Cove.

"It is a beautiful spot," Julia said.

"You loved Boston, but you left it for Dad."

She smiled, her chin in her hand. "I loved him more than I loved Boston."

"That's it," he said grimly, testing the coffee. "She'll never love me more than she loves this town."

"Maybe you're rushing her," Julia suggested.

"That's what I thought at first. But when we spent the night at a hotel..." He stopped to look at his mother's arched eyebrow. "You're shocked that I might have spent the night with a woman?" he asked incredulously.

Julia swatted his shoulder. "Of course not! I'm shocked that you patronized another hotel!"

He laughed. "That's a long story. Anyway...she seems attracted to me, then afraid of me."

Julia shrugged her plump shoulders. "That's just being a woman. We're as afraid of being consumed in a relationship as you men are."

"With her I think it's more than that. So I tried to back off. The plan was to act casual and create the need for me in her life."

Julia gave him a skeptical glance over her cup. "It didn't look like it was working too well when I came in."

"I keep forgetting to go slowly with her," he admitted in exasperation, "and she's such a hardheaded woman."

Julia's eyes twinkled. "She looked ready to slug you."

He nodded. "Your arrival was timely. I was so frustrated with her that I'm not sure what I would have done next, swatted her bottom or made love to her."

"She'd have probably welcomed either. She looked as miserable as you do. But what a lovely young woman."

"Isn't she? I bought her this dress when we were stuck in Portland to try to prove a point." He drew a deep breath as though the memory of her in it was more than he could stand. "It's the shade of purple that's closest to the horizon in a showy sunset."

Julia concentrated, trying to bring that image to mind, wondering at the sensitive intricacies of her firstborn son.

"I can't tell you how she looked in it except that the way I felt when I saw her walk out of the dressing room toward me exemplifies the way she's turned me inside out. There was that hot, wild hair, that naked white shoulder, and there's this ruffle that runs across her breasts." He made an awkward, masculine gesture to illustrate his description, and Julia bit back a smile. "I swear I heard music when she breathed. Mom . . . I may not be long for this world."

Julia laughed, reaching out to touch his face. "You'll live, darling, though you do have a terminal case. Maybe you need the clan behind you on this. Maybe if she sees how thoroughly delightful we all are, the thought of one day leaving Scannon Cove won't seem so distressful to her."

"Or she might run screaming in the other direction. She's not sure of me on my own. Imagine an evening spent with the four Mallorys?" He gave an eloquent shudder.

Never one to be diverted once an idea began taking shape, Julia frowned thoughtfully at her son. "You know, Will's birthday is coming up. Instead of meeting in Connecticut for it as we'd planned, why don't we meet here? We'll have a party and force her to wear that dress."

"Mom . . ."

"We can take over that room we reserve in all our hotels for small banquets." She was off the stool now, wandering around the living room in concentrated thought. "We'll have music, and David will prepare something extra special."

"Mom . . ."

"Matthew, I'm talking!" she said, as though her son were three years old and tugging at her skirt. He put a hand over his eyes as she continued. "Should we bring all the family in, do you think?

"Perhaps inviting your aunt and uncle and Jem—"

"No, Mother."

"All right. Just the four of us and our friends. But I'll plan something so special she won't be able to resist us."

Matt caught her hand as she gestured and pulled her to a standstill.

"No one could resist you, Mom," he said gently. "It's me I'm having trouble selling."

"For a business genius," she said, squeezing his fingers, "you don't understand the basic truth here. She's resisting you so hard because she feels something for you, something that threatens the stability she's built for herself."

"I do understand that," he insisted. "But what if, in the end, she votes for the stability and not for me?"

"She won't, darling," Julia assured him, patting his cheek. "She struck me as a very intelligent woman. Now, I'm going to bed to make some notes before I forget all the little details running around in my brain. Good night, Matthew. Don't worry. I'll take care of everything."

Alone at the bar, Matt leaned his chin on his crossed forearms. He was losing control here, and he didn't like it. And he wasn't sure that having Randy meet his family was a good idea. Will, though his brother, business partner and dearest friend, often behaved like a candidate for Bedlam. His father, brilliant tyrant that he was, would probably tell Randy to cut her hair and then ask her what in hell she thought she was doing messing with his son's car. He sighed. She'd already met his mother and survived, but the contact had been mercifully short. He'd seen strong men panic in the face of Julia's enthusiasm.

Matt groaned and pushed himself off the bar stool. He called the desk to tell them he was retiring but available if necessary. He turned off the lights.

Standing alone in the dark, he wondered for one fanciful moment what it would be like now to put his arm around Randy's shoulder and lead her to his bedroom. Impatient with his own vulnerability, he finally marched off alone.

RANDY WALKED SLOWLY around the blue Berlinetta. The new door had been flawlessly installed, the paint perfectly matched. The car was polished within an inch of its life, and she had filled the gas tank.

She walked away with a sense of satisfaction. Thank goodness that was taken care of. Now, perhaps, this troublesome Matt Mallory would be out of her life.

She wore a classic brown suit this morning and a creamy beige blouse with a tulip neckline. She had resurrected the blouse from her closet, determined to get a little wear out of it. At least that was what she told herself this morning as she was looking with a little more care than usual for something to wear.

Now, suddenly, she felt uncomfortable in the blouse. Well, she would simply hide in her office until Mallory had picked up his car and left.

She should have known his plans would not coincide with hers, she thought later as he walked across the showroom toward her office. He stopped at the doorway and leaned against it, smiling at her. Randy's heart jolted so violently that she wondered if it had shown through the blouse.

Matt's eyes rested at about the second button down, and she wished desperately that she were wearing the jacket.

"Nice," he noted. "Miranda, there's hope for you."

"And you, Mr. Mallory. You now have wheels."

"Well, that's a relief. Have you had lunch?"

She hadn't, and if he had an invitation in mind, she had a teasing wish to accept it. But she weighed the wish against the satisfaction of refusing him. Unable to decide, she asked instead, "Where's your mother?"

"Ironically," he said, "she's gone shopping with Katie to Fairview."

She nodded grimly. "I rest my case. Maybe next year if she comes to visit you, she'll have a mall right here in Scannon Cove where she can shop." Randy dropped a pencil into a ceramic holder and added on a note of forced lightness, "But then you won't be here next year, will you?"

He looked at her evenly. "Probably not. My father is in New Mexico negotiating for another site right now."

She shrugged her shoulders with nonchalance. "Then it'll be there for other guests drawn to the Mallory Inn."

"You didn't answer my question about lunch."

Randy leaned back in her chair. She hadn't slept well last night, and she suddenly felt very tired. "What would be the point of lunch, Mallory?"

"It's a lot like fuel in a car, Stanton," he explained blandly. "It allows the vehicle to operate. The point of lunch is to keep you going between breakfast and dinner."

She gave him a chiding glance. "You know what I mean."

"Yes, I know what you mean. Okay, so there's nothing between us, long-term or short-term. Then it should be fairly simple for us to be friends."

"Mallory." Randy leaned forward, her expression impatient. "Sexual attraction was all we had going for us. We don't even like each other."

He frowned. "That's your conclusion, not mine."

She stood, becoming agitated. "You disapprove of my clothes, my attitude, my driving and my need for security. You taunt me, torment me and—"

"But," he interrupted, moving inside the office to close the door as her voice rose, "I've never shouted at you when you were offering me your hospitality."

"That's because I've never tried to seduce you."

He laughed, almost more at himself than her. "You do it unconsciously every moment we're together."

"Then apparently being together," she pointed out, "is not a good idea."

"I have nothing against being seduced," he said, leaning against the closed door. His eyes scanned her face in sudden concern. "You're very pale today."

"Is it any wonder?" she demanded. "You make me crazy, Mallory." She prowled back and forth in front of her desk, feeling claustrophobic with him leaning against her only exit. Her breath was gone again.

"Didn't sleep well?" he guessed.

"No, I didn't."

"Dream about me?"

She glanced at him murderously as she paced to the window. She had—continuously. "No," she snapped. "There was a noisy party down the road."

"Liar."

She stopped pacing to face him indignantly, her color high. But before she could speak, he took hold of her arm and pulled her toward the door. "Come on. I'm taking you to lunch."

"I've eaten."

"One more lie and your nose is going to grow." He pushed her through the open door to the showroom.

"My jacket," she said.

"It's warm." He kept pushing her toward the outside door. "And you look gorgeous in creamy beige. Pale but gorgeous. Where's my car?"

"In the service parking lot," she sulked.

He headed off in that direction with a firm grip on her arm. The Berlinetta gleamed like something right off the assembly line. Matt did a turn around the car, then stopped, hands in his pockets, while he studied the door that had been replaced.

"Perfect," he concluded finally. "You *do* do the best body work for a hundred miles. Are you ready?"

"Matt . . ." she began doubtfully.

He laughed and opened the passenger side door, gently helping her inside. "No time for second thoughts. I've got a picnic basket in the back filled with David's shrimp and macaroni salad and other delights too delectable to mention until we can eat them."

"Where are we going?"

"I've found a very romantic spot," he assured her as he moved the growling car out of the parking lot.

"But our relationship is not romantic," she pointed out as he drove through town and took a turn that would lead them to the waterfront.

"You know it would be if you let it," he corrected.

"We've been all over this."

He glanced at her with a grin. "So why'd you bring it up again?"

Disgruntled, Randy folded her arms and prepared to have a miserable time.

But despite her impatience with his persistence, having a miserable time in Matt Mallory's company seemed an impossible accomplishment. The spot he'd chosen was one of her personal favorites. She'd been too busy lately to get out to the old cannery that stood in picturesque decay just outside of town. The weathered dock that stretched beyond the cannery was seldom used except by the few local fishermen who still dried their nets on it. Randy had come here often as a teenager to fish for suckers off the dock.

It was also hard to fight a beautiful, clear, early-summer day. The sea gulls dived, ducks paddled in wide circles and an occasional freighter went by in the channel, huge, rusty and magnificent.

At the farthest edge of the dock, Matt spread out a blanket he had brought and rolled up his shirt sleeves. The jacket of his brown suit had been left in the car. He opened a liter bottle of champagne that was wrapped in a chilled towel, and out of the basket came an array of elegant dishes from David's kitchen.

"Look at this!" Randy had never attended a gourmet picnic before. Matt unwrapped one sumptuous salad after another, then produced four fat, flaky croissants. "You are so spoiled!"

"I'm trying to spoil you," he said, handing her a glass of champagne. "I want you to know that David threatens to give up his career if this lunch doesn't weaken your resolve."

She frowned in puzzlement. "My resolve?"

"About our relationship." He saluted her with his glass. "To love and romance," he said.

She downed the contents of her glass, and he raised an eyebrow in surprise. "You've no objection to drinking to that?" he asked.

"Of course not," she said, holding her glass out for more. "You said 'love and romance.' You didn't say *our* love and romance."

He rolled his eyes, refilling her glass. "I'll bet you were an aggravatingly specific little kid."

"I was an aggravatingly unhappy little kid," she corrected, saluting him. "Everywhere else but here. To Scannon Cove."

"I'll drink to that," he said affably. "It's a nice town. I also had to promise David that I wouldn't bring any of this back, so you'd better be hungry."

They ate in companionable silence, backs turned to the water as they watched traffic move on Riverfront Drive. Old splintered pilings and several other canneries in a similar state of decay dotted the waterfront. Beyond them, on Scannon Cove's main street, modern buildings were interspersed with old Victorian ones. The pattern followed up the hillside, which lay like a jeweled mound against the bright sky as the early-afternoon sun sparkled on windows and passing cars.

"If your hotels are in places like Boston, Dallas and Seattle," Randy said, investigating a foil-wrapped plate and finding frosted brownies, "why on earth did you pick Scannon Cove as a site instead of Portland? Good Lord, look at these brownies! I don't have room to eat another bite, but I've got to have one.''

"They're in suburbs of those towns, and Dad just didn't like Portland, so he started looking farther afield. He liked it here.''

"But will you get enough business in Scannon Cove?''

"We've been full since we opened. Are you going to eat all of those, or can I have one?'' He indicated the paper plate held protectively on her lap while she devoured a brownie.

She licked her fingers. "I'm going to eat them all. You wouldn't like them. They have nuts in them.''

"I like nuts," he said with a chuckle. "I'm here with you, aren't I?''

She gave him a murderous side glance. "Whatever chance you had that I might save you one just disappeared.''

He put his glass down and looked at her threateningly. "I could wrestle you for it.''

She handed him the plate. "Barbarian.''

"You are such a coward," he accused teasingly. "I've never seen a woman so afraid of physical contact.''

"I am not!" she denied. "I just never wrestle in this suit. It's a Halston, you know. Cost me bucks.''

"Does Halston only make subdued, manlike styles?'' he asked. "Or do you deliberately select them to put men off?''

She shrugged, studying the last brownie on the plate, balanced on his folded knee. "Are you going to eat that one, too?''

Randy groaned as Matt picked up the remaining brownie, but he broke it in half and handed her a piece.

"This is very noble of you, Matthew," she said, snatching it from him before he could change his mind.

"Actually, when your livelihood depends on a dozen men doing their jobs without distractions, you don't wear anything that'll slow them down."

Matt considered that with a slow nod, then turned to her with a curious frown. "Yet you employ Vivian Payne?"

"She came with the business," Randy said with a smile. "I didn't have anything to do with that. And she's been a good friend to me. She's sort of unconsciously seductive. She was probably supposed to be twin girls and got both sets of hormones."

Randy giggled at that thought and leaned back against the slats that fenced off the dock. She was beginning to feel the effect of her champagne. She was pleasantly relaxed. Her stomach was warm, and her senses were heightened.

"Smell that river," she said, taking a deep breath and expelling it slowly as she analyzed everything that passed through her sense of smell.

"Evergreens, warm wood, a little salt from the ocean..."

"Fish," Matt contributed dryly, "diesel fuel..."

"Yeah," she agreed as though those additions were not unpleasant. "Some days the smell's a little fishier than others and the wood is wet and not warm, but basically it's always the same. It's such a comfort—the sameness."

Matt poured coffee into their cups from a steaming thermos and handed it to Randy, his expression suddenly sober. "How do you feel about me, Randy?" he asked, surprising her out of her pleasant wooziness. She sat up straighter and took a cautious sip of the hot brew. She had a sneaking suspicion that she knew where this question was leading.

"You're what is known in the trade as a 'live one,'" she said lightly. "You've got a gas-guzzling sports car, and you're in the market for an economical little number that's sitting on my showroom floor. I have to be nice to you."

He drew a knee up and rested his coffee cup on it. He gave her a censorious look. "Try to think of me in personal rather than business terms."

"You're a great procurer of foods," she said, indicating with a sweep of her hands the now empty picnic basket. She refused to relinquish her good humor. "And you're not bad company."

Matt studied her. She could sense impatience in his manner, and though she tried desperately to hold on to the light mood of their picnic, she could feel it slipping away.

"Will you be serious for a minute?" he asked.

She looked back at him with wide, reluctant green eyes. He put his cup down on the blanket, then placed hers beside it. He rested his forearm on his knee, his expression grave. "I'm falling in love with you, Randy."

For an instant that revelation was thrilling, and she began to smile. Then she remembered that he'd be moving on.

"It's just my slick sales personality," she tried to tease, gesturing lightly with her hand.

"Stop it!" He caught that hand in his own, giving it a gentle but firm shake so that she was forced to focus on the seriousness in his eyes. "You can't joke your way out of this or put me off with meaningless denials. I want to know how you feel."

Her troubled eyes looked into his, seeing temper but behind it a frustrated caring. She felt her guard lower.

The hand that he held relaxed, and she entwined her fingers with his.

"I'm falling in love, too," she whispered. The temper in his eyes fled, instantly replaced by a lazy warmth. "But—" She prepared to list her objections.

"Ah!" He made a halting gesture with his hand, then pulled her closer to him on the blanket, propping his knee up behind her to lend support. "Let's just explore that for a moment," he said, his eyes moving to her mouth with disturbing concentration. "No complaints, no conditions...just two people learning about love. All right?"

Cradled in his arms, her cheek resting against the cool cotton of his shirt sleeve, Randy found his mouth beginning to draw her attention. She forgot all the protests that were stacked up so neatly in her mind, and she put a hand to his smooth cheek. "All right," she replied.

His mouth was warm and gentle against her lips, moving only fractionally as he communicated the depth of tenderness he felt for her. Responding to that tenderness, she drew closer, running her hands through the coarseness of his hair as feeling began to swell inside her. He shifted his position, drawing his knee higher to hold her closer.

She drew away to look with startled eyes into his face, a trace of panic surfacing as she thought to remind him that only moments ago he was talking about friendship and now— But before she could form the thought, Matt took her lips again, the tenderness now tempered with a need to know that her feelings ran as deeply to passion as his. He had his answer in an instant when her lips parted for air and his tongue invaded. With a little groan she arched against him, matching the sudden hunger of his kiss with her own.

Randy had a vague notion of trying to keep track of his hands, since she and Matt were on a public dock in fairly plain view of passing traffic. But the possessive warmth of their wandering felt so delicious, she hadn't wanted him to stop. Until he trespassed under her skirt and along her stocking-clad thigh and a dangerous shudder began to build inside her. She pushed her hands against him, wedging a space between them while she gasped for breath. He let her sit up and took a moment himself to draw a deep draft of air.

"I have to get back," she said, still fighting for breath, her back to him.

When he didn't reply, she thought for a moment that he hadn't heard her. But when she turned to look at him, he was watching her, that sober expression she had seen a few moments before now back in his eyes, intriguingly combined with unsatisfied passion.

"I think we're coming down to a choice here, Randy," he said quietly. "Scannon Cove or me."

"You're being premature," she insisted. She tried to appear cool when inside every nerve ending was rioting. "It's not like we're on the brink of a commitment."

He studied her dispassionately. "You know we are. So what's the answer?"

She began gathering up the remains of their picnic and tossing it in the basket. "I don't have an answer."

"Well, that's hopeful," he said, getting to his feet. "Then there's a fighting chance you'll change your mind about leaving here." He was deliberately baiting her, he realized, but then he was getting desperate.

"I won't!" she denied, tossing her plastic coffee cup into the basket and facing him, hands on her hips. "Don't delude yourself into thinking I will."

"Then your choice is to let me go?" he insisted, squaring off to face her, arms folded across his white shirt.

She lifted her chin, her eyes and hair blazing in the afternoon sun. "No. I think I'll drug you and lock you in the old body shop in the basement. When I'm feeling frustrated and lonely, I'll come down and lay you on the worktable and have my wicked way with you—and drive you crazy like you're driving me crazy!"

Anger and impatience warred with humor as the quirk at the corner of his mouth fought to become a smile. He finally allowed it, quickly and with reluctance. "That might be a solution I could live with," he said.

Matt looked down into her spring-green eyes and knew he could never let her out of his life. In such a short time she had become woven into the pattern of his being, and he couldn't remove her without doing serious injury to himself.

On the drive back to Stanton Motors, with Randy silent and pensive beside him, Matt told himself firmly that he was going to have to be the one to find the solution to this dilemma, because Randy wouldn't be able to.

Matt pulled up in front of Randy's dealership. She reached for her door handle to get out of the car, but he stopped her, leaning across her to take her hand and place it back in her lap. "You can't leave till we settle something."

Randy let her head fall defeatedly against the headrest. "Mallory, you're going to push me over the edge!"

"You keep running from the problem," he pointed out mildly, "but it's not going to disappear. Now—do we or do we not want to do something about this relationship?"

"If the something is having a short affair, the answer is no."

"We settled that already," he said, grinning. "I'm talking about how to assure the permanence of it."

"Okay," she said, turning to face him. He leaned an elbow on the steering wheel and returned her steady look. "The plain truth is that we're the classic case of the irresistible force and the immovable object; only in this particular case, nothing is going to give. I can't leave, and you can't stay." She shrugged her frustration with an openhanded gesture. "It's...hopeless!"

He frowned, but his eyes were filled with amusement. "What happened to keeping me in your basement and driving me crazy? I was kind of looking forward to that."

"Real life," Randy said didactically, "runs on fact and facing things squarely."

"Love," he countered, "deals with truth as well as fact, facing things squarely and setting real life to music. It can't change the truth, but it can work with it to achieve an end never believed possible."

Randy eyed him warily. "Like what?"

"Like the possibility," he suggested, pulling her closer, "that I might be permanently assigned here."

She looked into his eyes as he drew her closer still, the scent of his after-shave and the lingering fragrance of the river surrounding her. Her heart seemed to stall, then give a few erratic beats. "You're kidding!" she whispered, her frail voice half hopeful, half doubtful.

"No, I'm not," he assured her quietly. "It's definitely a consideration." He studied her wide eyes. "Do you hear it now? The music?"

She nodded, still staring at him, her voice breathless. "A few...cautious notes. Yes." She swallowed. "Do you?"

"A frail piccolo," he said. "But I hear it."

"You'd really do that for me?" she asked. "I mean if it becomes...trumpets and cymbals?"

Easy, Matt told himself. No point in telling her he already heard the music in full orchestration, complete with cannon. "Yes," he replied steadily, "I would."

Randy, who knew that she would hold eternally to her decision to remain in place because her whole being needed that to survive, understood how generous he was to even entertain the thought of staying in Scannon Cove.

She flung her arms around his neck, holding tight. Tears burned behind her eyes. "You're a very generous man, Mallory."

His chest moved with a soft rumble of laughter. "No, I'm very selfish. If that's the only way I can have you..." He shrugged away the rest.

She leaned back to look into his face, her mouth quivering dangerously. "I think," she whispered, "that I could lose myself in you."

"No," he corrected gently, kissing the tremor. "I want you to find yourself in me."

THE FLAMBEAU PULLED UP in front of old Scannon Square, and Randy climbed out, squinting up at the old brick against the bright blue sky. She waited for Matt to tell her she was crazy.

The facade looked particularly deteriorated in the cheerful sunlight. Brick had kind of a somber look, anyway. The building looked forbidding and hopeless, with all its windows either broken or boarded up, the large wooden doors bearing a No Trespassing sign.

But Matt said nothing; he simply followed her as she unlocked the doors and pushed her way in to the tune of their mournful groan.

Inside the building, on her left and right, were tall, shallow display windows, their sills now littered with dead insects, their glass grimy and dull.

"Can't you see those polished up," she asked brightly, "and full of colorful wares?"

When he didn't reply, she turned to find him looking overhead, running his hands along the wall, staring at the floor, seeing things she was sure she didn't see. He walked past her into the wide, open bottom level that once housed an elegant restaurant and ballroom. With hands in the pockets of his jeans, he wandered across the wide floor, which was littered with trash. He looked up at the three floors of galleries that ran around the building and the frescoed ceiling supported by iron columns.

"Your nineteenth-century merchant had big ideas," he said with a surprised smile. "What on earth is this doing in Scannon Cove?"

She had to laugh at that. "Canneries and lumber mills were flourishing then; people were prosperous. In those days we were a pretty important port. Everyone thought we would develop into the key to Western shipping instead of Portland, which is another one hundred miles upriver. I'm not sure why they developed and we didn't when we're right here, practically at the mouth of the Columbia River. Now, one hundred years later, the postmortem speculation runs to everything from geography to political payoffs."

"Interesting," he replied. "Where are the stairs?"

Randy led him through a doorway and along a corridor past empty offices to a wide wrought-iron stairway. She began to run up the steps, but he pulled her back.

"Don't be overconfident," he cautioned firmly, taking her hand. "This building hasn't been occupied for forty years. Move carefully."

Randy hated being told what to do, but she stayed at his side gladly, thinking in confusion that his quietly spoken dictum had somehow felt pleasant to her ear. Suddenly, in this decaying, deserted hulk of a building, she heard a violin.

They spent an hour wandering up to the third gallery, finally stopping to lean on the iron railing and look down.

"I can see plants cascading from the galleries," she said dreamily, unaware that she had tucked her arm in his and joined her hands on his forearm. "And colors like your hotel—pink, lavender and sand. Lots of wicker and greenery, a kind of twenties' flavor. What do you think?" Her hair flared out as she tilted her head to look at him. It was shot with sun from the skylight and became molten, filled with warmth and movement.

Matt straightened and took her face in his hands, his blue eyes reflecting the same bright sun that flamed her hair.

"I think," he said, his eyes roving her face with such intensity that her cheeks flamed to match her hair, "that I hear a trumpet."

"The music rises," she responded, her voice sounding distracted as her eyes lost themselves in the depths of his, "I . . . just caught a violin."

"Then be quiet," he said, "and listen." And his head came down to blot out the sunlight. She became lost in the velvet vortex created by his lips, his hands, the simple magic of his very being.

In the shaft of gold dust coming from the skylight, Randy saw in Matt's eyes the love that he felt for her, and she knew hers sparkled for him. Though she had always been one who thrived on attention to detail, having every loose end tied, she found that she felt reasonably comfortable in this limbo state. That realization gave her the first unsettling thought about love. Was a metamorphosis taking place? Would she ever be the same Miranda Stanton again?

Easy, Mallory, Matt told himself. *Easy.* He wanted nothing more than to make love to her right now in the warmth of this sunbeam. She made him feel primitive and priestly all at once, as though he could love her on the marble floor of this gallery one moment, then do nothing more than worship her from a distance, feeling unworthy to touch her the next.

She laughed softly. "You look as confused as I feel."

He joined his hands behind her neck. Under the warm and silky fall of her hair he teased the nape of her neck with his fingertips. His smile was a little reluctant, as though things were not exactly the way he wanted them but that he would settle for the status quo.

"I'm not confused about the fact that I love you," he said, his voice quiet and solemn.

"Or I about you," she admitted, her hands reaching up to grip the forearms resting lightly on her shoulders. Incongruously, she thought, their weight made a lovely yoke. Then she sighed, knowing there was much to resolve before their love could bear expression. "I wish I could be different."

He kissed her forehead and pulled her close. "I can't be different. Why would I expect it of you?"

She snuggled into his shoulder, deliciously content. "Because it would make our relationship so much easier."

"Yeah, well. You know what they say about things that are easy."

She looked up at him. "That they're not worth having?" At his nod, she grinned. "I've always wondered about the reliability of that axiom."

He laughed, and holding her to his side, led her out into the bright sunlight. Matt stopped her as she headed for the car and looked up at the bright blue sky. "What a day!" he said, taking a deep gulp of the fragrant fresh air. Then he looked down at Randy and gently caught her neck in the crook of his elbow. "I'm going to kidnap you for a while longer, okay?"

"Sure," she agreed instantly. "Do you want to spend more time test-driving the Flambeau?"

He shook his head. "No, I want to walk." With his arm still around her shoulders, he led her toward the waterfront, and they began tracing a path parallel with the river. "I haven't had a chance to do much exploring since I've been here. Waterfronts are always so interesting whether they're on San Francisco Bay or in a little place like this. River activity particularly seems to bustle with such importance."

While Matt spoke, a small pilot boat chugged out to intercept a freighter coming into the mouth of the river from the ocean. Several sea gulls were catching a ride on a rusty tug pulling a log raft slowly upriver. A fish jumped, just an instant of silvery brilliance before it disappeared again in the ever-widening ripples of water. A black seabird swam toward them from the shelter of bushes that clung to the rocky riverbank. Matt stopped to watch it, pulling Randy with him. "What is that?" he asked.

"A cormorant," she replied, smiling up at him. "Weren't there any of these birds on the sound in Seattle?"

He shrugged. "I don't know. I have very little free time under the best of conditions, and that particular project was beset with problems. It seemed like I was on the job nonstop. Besides—" he squeezed Randy's shoulder and nuzzled her temple "—there was no friendly automobile salesperson there willing to tour me around, hoping to get my business."

"Poor baby," she said sympathetically, patting his cheek. "But the price of the Flambeau doesn't come down no matter how charming you try to be."

He feigned disappointment. "You're a hard woman, Miranda Stanton."

Smiling heartlessly, she nodded. "I know. Do you want to hear about the cormorant?"

"But of course."

They turned back to the smallish black bird with the long neck and hooked bill, watching his relaxed path upriver. "He's also called a hell diver."

Matt gave her a shocked side-glance. "My virgin ears, Randy!"

She rolled her eyes heavenward. "Tell me another one, Mallory. They're used a lot in Asia for fishing. The fisherman ties a sort of collar with a tether around the bird's neck so that he can catch a fish but not swallow it. He is allowed to keep every fifth or sixth fish just to keep him interested."

"He needs a union." Matt laughed and started to move on. Then they came upon a building built on stilts over the river. It could be entered from the riverbank, but a small dock built around it allowed entrance through a side door and held steps that led into the water. The windows were broken, and the siding was weathered and peeling.

"Bob McGraw's marine supply store," Randy said with a philosophical sigh. She led Matt along the narrow dock to the steps. "Boat owners could pull up right here and shout their order without leaving the vessel. Despite efficiency, honesty and hard work, he still fell victim to hard times. You can see why he gets a little fed up with greedy Eldon."

Matt nodded. "Must be tough to do everything right and still lose." Then his attention was caught by a wink of sunlight on the headland across the river in Washington.

"I wonder what that was," he murmured, leaning on the dock railing to peer out at the spot.

"That's a church," Randy told him, shielding her eyes with her hand. "It has a rose window facing us. It was built for a group of Chinese laborers brought to Fairview to work on the railroad. It's really very small and humble. It makes you feel like you should feel in a church."

"You've been inside?"

She nodded, her expression clouding. "Al and Donna renewed their wedding vows there on their thirty-fifth anniversary. They both passed away the following year."

"I'm sorry." Matt pulled her to him and turned her back to their path.

They followed the river another mile past the pilot-boat moorage, past a restaurant, an office building and a cannery that was the only one in the area still operating. They also passed a deserted train depot and railroad tracks that stretched ahead of them as far as they could see.

"Another victim of our times," Randy said, looking through the grimy window to the dim interior where an ornate counter was visible, behind which was a wall of pigeonholes and several old desks. "Burlington-Northern still uses the railroad to transport plywood from our mill to Portland, but the days of greeting relatives on the afternoon train are gone forever. That's sad, isn't it?"

"It is," he agreed, "but this is still such a lively little place. As long as there are people like Kurt Daniels and you who care about it, it'll live."

"That's why I think the square is so important," she said, her eyes igniting with excitement. "People passing through the town would love it! The best of our historic past and good shopping; that's a dynamite combination for tourists."

"I'm sold," he said. Then, putting a hand to his flat stomach, he added plaintively, "I'm starved. Didn't we pass a restaurant?"

"Right." Randy took his arm and started to lead him back the way they had come. "Right next to the pilot-boat moorage. It's called Andrew and Steve's, and they have the best home cooking in the county."

"I'm going to tell David you said that," Matt threatened, picking up his pace as her steps quickened.

"It's run by a wonderful Greek family. There are always fresh flowers on the counter from Harriet's garden and the best homemade pie anywhere. It's also generally known that if you didn't hear the current piece of news at Andrew and Steve's counter over coffee, it isn't reliable."

An hour later they were staring at each other across a table cleared of their hamburgers and pie. Matt was leaning on his forearms, watching Randy, who was absently stirring her coffee.

"You didn't put anything in that," he said quietly.

"Hmm?"

"The coffee. You didn't put anything in it, and you're still stirring up four-foot swells in it."

Randy sopped up a puddle of coffee with her napkin, then smiled guiltily at Matt, resting her chin on the palm of her hand. "I was just thinking that I hate to go back to work. I've never felt like that before."

The smile he returned was roguish. "And to what do you attribute this sudden irresponsible attitude?"

"You," she admitted softly. "I enjoy being with you. No..." She thought about that a moment and amended, "I love being with you. You're crazy, but you can be trusted with my most carefully held thoughts and feelings." She sighed and leaned back against the booth, a soft light in her eyes. "I guess you know that you're in love when the thought of losing someone is too painful to contemplate."

Matt stretched his arms across the table and held his hands palm upward. She placed hers in them, and his closed over hers like a warm glove.

"If you want me," he said, "I'll be here."

"Forever?" she challenged.

He gave her a look that melted her doubts and revved her already strained heartbeat. "Would forever be long enough for us?" he asked.

Drowning in the wonderful warmth of his eyes, she thought absently that eternity did seem a pitifully short time for all the possibilities she could foresee.

"More coffee?"

Randy heard the question but couldn't quite divert her attention from Matt to form an answer. Reluctantly, Matt pulled his eyes away from her and smiled into the friendly face belonging to the waitress bearing a coffeepot. "No thank you," he said. "I'm afraid we have to leave."

The waitress swatted Randy's shoulder with her free hand. "Would you wake up and introduce me!"

Randy came swiftly to awareness as the sound of the familiar voice registered. She looked up sheepishly at the waitress with whom she'd been good friends in high school. For frequent patrons of Andrew and Steve's, the day wasn't complete without Effie's friendly harangue.

"Eftaxia Karakalos," Randy obliged, "this is Matthew Mallory. Matt, my friend Effie. We went to Scannon Cove High together."

Effie smiled at Matt. "And I suppose you think that this sweet, innocent smile she's wearing reflects the real Randy."

Matt folded his arms, looking interested. "You mean it doesn't?"

Effie sat down next to him, leaning toward him conspiratorially. "Ask her about Louie Maloney."

Matt grinned and fixed Randy with a probing look. "Do you want to tell me about Louie Maloney?"

"Only that he had it coming," Randy replied feelingly.

"That's intriguing." Matt turned to Effie. "Maybe you'd better tell me."

"Louie was a senior," Effie explained, putting down the coffeepot as she warmed to her story. "Randy and Debbie and I were juniors. One night he took Debbie out, and Randy and I went to a movie, grousing about how Debbie had a date and we didn't. When we were driving home, we saw Debbie walking. Randy stopped to pick her up, and Debbie told us Louie made her get out and walk because she wouldn't ... you know." Effie gave an eloquent shrug.

"I follow," Matt said.

"So," Effie continued, "we took Debbie home, and when Randy drove back across town to take me home, we saw Louie's car parked in front of the Pizza Pirate. Randy pulled over, ran to his car and pulled out the..." She looked to Randy for help.

"Distributor rotor," Randy provided.

"That's it. He had to walk home and everywhere else for the next couple of days. Louie wasn't very smart mechanically."

Matt laughed, raising an eyebrow at Randy's defensive expression. "You little devil, Miranda."

Effie went on. "Then she left the...the distributor thingie in his mailbox three days later with a note warning him to be careful how he treated the friends of—" she dropped her voice to a dramatic bass "—the Masked Mechanic!"

Matt put a hand over his eyes. "The Masked Mechanic?" he repeated painfully.

"I know," Effie agreed. "Corny. But it worked. Louie now has a lovely wife and kids, comes in here all the time and leaves large tips. He even lets Randy work on his car."

"How did he know the Masked Mechanic was Randy?"

"Everybody knew Randy was better than any guy with cars, even then. And she was a friend of Debbie's."

"And you signed our names in lipstick on the windshield," Randy reminded.

Effie looked thoughtful. "That may have had something to do with it. Well..." She stood suddenly and picked up the coffeepot. "It's been a pleasure meeting the man who's put such a glow on Randy's face." Then she winked at her friend. "See ya."

Arm in arm, Matt and Randy walked slowly back to the Flambeau, which was parked in front of Scannon Square. "You do have a glow," Matt said, studying her face as she leaned against the car, waiting for him to open the door.

She laughed softly. "It's a reflection of a lovely morning." When his look became too intense for her to deal with, she asked briskly, "So what do you think of the Flambeau?"

Acknowledging her ploy to distract him with a light kiss on her lips, he helped her into the car, then slipped into the driver's seat.

"If we could come to terms with the redhead that's supposed to come with it, you'd have a sale."

Randy ran her finger studiously down the list of accessories affixed to the passenger-side window. "There's no redhead on the Monroni sticker," she said.

He put the key in the ignition. "Probably because you're priceless."

Randy moved closer to him, seduced by his good humor and gentle flattery. "Of course, I am the boss. And there are dealer-installed options available." She leaned forward to plant a light kiss on his lips, her eyes suddenly stormy with emotion. "I love you, Matt."

He kissed her back, his eyes reflecting the turmoil in hers. "Then I'll sign the order."

Chapter Seven

"You don't have to tell me, you know," Viv was saying, moving her knees as Randy reached into her side drawer for an envelope. "What's two whole years between friends, several paychecks that were a couple of days late, several blind dates that were backed out on, several books that were never returned, sev—"

"Vivian," Randy interrupted firmly, "there is nothing to tell yet."

"But you were cuddled up to him when he brought you to work the other day."

"We're . . . getting along," she evaded.

"Rather well, it looks like."

She smiled. "Yes."

Vivian's "Yahoo!" brought Gordie and Eldon to the doorway of Randy's office with expressions of concern.

"Just Vivian," Randy explained with a roll of her eyes. Understanding Vivian, they walked away.

"So you haven't made love?" the bookkeeper inquired.

Randy shook her head, finally exasperated. "No."

"Are you going to?"

"Viv . . ."

"Well, I'm just concerned. You're such a Victorian."

"Victorian women did not run automobile agencies."

"They ran the men who ran the automobile agencies...or horse-and-buggy agencies," Viv philosophized. "Same difference. I'll bet nobody runs Matthew Mallory."

Randy nodded. "That's probably safe to say. Although he's close to his family and as involved in their business as if it were his alone."

"Loyalty's not a bad trait," Viv said.

Randy smiled dryly. "Tell me about it." No one knew better than she how precious a trait loyalty was.

"Vivian," Randy said, suddenly brisk. "I've got to get these checks off, and you must have something else to do."

As Vivian left Randy's office, the telephone rang.

"Stanton Motors," Randy answered, her voice betraying her preoccupation with her bill paying.

"I'm dissatisfied with a purchase I've made through your dealership!" an angry male voice complained.

"Oh?" Randy pushed the checkbook aside and tried to sound conciliatory. "What's the problem, sir?"

"You haven't followed through on your promise," the angry voice went on. "I'm short an accessory, and no one has called me to see whether or not I'm a satisfied customer."

"Sir..."

"So what do you intend to do about it?" the voice demanded. "Or do I have to get in touch with the Better Business Bureau?"

A deep note in the male voice suddenly struck a chord in Randy, and she finally identified the caller.

"I could call on you tomorrow, Mr. Mallory, and give you Stanton Motors' personal attention."

"Mmm," he said thoughtfully. "That sounds exciting. About my accessory..."

"The redhead?"

"Yes."

"I'm sorry. We had only one left in stock, and she's been sold."

"Aw." He sounded crushed. "To whom?"

"The IRS in lieu of quarterly taxes."

His rich laugh came to her ear like a piece of music. "Thank God I have an accountant to do that for me. Where were you at lunch today?"

"I didn't have time for lunch today. Did you miss me?" She was fibbing. She had picked up a salad and brought it back to her desk just to have time to think. He'd given her little time during the past week to do anything but drown in his eyes, get drunk on his kisses and decide that the Mallory touch was even more powerful than the Midas touch he was purported to have.

When Matt touched her, she did not become a gold statue but rather molten gold to form in his arms in any way he chose. She loved him—she knew he loved her—but the power he had over her was frightening.

In the short six days since their tour of Scannon Square, their relationship had accelerated with whiplash suddenness. And she was trying desperately to hold on to her senses. But Matt seemed to make her forget that she was at heart a sound and sensible woman.

His voice also seemed able to make her forget her senses. Something inside her chest was quivering, and it was hard to form a coherent thought.

"Then that must mean you'll be hungry for dinner."

"Yes." She had eaten none of the salad but had spent the entire hour thinking of him and where their relationship was going.

"Good," he said. "My father and brother are here. Mom would like you to join us for dinner."

There was a long moment of silence; then Randy asked hesitantly, "Do...do you think that's such a good idea?"

Silence again. Then Matt demanded, "What kind of a question is that?"

"I mean..." She couldn't explain the vague fear that had haunted her this past week. "Well, what are they doing here?"

The question came out aggressively, as though she felt they had no right to come to Scannon Cove.

"It's Will's birthday," Matt answered patiently. "We always try to be together on birthdays. I told you that. Randy, what's the matter?"

"Nothing," she said quickly. "Of course I'll come. What time?"

"Seven o'clock."

"All right. I'll be there. I've got to go, Matt. I'm in the middle of closing a deal."

As she replaced the receiver in its cradle, she looked around herself at her empty office. She had no deal to close. The truth was that she was afraid of Matt's family, afraid that they would never let Matt be assigned here.

Now that the hope that she could have Matt had been dangled in front of her eyes, she didn't think she could live without him. She looked out her window at the mid-afternoon bustle of cars and people and children going home from school, and her vague fear became panic.

For the first time in her working life Randy Stanton went home early, slipped into her robe, put the teakettle on the stove and lay on the sofa, staring at the ceiling.

She was brewing her tea when the doorbell rang, and she knew who was calling. Reluctantly, she opened the door. Matt stood there, his expression grim. He walked into the house without being invited in.

"What are you doing here?" Randy asked, closing the door behind him. He stopped in the middle of the living room and turned to her impatiently.

"What are you, director of transportation all of a sudden? What are my parents doing here? What am I doing here? I'm here because I didn't like the way that you sounded on the phone. So I called back and learned from Vivian that you'd gone home early."

"I am the boss, you know," she pointed out, sinking into a corner of the sofa and hugging a throw pillow to her chest. "I can do that if I want to."

"You can do whatever you want concerning your business," Matt said, unbuttoning his suit coat, "but when it comes to us, I wish you'd be honest with me."

She looked up into his concerned frown and patted the cushion beside her with a sigh. "That's fair," she said. "Sit down." When he complied, she clutched the pillow a little tighter and began. "Something's been bothering me all week."

"What?" he asked.

She leaned an elbow on the back of the sofa, still clutching the pillow with her other hand. "Matt, what if you hate Scannon Cove?"

He frowned. "I don't hate it. I like it."

"I mean after...later. You're used to big cities, big decisions. Scannon Cove is so small. What if we get married and you hate it?"

Matt looked a little relieved and sat facing her, gently stroking her arm. "This might be hard for you to understand if you've never felt completely loved. But however things turn out, I'll be happy if you're with me, wherever I am."

"Okay," she said, her voice coming out high and small. "I've never been in love before. But this... this... excitement, this music we're both hearing... it'll pale, won't it, when we have to do the everyday things? I mean, we'll love each other, of course, but the newness that makes you think you'll be happy forever will wear off. How will Scannon Cove seem to you then?"

"Randy," he said, exasperated. "We're not infatuated with each other; we're in love. That doesn't pale; it deepens. You will never be less beautiful to me, less appealing, less critical to my happiness, than you are at this very moment."

"Oh, Matt," she groaned, getting to her feet and tossing the pillow down. He watched her as she paced across the room, then spun around to face him.

"Even if you're happy to stay here, how are your parents going to feel about it? It sounds like you're the motor in their organization. What's your father going to think when you ask him to assign you permanently to a little backwater town like Scannon Cove?"

"I've already told him," Matt said, catching her hand as she paced by him. He pulled her into his lap, concerned blue eyes looking into hers. "He was surprised, and... frankly, he was upset at first. But he knows that's the way it's going to be, and he's accepted it."

"But if he's upset, it's starting already," Randy said in distress. "I don't want to come between you and your family."

Matt laughed. "My father likes to have his own way, and he gets upset every time anyone thwarts him. That's how he is—that's what's made him so successful. He doesn't understand the meaning of the word no."

Randy gave him a knowing glance. "He reminds me of someone else I know. Matt, do you see what I'm saying?

He may say he's accepted it, and he may even want to. But he'll eventually resent you for marrying me and staying here; then he'll resent me. What'll that do to our relationship?'' When he said nothing, she pushed away from him and walked to the window. "This isn't going to work until we resolve everything.''

"I don't think any man and woman ever resolve everything." Matt said quietly. "There are some things you just have to live around. I don't think my family would ever resent either one of us. I'm sure we'll have other problems, but we can still have a durable relationship.''

"Durable." She repeated the word, glancing at him over her shoulder. "That doesn't sound very romantic.''

"I thought security and durability were what you wanted most out of life,'' he reminded.

She had said that, hadn't she? She had thought that. Why did it not sound like enough now? Turning away from the window, she walked toward him. "Is the fact that you've decided to stay here the issue we'll have to live around.''

"No,'' he said without a pause. "I've made that decision, and it won't make me unhappy.''

"Then what is it that will be a problem for us?'' Randy wondered for a moment what she was doing probing him when only a moment ago she had said that too much remained unresolved between them.

He studied her thoughtfully, his expression making him more of a stranger than he'd been that day she'd confronted him on the showroom floor. He was no longer the kind, witty, understanding friend he'd been since they met but someone entirely different. He looked grave and just a little impatient with her.

"Sit down," he said finally, pulling her down beside him.

Matt looked at her bright eyes and reached out to touch the hair he dreamed constantly of being entangled in as they made love. He hated the thought of hurting her. But he hated, too, what she was doing to herself.

"I don't want to see you make a decision out of fear," he said, his voice quiet but unyielding.

"Fear?" she repeated. He saw the instant confusion coupled with hurt in her eyes. "What do you mean? What does our relationship have to do with fear?"

"Not our relationship," he corrected. "I'm talking about your decision to stay here."

"But I explained that," she said anxiously. "I like it here. I feel secure here. A lot of my effort and energy has gone into this community."

"I understand that."

"Apparently you don't!"

Matt drew a deep breath and forced himself to relax, hearing the temper rising in her voice and knowing he could do nothing but let it take its course.

"I told you about my mother and all the foster homes," she went on, pulling back from him so that they no longer touched. "I was happy in Scannon Cove with the Curtises for the first time in my life. I love this place; it has nurtured me. Can't you understand that?"

He knew he was about to lay his head on the block, but now that they had gone this far, there was no holding back.

"How true is that, Randy?" he asked quietly.

"What?"

"I know it's all true about your mother and the moving and the Curtises," he said. "I know you love it here and that you want to stay. But how much of the reason behind it is love of this place and how much is fear of the outside world?''

''What do you mean?'' she demanded.

''I think you've mistaken security and stability as a place outside yourself,'' he replied. Then he reached out to gently tap his index finger against her sternum. ''Instead of inside.''

She slapped his hand away and sprang to her feet, screaming down at him. ''How would you know? You've probably never had an insecure moment in your life! Maybe when people love you and you're strong and competent, you've got enough inside you that you can cope anywhere. But there are those of us who haven't been so blessed! We need a little outside help, and mine is Scannon Cove.''

''Randy, that's a crock,'' Matt retorted calmly. ''I've never met a woman more competent, more intelligent or more determined. You can delude yourself all you want. You can call on your past for a crutch, but the truth remains that you're afraid. You don't have to admit it to me, but you'll never have a moment's peace until you admit it to yourself. Scannon Cove is a beautiful place, but the world is filled with them, and you're closing yourself off from all it has to offer because you're afraid of it.''

Randy's complexion blanched with temper. ''And what about you. Won't you admit that now that you've said you'll stay here with me, you're afraid that I'll take you up on it?'' She drew a shaky breath and looked at him with eyes that knifed him. ''Aren't you regretting that promise now that you might be faced with keeping it?''

''No, I'm not. I'm going to marry you, and we're going to stay here and be happy. But I'll be happy because I love you and because I know that what I'm missing, I'm missing because I made the conscious choice myself. You'll be happy because you don't have to take a chance outside the world in which you're comfortable.''

Tired of hearing that, Randy turned away from him and went to the window. ''Maybe you'd better leave,'' she suggested angrily.

''All right.'' She heard him stand and walk across the room to the door. He opened it and paused. ''You can prove that you mean that in the temporary sense by meeting us for dinner in the small banquet room at seven o'clock. I won't come for you. I'll take your appearance at the hotel to mean that you love me and that you want to marry me. If you don't come, I'll understand. Whichever way it is, I love you, Randy.''

The door closed behind him, and she heard his footsteps as he went down the walk to his car.

Randy spent the next hour thinking that Matthew Mallory was finally out of her life forever and good riddance! It would be a cold day in hell before she showed her face at the Mallory Inn again, much less in the small banquet room to meet his family.

Thank goodness she had finally seen that he only pretended to understand her need to remain in Scannon Cove. He really thought the need was some emotional aberration over which she malingered.

Wandering across her living room with a cup of tea, Randy replayed their conversation in her mind. The world beyond her window was caught in early-evening traffic.

''I think you've mistaken security and stability as a place outside yourself,'' he had said, ''instead of inside.'' And he had tapped her breastbone.

She sat in the wooden rocker near the window and tried to recall why that had upset her so. It was that tapping gesture, she thought, the one he always used when indicating the woman who lived inside her. The one she hid so carefully and sometimes wanted so desperately to set free. Was she angry that he understood her so well?

She spent the next hour analyzing her response to Matt. She had accused him of never having known an insecure moment and of wanting to renege on his offer to stay in Scannon Cove.

But recalling the times they had spent together, she had to admit that he had never been anything but sincere. And he had treated her fears with the utmost compassion and patience. As angry as she was, she could not believe that his concern had been an act.

Then she remembered that his last words before leaving her this afternoon had been "I love you, Randy." She then put her teacup down and looked at her watch.

Chapter Eight

By the time the salad was served in the small banquet room, Matt was convinced that he would never see Randy Stanton again. He had circulated during the cocktail hour, absently visiting with friends and the staff. He had kept a surreptitious eye on the door, but futilely, because Randy had not appeared.

As they took seats for dinner, he wondered if he'd had the right to say what he had to Randy. To make her take a hard look at herself when he spoke from a position such as this one, surrounded by family and friends. She was right. He had never known a lonely moment, and she had struggled through many to be what she was today.

It was just that there was so much he wanted to see and do with her that couldn't be done in this beautiful but confining little town.

If she would only walk through that door, he thought, he would love her so hard she would never suspect that the world had anything else to offer her but his arms. And he would never long for more than Scannon Cove if he could simply hold her.

His father was talking about New Mexico, looking amazingly fit for a man in his mid-sixties who had had a serious heart attack just one year ago. His thick red hair was liberally flecked with gray, but his square-jawed, freckled face was lively and robust. His blue eyes, the same color as his son's, looked across the table at Matt.

"Well, where is this young woman that I've heard so much about from your mother?"

Unwilling to admit defeat, Matt glanced at his watch.

"Probably primping for us," Julia said, patting her husband's hand. "Slow down on that salad, dear. Remember your diverticulitis."

Duncan Mallory looked at his oldest son. "Will you tell her to leave me alone! She's been watching me like a hawk ever since I arrived."

"We could sell her to the Hiltons," Will suggested. "Let her drive them crazy. Who is that?"

Matt looked up at his brother's exclamation, silently repeating the words himself as he saw Randy on the threshold of the small banquet room, looking over the crowd. She was wearing the lavender dress, and she had never looked more beautiful. Her hair was swept up, but there were wisps of that copper silk all about her face. The hint of a swell of breast where the ruffle crossed her chest drew his eye. It was a moment before he could stand and walk toward her.

"What . . . ?" Will watched his brother rise and noted his expression. He saw the woman notice Matt, and connoisseur of women that Will was, he noted her expression also. He looked across the table at his mother.

"Tell me that angel isn't Matt's girl," he demanded in feigned disgust.

"That would be a lie," Julia said, putting down her fork. "That's Matt's girl. Behave yourself, darling. I'd hate it if your brother killed you."

"Well." Duncan looked over his shoulder to see the object of his family's discussion, then stood as Matt and the young woman came toward him.

Will stood also. "How does he always do that?"

"What?" Duncan asked.

"Get the best. In service, in loyalty from his employees, in women."

"It's the Mallory touch, Son," Duncan said quietly as Matt and Randy approached. "You're just a slow learner. Well, Matthew. This must be Miranda."

Fighting down her rising panic, Randy concentrated on Matt's hand at her waist when she shook hands with his father.

"Duncan Mallory, my father," Matt said. "And Will, my brother."

"Listen to me!" Will said urgently, holding her firmly by the shoulders.

Randy looked up into eyes that were dark, like Julia's, and filled with the devilment that often came and went in Matt's eyes. But it looked like a permanent fixture in these dark ones. He was slightly taller than Matt, a little leaner, darker featured.

"Yes?" she inquired, her eyes catching his silliness because she was suddenly extraordinarily glad to be here.

"Everyone thinks he's the smart one." He inclined his head toward Matt, who was giving his father a long-suffering look. "But it isn't true. I am. I mean, all he does is make the hotels run, but I put them up. How could he run them if I didn't put them up?"

"True," she admitted, nodding gravely.

"I'm better at tennis, too. Do you like tennis?"

Randy nodded. "Love it."

"Well, it's settled, then!" Will smiled triumphantly.

"Sorry," Randy said consolingly, "but I love *him*." She shrugged carelessly in keeping with Will's teasing but glanced at Matt with a look that told him just how serious she was. The look he returned her brought hectic color to her cheeks.

"Well..." Will pretended to bluster. "If you want to bring love into it..."

"William, sit down," Julia said firmly.

"Yes, ma'am." Will instantly complied, patting the vacant seat next to him on his right side for Randy to sit down.

"You look lovely, Miranda," Julia said, smiling at her from across the table. "That dress is exquisite."

"Thank you." Randy returned her smile as Matt pushed her chair to the table. "Your son chose it for me."

"I heard about that," Duncan said, pouring wine into her glass and beckoning a waiter for her salad. "My son has always had impeccable taste, in women and in clothes. Takes after his father." He reached out to pat Julia's hand, and the woman turned her hand to clasp his fingers.

"I'm in love with an aerobics teacher who pumps iron," Will announced, peppering his salad. "She has a Wimbledon-quality backhand."

"On the tennis court or in the bedroom?" Matt asked.

Will glared at him. "You're supposed to be nice to me. It's my birthday."

"Does that mean you're going to grow up?"

"Nope. Just because you were born ready for Princeton, it doesn't mean the rest of us have to join the ranks." Will leaned toward Randy conspiratorially. "He is absolutely no fun."

"Oh?" she asked, tossing a suggestive glance Matt's way. "I haven't found that true at all."

"William, be quiet," Julia said.

"Yes, ma'am." Will went back to his plate with concentration.

"Matt called a board meeting yesterday," Duncan said, fixing Randy with a probing expression. "He told us he wants to be permanently assigned here in Scannon Cove. Were you aware of that?"

Randy nodded, surprised that the subject was to be brought up at the dinner table. But then Duncan Mallory didn't look like a man to skirt an issue when he wished it to be discussed. She swallowed.

"I'm aware of it. I suppose you could say I'm responsible for it."

Duncan nodded. "Matt's explained the situation to me. But do you realize how valuable he is to me in his capacity? His cousin might be as good one day, but right now he's very young and doesn't have Matt's instincts for the business."

Randy looked at Matt for help, not knowing what to say.

"I thought we settled this discussion earlier?" Matt frowned at his father, and Randy saw Julia and Will exchange a glance.

Duncan shrugged. "You had your say. I didn't." He eyed his oldest son levelly. "And what if I say no?"

Randy felt a lump of dismay rise in her throat, but to her surprise Matt just smiled.

"What always happens when you say no?"

Duncan fought back a grin. "You do what you damn well please, anyway."

Matt shrugged. "Then why are we discussing it? Eat. But stay away from the salad. Remember your diverticulitis."

It was later, while a small band played mellow music, that Duncan asked Randy to dance.

"I'll forgive you for depriving me of the best trouble-shooter I've ever had in the company," he said, holding her in a grip that reminded her of a gentle bear hug, "if you promise me that you'll never do anything to hurt him."

The horror Randy felt at the very thought of hurting Matt showed in her eyes. "I wouldn't. I love him very much."

"And apparently he feels the same way. He's always loved the challenge of putting our houses on their feet. I know he doesn't put that aside lightly for just anyone."

"Scannon Cove is a wonderful place," Randy said. "He'll be happy here, Mr. Mallory. I promise."

"I'll hold you to that," he said. Then he began talking about Matt's new Flambeau and asking her about fleet prices.

Will cut in as the band struck up a cha-cha.

"I don't think I can do that," Randy protested as he swept her away.

"I'll teach you," he said, pulling her into a corner of the room, away from the crowd of dancers. "I learned the cha-cha while putting up the Mallory Acapulco in Mexico."

"I didn't know there were any foreign Mallory Inns."

"Only in Mexico and Canada. Now pay attention."

In a few moments Randy was following his lead in the bouncy dance.

"Matt says you run an automobile dealership."

"Yes." Randy stared at her feet, concentrating.

"Are you going to stay with that after you're married?"

"Uh-huh."

"And Matt really agreed to that?"

She looked up at him in surprise, forgetting to cha. He bumped into her.

"Of course," she said.

Will shook his head at her as though she were the eighth wonder of the world.

"I'd have thought that he'd never settle down. He's like Dad—full of guts and daring. Always looking for a new hill to climb." He smiled. "You have him bewitched, haven't you? You've put a spell on him."

"Yes." Strong arms closed around Randy from behind and held her fast against a body that was now so familiar to her that it made hers react immediately to its touch. She put her hands up to clasp Matt's arms. "She does have powerful magic." He leaned down to ask her in a stage whisper, "Can you make him disappear?"

She leaned her head against Matt's shoulder to look up at him. "Couldn't I just send him for champagne?"

"That wouldn't take long enough."

"Nice guy," Will grumbled, mockingly offended. "If you want her to yourself, just say so. I can take a hint. Don't beat around the bush. Just—"

"Leave now, Will," Matt said mildly.

"I'm going." Will snatched the arm of a young lady serving drinks, steadying her laden tray as he looked into her surprised dark eyes, and began an outrageous line of conversation.

Matt watched him go with a fond smile. "I was thinking of introducing him to Vivian."

Randy pulled out of his arms and looked at him in surprise. "You know, that sounds like a great idea."

Matt laughed. "I thought that you might think so. They certainly would make a unique couple."

"True. And they probably would hit it off immediately."

"We'll see what we can do with some matchmaking."

It was their first opportunity to speak alone together since Randy had walked across the room toward him earlier in the evening. He held her close, his hand at her back firm and proprietary.

"Do you have any idea," he asked gravely, "how happy I am that you decided to come?"

She leaned her forehead against his chin. "I hope you're as happy as I am. But..." She pulled back to look into his face, her eyes dark with doubt.

"What?" he demanded.

"Your family isn't very pleased that you'll be staying in Scannon Cove."

"They'll just have to get my cousin Jeremy ready faster than they had planned."

"No. It wasn't just concern for the business," she said, her distress deepening. "It was concern for you. As though they didn't really believe you could be happy here."

He smiled down at her. "Do I look unhappy to you?"

She studied his face, his deep blue eyes, which could be very guarded or very expressive, depending on how private his thoughts were, and the line of his mouth, mobile in laughter or lovemaking, taut in concentration or anger. Matt seemed very open tonight, as though he held nothing from her; his smile was easy, relaxed.

"No," she said, wanting to be convinced. "You don't."

"Then I'm getting weary of that subject. Come on outside. I want to tell you something." He put an arm around her to guide her toward the French doors that led out onto a patio overlooking the river.

The evening air was deliciously fragrant but cool. Randy took a deep, steadying breath while wrapping her arms around herself as protection against the river breeze.

"Here." Matt walked her toward the railing that looked out on a ten-foot drop to the river. Channel lights winked at them from the darkness beyond that seemed to contain nothing but the gentle lap of water against the grassy bank.

Then Matt's suit jacket, warm from his body, enfolded her back and shoulders and was gathered around the front of her as he perched on the railing and pulled her to him.

"I'll be by early for you tomorrow. We're taking Will to Scannon Square."

She looked up at him in surprise. "Why?"

"Will and I do our own thing, apart from the Mallory Inns. Will's got a real knack for restoring and remodeling buildings as well as starting from the ground up."

"You mean..." She brushed impatiently at a tendril of hair the night breeze whipped across her face. "You mean that you're considering doing the square?"

"I'd like to hear what Will thinks," he said noncommittally. "I think that it'd work, but I'll leave the final say to him. He knows what's possible and what isn't."

"Oh, Matt!" she gasped, feeling a squeal of pure delight building inside her.

"Right now it's just a consideration," he said. "So don't get your hopes up." Then he pulled her back to him and kissed her hair. "It'd be a good project for the summer. By fall we'd be ready to move indoors and then have it put together by early next year."

The squeal erupted, and she leaped at him, her arms around his neck. "Oh, Matt! I'd love that! Imagine if we could present you and Will to the council as caretakers of the project!''

''We'll see what Will says,'' he cautioned again, bracing himself as she hung from his neck, then added dryly, ''I'm sorry you don't care for the idea.''

''To know that it might be done,'' she said, now calmed but breathless with awe. ''And that it would be done with care by skilled craftsmen.''

The strains of the birthday song drifted out onto the patio, and Matt looked toward the dining room with a reluctant sigh.

''We'd better get back. No telling what Will might do under the influence of birthday cheer if I'm not there to stop him.''

Randy laughed. ''Your mother seems to have him well in hand.''

''It's a game they play,'' he explained as they drifted slowly toward the party. ''Because he was such a brat as a kid, he's trying to make up to her for the gray hairs he's given her.''

''Did you?''

''Give her gray hairs? No. I thought she was an angel incarnate. But my father and I were always fighting and still often do. It's the old story of being too much alike. We've each got our own ideas and want to see them implemented now.''

''Your father seems to have a deep respect for you, though. Your whole family does, Will included.''

Matt smiled. ''Will and I, though very opposite, work well together. We have respect for each other's abilities.''

''I'm jealous,'' she said sincerely.

''Don't be.'' He winked, pushing the doors open. ''You're about to become one of us.''

MATT AND RANDY stood at the gallery railing, looking down on the vacant main floor of Scannon Square, much as they had done a week ago. There was no sun slanting in on this rainy day, but the many windows still unboarded made it light enough for careful study.

With Matt's arms and body enclosing hers as she held the cold iron railing in her hands, Randy struggled to remain quiet. Will had followed them through the building for an hour, studying everything and saying little except to throw an occasional question at Matt or Randy. Impressed by this metamorphosis of the clown of last night, Randy watched Will's set features as he looked around slowly, then leaned his forearms on the railing several feet away from her and Matt.

He turned to them and said matter-of-factly, "It'll work."

"It will?" Randy demanded. As he nodded, she turned to Matt, her voice rising. "It'll work! He said it'll work!"

Matt nodded, smiling. "I heard him." He caught her waist as she threw her arms up in delight. "When does the New Mexico project begin?" he asked Will.

"Not until next April. There's time."

"When can you start?"

"Right after the wedding."

"You're getting married!" Randy teased.

"No, you are," Will corrected. "And to the wrong brother. But you're the one who has to live with the decision."

Randy smiled up at Matt as they started for the stairs. "What a delicious fate."

AT THE NEXT MEETING of the Scannon Cove Downtown Development Committee, Matt and Will both appeared with Randy, and even she was left speechless by the thoroughness of their preparation. She watched Matt spread a blueprint on the table, distribute bound reports on the costs and timetable for completion should the committee vote to take the project to the city council.

Grissom challenged their ability to actually complete such a project despite their report. But another member of the committee, a Coast Guard officer who had previously been stationed in Boston, cited a section of Beacon Street that had been restored by Mallory Brothers.

"It was done tastefully, true to history, within budget and on time."

The blueprint was passed from hand to hand once more; then Will produced an artist's rendering of the completed structure, something even Randy hadn't seen. As it passed from the Coast Guard officer's hand to hers, she swallowed back emotion.

There it was, Scannon Square in all the glory of its Italianate architecture. It was just as she had seen it in her mind's eye and in her dreams. The brick cleaned, arched windows winking light, the scrollwork under the eaves and on top of the columns restored to fussy perfection. The artist showed the block landscaped and with throngs of people coming and going through its open oak doors.

She looked up at Matt, her eyes showing him everything that he meant to her. He had realized her dreams for Scannon Square and for Miranda Stanton.

They stared at each other for a long moment; then Kurt Daniels broke the confusion in the room by calling for a vote.

Chapter Nine

Matt and Randy were married in Portland with Will and Vivian in attendance and Duncan and Julia watching from the first pew. Then they drove to the airport to watch Matt's parents take off for Connecticut.

"I know how you feel about leaving Scannon Cove," Julia said, embracing Randy, "so I hope you won't mind if we invade once in a while. I'm always ready to take a trip."

"I'd love that," Randy assured her, reaching up for her new father-in-law's hug.

"You two are going to be pretty busy with your respective businesses and watching over the Scannon Square project. You won't have a moment to call your own until next year."

Julia elbowed him in the ribs. "Then we'll come back next year. Come on, darling. They're calling our flight."

In the airport terminal, Will and Matt shook hands. "See you in a few days," Will said.

Randy looked up at Matt in inquiry. "I thought we were all driving back together."

He put an arm around her shoulder, holding her to him. "You were mistaken," he said with a smile. "Will and Vivian are driving back together. You and I are staying for a brief but wild honeymoon.''

''How brief?'' Vivian challenged.

''How wild?'' Will asked with interest and a wicked lift of his eyebrow.

''Three days tops,'' Matt replied. Then, leaning down to give Vivian a hug, he added, ''And the rest is censored. Drive safely, you two.''

''But how are they going to get back to Scannon Cove?'' Randy asked.

''They're going to rent a car,'' Matt explained with a grin, pointing to the automobile rental booth to which Will and Vivian were headed, hand in hand. ''Only not from Stanton Motors, because then we'd probably have to rescue them from somewhere, and I don't want my evening interrupted.''

''But I told my crew I'd be back tomorrow morning!''

''I know.'' Matt nodded, pulling her across the terminal toward the wall of doors leading to the parking lot. ''But I told Walsh not to expect you back till Wednesday.''

Randy halted in her tracks. Matt pushed her through the open door, then caught her hand and started toward his car. ''Can't you just picture,'' he asked over his shoulder as she ran to keep up with him, ''a nice quiet dinner at the Benson, just you and me, then the room you had the night we were stranded there?''

Her heart was racing, and it wasn't just from the effort to match his steps.

''But your hotel . . .''

''Will's in residence now. He can take care of things until we get back.''

''Okay.'' Her tone was slightly strained. As Matt stopped at the Flambeau, he pushed her up against the driver's side door, warm from the hour in the sun, and put a hand to the roof on either side of her.

"Aren't you anxious to spend a little time alone with me?" he teased, running a tantalizing finger along her jawline. "Scannon Cove will be there when we get back, I promise you. But for three days there will be no hotel emergency infringing on our time, no battle between your salesmen, no Jake running over cars before you even get them prepped. Nothing..." He reached down to kiss her lightly, the sun catching the deep blue of his eyes, turning them to aquamarine. Randy felt blinded by the light, by her love for him and his for her, by the brightness of the future that lay ahead. "Nothing to distract us from each other."

She smiled a sigh. "That does sound wonderful."

He unlocked her door and led her gently inside. "Then get in. We're wasting precious time."

RANDY WAS NERVOUS. The hotel room was touchingly familiar in its Victorian warmth and brought a flood of memories that flushed her cheeks and made her watch the closed bathroom door with a little trepidation.

She was supposed to be putting on her makeup, getting dressed for dinner. But instead, clad in a wispy white slip, she was alternately staring at her reflection in the mirror over the fussy vanity and watching the bathroom door, waiting with pounding heart for Matt to emerge.

There had never been time in her life to be intimate with a man. Those who weren't frightened by her aristocratic looks and her intelligence were skeptical of her profession and kept their distance.

Looking around at the Victorian setting, she thought dryly that she felt as fearful of this night as a nineteenth-century maiden about to lose her virtue to some powerful, experienced and slightly wicked merchant.

The bathroom door opened, and her eyes deep green and wide with alarm, Randy swung around to stare as Matt emerged. He wore only his slacks and carried his belt and watch in his left hand. His blond hair was wet and neatly combed, though curling already as it began to dry.

At the sight of her expression, he stopped to look back at her. "Tell me that there's a ten-foot grizzly bear behind me," he said, frowning at her, "and that that look of terror isn't for me."

His humor relaxed her in a small way, and she pretended to crane her neck to look behind him. "No," she reported with a smile. "No grizzly. And it isn't terror."

He returned her smile, tossed his belt and watch on the bed where his shirt lay and moved to the vanity. He sat on the edge of the small table and looked down at her.

"What is it?"

His expression was open, relaxed, his easy grin warm. Her breath fled. Those features had always seemed to her his sexiest qualities, even more appealing than his considerable good looks, and his lean, athletic body. His naked chest, tan and burnished by the small light in the corner, was gorgeous, admittedly; but right now her eyes kept wandering back to his face. How odd, she thought absently, that so few people realized how much sex appeal there was in kindness.

She came back to awareness as he caught her chin and tilted it up. "The fact that we're in a Victorian room," he said quietly, "does not mean you can go into a brown study."

She lifted a shoulder in confusion, her face a little flushed. "I was just wondering...how to explain."

He was still, waiting for her to go on. How did a twenty-seven-year-old woman explain to a man who had probably seen and done everything in every corner of the world that she was still a virgin.

She looked up at him, and he was still waiting, his eyes quiet. Suddenly she wanted him more than anything in the world, but she was a woman who felt comfortable only with that which was familiar to her. She was still afraid.

She stood to loop her arms around his neck, leaning her body in its light slip against the warmth of his chest. With her standing as he sat, she had a slight height advantage, and she looked down at him with a rueful smile.

"I've never done this before, you know," she finally said.

He arched an eyebrow. "Gone to dinner?"

She saw in his eyes that he knew what she meant, and she tugged gently at the back of his hair. He laughed.

"Made love," she said.

He nodded, the quiet now disturbed in his eyes, something brewing there. "I know."

She gave a small, embarrassed laugh. "And I thought I'd been so sophisticated. What gave me away?"

"I'm not sure." His hands settled on her hips, and he stroked ever so gently. "Some new radar I have, I guess. I've never sensed that about a woman before."

"Well . . ." She leaned down to kiss him gently on the lips, smiling as his smiling mouth awaited hers. "I just thought I'd warn you. In case I get hysterical and start screaming or something."

He chuckled. "Do you think you might?"

"I'm trembling," she said, her voice very soft, her eyes enormous. "I'm a little scared."

His warm hands ran up and down her back, pulling her closer as they cleared the silk of her slip and found the satiny smoothness of her shoulders. He kissed the swell of her breast atop the lace, then grazed his chin teasingly against hers.

"I can feel you trembling," he said. "But are you sure it's fear?"

She stood still to assess, to evaluate. And as she did his hands moved over her silk-clad hips, molding her thighs, bracketing her waist to ride up her rib cage. His thumbs applied light pressure across the tips of her breasts, and through slip and bra she felt the constriction of her nipples. When he pulled her to him again, her heart was rocketing, the slow movement of her blood, which she had thought was fear, now like the pulsing through her veins of warm honey or molten gold.

He stood slowly, lifting her in his arms as he did so. She looked into his eyes, fascinated by the vortex of passion beginning to build there.

"That isn't fear, Randy," he said softly. "That's excitement."

Leaning down, Matt swept back the spread and blankets with the hand under her knees and placed her on the cool sheet. She sank into the feather bed, holding her arms up for him as he sat and leaned across her.

"Does this mean dinner's off?" She giggled, her fear evaporating.

He had pulled her slip off and was studying her long, slim form in pearl gray panties and bra. "You may not eat until Wednesday," he said, leaning to plant a string of kisses at her waist.

Then he lay down beside her and gathered her in his arms.

Randy felt spellbound by his touch. His large, warm hands, gentle and blessed with magic, stroked her shoulders, her back, the length of her arms, then moved over her shoulders again and down her back to stop at the fastening of her bra. He loosened his hold on her for a moment, just long enough to flip the bit of lace over the side of the bed. Then he studied the small, firm globes of her breasts, ivory and pink in their invitation.

He looked up into her face, the storm in his eyes now raging. "How can every little inch of you be so beautiful?"

She smiled, molding his strong shoulders in her hands. "I think it's a case of the eye of the beholder."

It wasn't, of course, Matt knew. How many times had he looked down like this at a woman? Yet how many times had there been this magic combination of long-limbed elegance, blessed by the wonder of innocence, coupled with the fire building in a pair of sage-green eyes?

His eyes went to the flame of her hair, flared out on the pillow, and traced the long, ivory line of her body. He felt a fullness not only in his masculinity but at the very heart of him, as well. She was his to make love with at last.

Fascinated by the warmth and muscle under her fingers, Randy tentatively ran her hand lightly across Matt's chest, following the tangle of golden hair to his waist. She felt his muscle react and drew her hand away, smiling guiltily.

"Are you ticklish?"

He laughed softly, placing her hand back at his waist and holding it there with his own. "Yes, but don't stop."

He lay back and tilted her up over him so that she could work her hand carefully over every inch of his bare chest. Remembering how delicious his mouth had felt on her skin, she leaned down, her face hidden by the curtain of her hair as she planted kisses along his flat, broad waist. As she reached the concave indenture near his stomach, a fractured sigh escaped him. He reached down to tuck her hair behind her ear, and she smiled shyly at him, knowing she had pleased him if only in a small way. She had been so afraid that her innocence against his experience would leave him wanting.

Her eagerness to please wrenched at Matt and warmed him at the same time. He pulled her up beside him, taking a moment to remove his slacks and briefs. When he turned back to her, her arms were open for him, and he went into them, her generosity helping him hold tight to his unraveling control.

As he leaned down to kiss her, her hand roamed along his back, feeling the tapering of his waist, the tight muscle in his hips and sinewy thighs.

Matt's lips moved to her breasts, and Randy's exploration of his body stilled. She found herself suddenly unable to concentrate on anything but herself. Pressure was building in her chest, a strange spiral of feeling that flew out from a central point, then closed in again, teasing her to a new level of personal awareness. A delicious tremor was building in her lower limbs. Had she really lived in this body so long, she wondered, and been so unaware of its secrets?

Matt's lips traced down her rib cage and across her stomach. He encountered the barrier of her panties and disposed of it. He bent her knee up to kiss it, then follow the slender line of her thigh upward.

She gasped, startled by the intimacy, though wanting it. His hand replaced his lips, and she held him close to her, afraid that this wild raging inside would abate if she did not. The spiral tightened, diminishing its circumference with the narrowing movement of his hand until it was twirling in on itself, leaving one hot pinpoint of desire that made her see color and light and things beyond imagining.

He hesitated over her for a moment, and she moved to accommodate him, her eyes loving, waiting. He entered her surely, firmly, breaching her body's resistance, stifling her cry with a kiss of reassurance.

"It's all right," he said gently, combing the hair back from her eyes with his fingers. "It'll be all right in a minute."

She smiled up at him, her eyes languorous with passion. "It's all right now, Matthew. I love you."

"And I love you." He reached a hand under her to hold her fast against him. "God, I love you."

Randy was surprised to find that the wild longing she thought would end with his entry had only begun. The pressure within her renewed itself again. Even stronger this time as he moved her with him in an undulating rhythm that served to accelerate the tremor inside her until she thought she would fly apart. And then she did, body shuddering, pulsing, closing and opening like a bud in a warm winter. As the spiral finally loosened its grip on her and the world began to settle into place, Randy knew the metamorphosis was complete. She would never be the same again; Matt's touch had changed her forever.

Matt pulled the covers over them, settling her in the crook of his shoulder. He lay quietly, holding her tightly against him, marveling at her reaction to him and his to her. Love made the difference to the union of two bodies. This woman, he thought, clutching the slender bone of her shoulder in one hand, had diverted his future in a way he would never have chosen. But what she had given him in return was beyond all he had ever imagined possessing.

Astonished green eyes looked up at him. "Is lovemaking always like that?"

He smiled gently, shaking his head. "It was never like that before."

"Really?" she asked, seriously searching his face. "Even though I'd never made love before?"

"Candidly," he replied, kissing her forehead and settling down with her into the pillows, "what you lack in experience you make up for in aptitude."

"Oh, good." Liking the pleased sound of his voice, she snuggled into him, suddenly feeling a desperate need to sleep. "I feel wonderful. Sleepy but wonderful. How do you feel?"

"Wonderful," he replied. "Hungry but wonderful."

She raised her head, frowning at him with eyes that were heavy with weariness. "Do you want to go eat right now?"

"No." He pulled her back down to his shoulder. "Sleep for a while. We'll eat later."

Needing little encouragement, she burrowed against him, and as she fell asleep, Matt lay quietly, marveling at the wonder of life's intricate design.

Matt and Randy spent the next three days walking hand in hand in downtown Portland. They paid special attention to the restored riverfront and the historical section near the Burnside Bridge, where many old buildings of the same Italianate construction as Scannon Square had been restored.

One entire day was spent wandering through an old building, now called New Old Town. It was filled with shops and restaurants, much as Randy had envisioned for her own project. They took notes and had long discussions about color and design for Scannon Square.

They visited the Frederick and Nelson Department Store again, and Rayanne, recognizing them, was anxious to help in the selection of dresses.

"Suits are still the most practical thing for work," Randy insisted to Matt in a whisper.

"Fine," Matt whispered back, "but I refuse to look at them at home."

"I wear jeans at home."

"I've seen them. They're baggy. Dresses."

"Matt . . ."

"Randy, you've got great legs. Why cover them up or wear something that doesn't flatter them?"

She kicked a leg out and did a graceful turn of her ankle. "You really think so?"

"That's why I married you."

"Really?" She looked innocently surprised. "I thought you married me for my fleet of rental cars."

"Cute. Rayanne's calling you."

Four dress boxes later, they emerged onto the busy, sunny sidewalk.

"You know what else I'd like to do?" she asked.

He smiled indulgently, squinting against the afternoon glare bouncing off automobiles and store windows. "What?"

"Get my hair cut," she said, enthusiasm sparkling like the afternoon sun.

"No," he replied.

"Not short," she explained. "Just trimmed." She indicated a length that would skim her shoulders.

"No," Matt repeated.

She faced him squarely, her jaw firming, though her green eyes remained calm. "It is my hair."

"Most of the time," he conceded with a grin. "But in bed it's my hair. It wraps itself around my senses until you're as much a part of me as my own heartbeat." His eyes turned her spine to oatmeal. "Please don't cut it."

Unable to find an argument against his touching plea, Randy took his arm and began to lead him away.

"All right. But you have to take me to Le Panier and buy me the gooiest pastry they've got."

"Done."

THEY RETURNED to Scannon Cove on Wednesday, and as they drove through the downtown area on their way to the hotel, Randy could not remember ever being happier. She had Matt, and better than that, she had him in Scannon Cove. Because he preferred to be in residence at the hotel in this critical first year of operation, Randy agreed to move out of her cottage and into Matt's suite, provided that they keep the cottage for rare holidays.

"Home," she said, stretching her arms in front of her as far as the dash would allow. She dropped her hands in her lap and turned to smile at him.

"Will and Vivian seemed to hit it off."

Matt laughed, pulling into the Cove Mallory parking lot. "Talk about two of a kind."

"Wouldn't it be fun," she suggested over a laugh as Matt turned off the motor, "if they got married and Will moved here permanently?"

He pushed his door open and glanced back at her dryly. "If you had to be around Will permanently, you'd be wanting to move to Connecticut."

Just for a moment the very thought alarmed her. But when she looked into Matt's eyes and saw the teasing light as he came around to help her out of the car, she was able to smile back.

"Funny, Mallory." Then with an air of seriousness as he opened the inn's large double doors for her, Randy asked, "David is on duty tonight, isn't he? I feel like celebrating our being home."

Matt watched the girls behind the desk cluster around his wife, offering their congratulations, hugging and giggling. And he wondered how he would get her back to Connecticut for Christmas much less for a month during the summer when the family always gathered. Dismissing it from his mind, he forced his way into the feminine circle to be pleasantly bombarded himself with kisses and congratulations.

LIFE RESUMED a normal pattern. Though Will now also lived at the Cove Mallory, Matt and Randy were deliciously private in the large suite. Randy made breakfast every morning before leaving for the dealership. They ate dinner in the dining room or used room service and spent long, quiet evenings learning all the things about each other there hadn't been time to explore before.

Will occasionally joined them for dinner, sometimes in the company of Vivian, whom Randy diagnosed as obviously, painfully in love.

"You're playing Cupid," Matt commented lazily. They were sitting on the floor on either side of the coffee table, a board game spread out between them.

"I thought I was playing Trivial Pursuit. Where are the most expensive seats at a bullfight?"

He thought a moment. "In the bordello next door?"

She glared across the table at him. "In the shade! Don't you think that they're cute together?"

"The bulls?"

"Will," she clarified, "and Vivian."

"It's hard for me to think of my brother forever married to a sexpot." He looked up into Randy's expression of injured feelings and added quickly, "Even though I am."

She kicked his shin. "Viv has a heart of gold."

"Raquel Welch probably does, too, but I wouldn't want her for a sister-in-law. Who was the movie industry's biggest male box office attraction in 1980?"

Randy didn't even have to think about that. "Burt Reynolds. Why not?"

He shrugged. "I don't know. It'd be too distracting."

She slapped the card from which she had been about to read his question on the table and faced him with a pout. "You mean you'd rather watch her than me?"

"Never!" He looked properly horrified, but his lip was twitching.

Randy stepped over the coffee table by planting a foot in the middle of the game board. She pushed Matt down to the carpet, pinning him there and kneeling astride him.

"Have you read the article in the Oregonian about family violence?" he asked seriously, his voice strangling as she leaned her elbows on his chest.

"No, but you're going to be the subject of tomorrow's article if you don't explain to me why you find Vivian more appealing than me."

"I didn't say she was more appealing, I . . ."

"You said that you would find her distracting," Randy reminded, leaning a little harder on her elbows, "and she would be distracting you from me—I'd like to know why she'd be able to do that."

He appeared to consider the question and replied gravely. "I think it's her subtlety."

Randy's forearm was now at Matt's throat. "There's nothing subtle about a thirty-six D."

"You're right," he gasped. "Subtlety isn't everything. Is your CPR training current?"

Suddenly, Matt was uppermost, and Randy was pinned to the carpet.

"Now," he said threateningly, sweeping her up in his arms, "just to prove to you that Vivian does not hold more appeal for me than you do..."

"We just did this an hour ago," she pointed out softly, passion beginning to stir in her eyes.

"You've never heard of seconds?"

"In increments of time, in dueling, in servings," she said. "But in sex?"

"Of course. I think that we should spend the rest of the evening making our pursuits a little less trivial."

Chapter Ten

It was late October. The outside of Scannon Square looked much as it must have years ago except that now its Italianate shoulders were squared with the character lent by time. Its bricks were glowing with the patina of age. Among its contemporary neighbors it had the grace of an old woman in a crowd of debutantes. The general public appeared to watch with interest as Mallory Brothers Builders progressed, and the local newspaper covered the evolution of Scannon Square with regularity.

Even Grissom was planning to set his daughter up in a flower shop on the second level. Randy had all the prospective businesses signed to contracts, and they were anxiously waiting the precious next few months while the crew went inside to clean, reconstruct, partition, paint and paper.

Randy's excitement grew daily, and she spent more and more lunch hours at the site, watching the progress. Her respect for Will as a brother and as a builder grew by leaps and bounds. He treated her with genuine affection, and though she knew that he still wondered about Matt's decision to settle in Scannon Cove, he never mentioned it or the life Matt had led before.

Listening to his teasing banter from the shelter of Matt's arms one evening after dinner, Randy came to the conclusion that she could not think of one thing more to ask of life that she did not already have.

"I understand you're hiring another accounting clerk for Harper's office," Will said.

"Yeah," Matt replied. "I was looking at applications this afternoon."

"Why don't you hire Vivian?" Will suggested with all apparent sincerity. "She keeps books."

Randy laughed. "Now there's an idea."

"True," Matt agreed dryly. "A bad one, but an idea nonetheless. Can you imagine how having Vivian around here would slow down Will's progress at the square?"

From his perch on the arm of an overstuffed chair, Will cast a condemning look at his brother, who was seated in a corner of the sofa, his arm around Randy, who reclined against him.

"You two have not been the epitome of efficiency since you got married. Case in point: the laundry was three feet deep in suds, and where was our illustrious Cove Mallory manager?"

Randy blushed as Matt looked back at Will with an unabashed grin. "I had taken an hour off."

"And apparently so had Randy," Will noted. "Because I went to the dealership to offer to take her to coffee and Viv told me she had run home for an hour to, ah, freshen up."

"It was very refreshing," Matt said. "Thank God for Randy's cottage."

"Very," Randy seconded. "And the janitorial crew handled the problem just fine even though Matt couldn't be found."

"Dad would be horrified," Will teased.

"No, he wouldn't. He just operated on a different schedule. I've covered more breakfast meetings for him because he had . . . better things to do."

"Well, then, if you hired Vivian and I spent a lot of time here, I'd just be following a family tradition, so to speak."

"William," Matt said with a sigh, "isn't it time you went home?"

"If it wasn't for your sweet wife, I'd be discouraged from visiting by your rudeness."

Matt walked Will to the door with a fraternal hand on his shoulder. "How can I break it to you that I could live without your visits?"

Randy smiled to herself the next moment when Will brought up the subject of light fixtures that had been ordered for the square. Apparently they were lost somewhere between the manufacturer and the Portland freight service that would have shipped them to Scannon Cove. Suddenly Matt and Will were all seriousness, leaning in the front doorway as they discussed a solution. On rare occasions the incessant, friendly harassment that pervaded their relationship was pushed aside and the depth of their friendship became apparent. It made her feel warm to know that they were brothers in spirit as well as by bond of blood.

"Okay. See you two tomorrow." Will clapped Matt on the shoulder and blew Randy a kiss.

As Matt closed the door behind Will, he flipped off the light switch, leaving only the hall light to guide his way to Randy, who was still sitting on the sofa. He held a hand down to her.

"I'm beat. Are you ready for bed?"

As Randy slipped under his arm and leaned against him for the short walk to the bedroom, she thought contentedly, *This is it. Finally. Life as I've always dreamed it—solitary Randy in a loving man's arms, forever content, forever secure.* She breathed a silent prayer of thanks.

RANDY WAS CROSSING from the main showroom to the used-car lot the following day when she spotted Matt's Flambeau rounding the corner with Will in the passenger seat.

With a smile and a wave, she ran toward them, slowing as Matt got out of the car in casual clothes, not the three-piece suit in which she had seen him this morning. He ran around the car toward her with a look that told her instantly that something was wrong.

He caught her arms as he reached her and leaned down to hug her to him.

"What is it?" Randy asked, unconsciously bracing herself.

"My father's had a heart attack," he said, his eyes dark with concern, his mouth set in a grim line.

She clutched his forearms, feeling his pain. "How bad?"

He shook his head. "Bad. But I'm not sure about details. Mom wasn't too coherent. Randy, I've got to go to Connecticut."

"Of course," she said firmly.

"There's a flight out at seven p.m., so we've got to go right now to the airport." He held her close again, and she could feel the anxious thrum of his heart. "I love you."

"I know, darling." She pulled his face down and kissed him thoroughly. "I love you, too. And don't worry about anything. I'll keep my eye on the hotel and the square."

"I'll call you as soon as I know more," he promised as she walked him back around the car.

"Drive carefully," she cautioned, leaning into the car as Matt opened the door. "Bye, Will. Please take care of him for me."

"Always," he promised with a thin smile.

Randy held Matt one more time, absorbing the warm, safe feeling of being enclosed in his arms, then stepped back to let him get into the car. With a wave, he drove off, and Randy stood at the curb until he was out of sight, the late-October wind swirling the skirt of her brown wool dress, making a flaming banner of her hair.

THE TWO WEEKS that followed were the longest of Randy's life. Not a stranger to being alone and lonely, she now found solitude harder than ever to bear. Accustomed to Matt's warmth and vitality, his unfailing humor and constant strength, she felt his absence like an amputation. The suite seemed to echo emptily; their bed was vast and cold without him.

Randy went to the dealership early and stayed late, spending her lunch hour at the square. Though she had made it known to the hotel staff that she was available should she be needed for any reason, she tried to stay out of the way.

Katie Kaufman was in charge in Matt's absence, and he had obviously trained her well. As far as Randy could tell, everyone performed as though Matt were looking over his shoulder.

Matt called every few days, keeping Randy abreast of his father's gradual recovery. For the first week Duncan's progress was slow, his condition guarded. By the end of the second week he was out of intensive care and threatening to leave the hospital with or without the doctor's approval.

"Does that mean you're coming home?" she asked hopefully.

"Yes, we'll be coming in on Saturday." Matt ended their conversation with the "I love you" that she lived on from phone call to phone call.

AT THE MALLORY HOME on the outskirts of Hartford, Connecticut, Matt leaned against a small-paned window, looking out at the dark blue of early evening. Flame-colored leaves that reminded him of Randy's hair lay in purple shadow on the broad expanse of lawn.

"You didn't tell her," Will said from the stone hearth across the room, where he stoked a recalcitrant fire.

"I'll tell her when I get home," he replied absently.

"Do you think that she'll come?"

Matt heaved a sigh, fogging the small pane at eye level that provided his view outside. Ironically, he thought, that misted square of glass exemplified his view into the future.

He knew Randy's features by heart and saw them in his mind's eye every waking moment. He knew every curve and contour of her body and felt them react to his touch in his dreams. He knew what pleased her and what hurt her. But he couldn't hazard a guess on how she would react when he told her that they would have to come back to Connecticut to live.

Though mending satisfactorily, his father would have to play a much smaller role in the company if he was to live to be an old man. And there was no one but his oldest son at this point to step in.

Randy had made her feelings about leaving Scannon Cove more than clear, but that had been before they were married. She seemed to need him and want him so much, to love him more than he had ever hoped.

Yet there was that impassioned devotion to Scannon Cove—the place where she had finally found a home and then found herself. He had tried to understand that about her, because his growing up years had been so different. The Mallorys had been on the move continually, but the place hadn't mattered to Matt so much because he had the people he loved. But Randy hadn't found the people to love her until fate had placed her in Scannon Cove.

"Does that mean you don't know?" Will interrupted Matt's reverie, still waiting for an answer.

Matt turned to walk toward the fire and spread his hands over it as the flames began to dance.

"I guess it does. It's hard to admit, but I don't know if she'll come back with me or not."

"She loves you very much," Will said with a gravity unusual for him.

"I know." Matt nodded pensively. "But she came up a lot differently than we did. She married me because I promised to stay in Scannon Cove; my gypsy life-style couldn't provide the kind of security she feels she needs. Now I have to renege on that promise."

"If you don't, thousands of employees and hundreds of thousands of guests will have their jobs and their comfort in jeopardy."

"I know that, too." Matt stared moodily into the fire. "It's at times like this that I wish I'd stayed in food service with David."

RANDY SENSED that something was amiss the moment Matt took her in his arms in the middle of the used-car lot. She looked into his face, hoping to read the answer there, but it was hidden. His eyes were clear and deep with his love for her, his smile genuine. He spun her off her feet, then kissed her thoroughly with little regard for the whistles and applause from the lineup of mechanics taking their coffee break.

He asked about the hotel and the square as they drove home, then lingered at the desk in the lobby for a few minutes to talk to Katie.

"Go on ahead, sweetheart," he told Randy, giving her a gentle shove toward the elevators. "I'll be right up."

In the suite, Randy set the small table in the kitchen and checked the casserole that she had left in the self-timing oven. It was done to perfection. She tossed a salad and opened a bottle of Gewürztraminer, trying not to think about what might be on Matt's mind. The possibilities were too frightening.

She knew him intimately enough to realize that something was obstructing the easy camaraderie that had become such a blessing in their marriage. And she had the most terrifying feeling that the obstruction was the very thing that she had refused to lend thought to in his absence.

Randy was fussing around the kitchen like a madwoman, though everything was done, when Matt finally entered the room. A bellman followed with his bag, telling him a joke.

The door closed behind the departing bellman and Matt emerged from the bedroom in a blue sweater and an old pair of jeans.

"Smells good," he said, coming to wrap his arms around her and plant a kiss behind her ear. "Mmm, and so do you."

"*Eau de* overhaul." Her laugh was brittle, and she squirmed out of his arms to place the casserole on the table.

"Chicken Divan?" he asked, crossing to the table to sniff.

"David got it all ready for me, and I just put it in the oven. I thought that you'd want to keep dinner simple after eating on the plane and probably being inactive all day."

Matt stood at the table and poured the wine. "I walked for miles in Connecticut. Our property fronts a lake that meanders through the greenest, hilliest—"

"What was Katie's report on the hotel?" she interrupted, going back to the refrigerator for salad dressing.

After filling their glasses, he put the bottle down and leaned a hand on the back of his chair to study her frantic movements. She filled the coffee maker as though she were performing the Japanese tea ceremony, then looked about.

"Do I have everything?" she asked with exaggerated casualness. "What did Katie say? Is everything okay? It looked like it to me."

"The only thing not on the table is peanut butter," he replied a little tightly. "Katie said everything is fine, and it appears that it is. Now can we eat?"

Randy walked to the table, her nerve endings screaming. She looked at Matt with an arched eyebrow. "A little testy, are we?"

Matt pushed his chair up to the table with annoyance. Then, as Randy jumped, he looked into her anguished eyes and expelled a ragged breath, tightening his grip on the chair as he forced himself to remain calm.

"Yes," he admitted. "I am testy, tired, worried and just a little scared."

Randy faced him across the table, her hands, too, clutching a chair back. "What would frighten the Midas-touch Matt Mallory?" she asked coolly.

He looked into her eyes, his expression judicious, and she had to look away. "I think you know," he said.

When she said nothing, he poured more wine into her glass and then his. "Can you put that back in the oven for a few minutes?" he asked, indicating the casserole. "I'd like to talk to you."

Randy did as he asked, her heart hammering against her ribs. He handed her a glass of wine, then led her gently to the living room. She had a fire going in the fireplace, and they sat on the sofa, facing it. But instead of their usual cuddle in one corner that always followed dinner, they sat at opposite ends, Randy tucking her feet under her, Matt stretching his legs out as though they were still cramped from the plane.

"So, how is your father?" Randy asked before Matt could speak. Her stomach was churning, because now she knew beyond a doubt what was coming.

"He's out of immediate danger," Matt replied, staring into the fire. He did look tired, Randy noted. For a moment she let herself imagine what that trip home must have been like for him—seeing his father's life in danger, consoling his mother, making all the decisions Duncan should have been making and couldn't. Then she put it out of her mind, selfishly holding to her own concerns before he overrode them. "But if he's to live to be an old man, he has to relinquish a major part of his responsibility in the company." He turned to Randy, his eyes revealing the reluctance with which he spoke. "At this point in time, I'm the only one who can assume it. I'm afraid that your worst fears are realized, Randy. We have to go back."

"Surely there's someone else," she suggested weakly. "I mean, you're always telling me that you surround yourself with the best people."

"I do," he agreed readily, "but this is my job, not theirs. This is a family-owned company, and there's got to be a Mallory at the top. My uncle is older than my father, and my cousin is young and untried. Administration just isn't Will's thing. It's got to be me."

"Does it?" she asked stiffly. There was just enough suspicion in her voice to make him stiffen. Anger suddenly overrode the patience that he'd been trying so hard to maintain.

"What does that mean?" he asked quietly.

She gave him a level look, her own anger mounting, swamping her fear. "I find it hard to believe that among all the highly paid members of your father's staff there isn't someone who could step in instead of you." She took a sip of wine and added with a touch of bitterness, "Of course, you're the one with the golden touch."

He laughed mirthlessly, downing the contents of his glass in one long swallow. "Meaning that I've chosen to take on the welfare of twenty-seven hundred employees, the management of a staggering financial burden and an eighteen-hour-a-day schedule for reasons that are selfish?"

"Burdensome as that all is to contemplate," she said, looking at him evenly, "it'll keep you from staying here, won't it?"

He stared her down for a long moment, but she refused to flinch.

"Right," he said finally, getting to his feet. "And I arranged my father's heart attack so that I'd have a valid reason to leave. Valid to some people, that is, though not to you. Family matters aren't important enough to make you change your plans."

"I've never had to consider a family before," she pointed out.

He wandered to the fireplace, hands jammed in his pockets. "Yes, I know. Poor little abandoned girl. Moved from pillar to post and hating everyone she came in contact with whether or not they were responsible for her circumstances." He spun around, his bristling anger outlined by the fire behind him. "Hell, Randy! Are you going to trade on that for the rest of your life? I'm sure it was ugly and horrible, and I'm sorry that it happened to you. But that lonely fourteen years out of your life ended when you came here to live. The future waits with limitless possibilities and a million promises that you're hiding from because you're holding so tight to those years. Let them go! Live now and stop being afraid."

Angry and hurt, she swallowed a painful lump in her throat, holding tears back through clenched teeth. "Easy for you to say..." she accused.

"Oh, God!" He threw his head back in exasperation; then he walked back toward her, his eyes snapping impatience. "Maybe it is easy for me to talk. But I'm tired of having to excuse or qualify everything that I think and do because you were abandoned and I wasn't! I was loved and spoiled and given the best of everything because I was the product of my parents' love, and because we were a family. But let me tell you something about that. You don't just get from a family, Randy—that feeling that you've missed so much, the fuzzy feeling that means that you belong. You have to give to get it. You have as much responsibility to fulfill their needs as they have to answer yours."

Her mouth quivered, and the tears fell. "I thought you and I were a family."

He sank down beside her again, his eyes drained of anger. There were dark circles under them, and she noticed for the first time in the dim light of the living room that his face looked a little thinner.

"I wonder now if we are," he said heavily.

Hearing him voice that doubt, Randy felt her stomach fist. "So where do we stand?" she asked.

He looked at her for a long moment, then got wearily to his feet. "If we were a family," he said, looking down at her, "we would stand side by side. As it is, maybe we're just a couple of lovers playing at propriety." He turned away and stopped at the door. "I'm going down to the lounge. You take the bed; I'll sleep on the sofa."

"Matt!" There was desperation in her voice, fear and sadness. But he didn't hear it.

The night passed even more slowly for Randy than the two weeks that Matt was away. She argued with herself, cried, railed against her husband and shed more tears. It wasn't fair. Finally, she had things the way she had always dreamed they would be, and her sunny future was being destroyed.

She knew, of course, that Matt had been powerless to prevent his father's heart attack or the administrative gap Duncan's absence would leave in the company. But she couldn't push away the thought that Matt had leaped a little too eagerly at the prospect of going back to Connecticut.

By morning Randy had cried away her anger and forced herself to face the facts. Matt had to go back; he had no other choice, and she had come to love him too much to let him go alone. She wasn't sure she could handle being away from Scannon Cove. But if Matt would let her accompany him on the condition that she could return home if she found it too difficult, she knew she had to try. It was a feeble solution at best, and possibly only temporary, but it was a plan.

Implementing it immediately was impossible, however, because Matt had not returned to the suite the previous night.

Heavyhearted, Randy went to work feeling as though she slogged through honey as she tried to add figures, answer questions and hold the shreds of her composure together.

She called their suite several times during the day but got no answer. As Randy prepared to close the shop, a query of the switchboard operator revealed that Mr. Mallory was out and wasn't expected back until late.

With a defeated sigh she locked the doors after Gordie, turned the lights off in the showroom and wandered through the dark corridor to the shop.

The silence of the garage at night and the faint, familiar odors of oil and paint had always been a balm to her spirit in the past. Tonight the emptiness seemed only to exaggerate her loneliness.

The Morrisons' truck was in again, she noticed, hoping it would be serviced without further damage being done to it. Looking around, she saw several vehicles that were regular customers. She felt a sense of pride that she had been able to maintain the reputation of quality service the shop had built up over the years, before she had purchased the dealership.

A new station wagon stood against the wall, waiting to be prepped. Her own demonstrator sat beside it, needing a new headlight, thanks to Jake and the wrench that inexplicably flew out of his hand while he worked on a car on a nearby grease rack.

With a sigh Randy pulled her coveralls off the wall peg, removed her skirt and slip, then stepped into the rough garment, zipping it over her teal-blue panties.

She was sitting cross-legged on the concrete floor, pulling at the box that contained the new headlight unit, when she heard a sound behind her. Her heart leaped to her throat as a large male hand reached over her shoulder to snatch the box from her.

She turned to see a pair of long legs in familiar brown cords. Her eyes flew up as Matt gave one hard yank to open it, then got down on his haunches to hand it back to her. Remnants of anger still smoldered in his eyes, along with a trace of regret and obvious weariness. As his gaze ran over her pale face, she thought she saw longing take its place in the complexity of emotions there.

Overwhelmed by his nearness and the scene last night, Randy felt a tightness develop in her chest and a faint tremor in her hands. She put the box down on the cold concrete floor.

"I . . . tried to call you today," she said, staring at the box.

"I know," he said quietly. "I got the message when I came back tonight. When you weren't at home, I was pretty sure I'd find you here." There was a moment's pulsing silence; then he asked quietly, "What did you want?"

"I wondered . . . how you were." Tears were building in her throat, because she had missed him so much during those interminable weeks. Yet he hadn't seemed as far away from her then as he had last night, as he did at this moment.

"I was fine," he replied, his expression, when she glanced up at him, still too complex to understand. "I was walking, trying to think. I must have covered Scannon Cove from end to end at least three times." Then he seemed to become distracted, and his eyes sharpened on hers, love suddenly unmistakable in their bright depths as he rose, pulling her to her feet. "Do you have any idea how much I missed you while I was in Connecticut?" His voice was raw with emotion, filled with the strain of painful honesty. "All the difficult things I had to do were doubly difficult, because when I turned around to share a thought with you, to ask your opinion or to just . . . to just look at you—" he swallowed audibly "—you weren't there."

Randy flew into his arms, sobbing noisily. The warmth and solidity of his embrace closed around her, his delicious mouth finding hers and setting her life back on its feet. He did need her; everything they had together was still intact.

"I missed you so much," she told him as he rained kisses on her cheek and behind her ear to the collar of the coveralls. "It's all so black without you. I'm sorry I hurt you."

He raised his head to look at her, his easy smile sparking hers after what had seemed like such a long, grim darkness.

"Get out of the coveralls," he said, "and let's go home and finish this conversation."

As he put her gently away from him, she noted the smudges of grease on his jacket, the long streak on his cords. "Oh, your clothes!" she groaned. But she had started to step out of the coveralls and the last thing that Matt wanted to look at was his stained clothing. His eyes went from her long, stocking-clad legs to her eyes, one eyebrow raised in question.

She shrugged a delicate shoulder. "These can be worn over pants but not over a skirt."

"Ah." He nodded with understanding and took her hand to steady her as she stepped out of the greasy puddle of coveralls.

"My skirt is over—" She began to say, pointing behind her to the workbench on which she had left it, but Matt was shaking his head and grinning. "For two weeks in my lonely bed I've had wild dreams about those gorgeous legs. Now that I've seen them, I'll never make it back to the house." He looked around himself for a solution, and his eyes stopped on the station wagon. He turned back to her, his eyes wicked. "Do you feel adventurous?"

"That isn't even prepped yet," she said, laughing. Then, caught by the outrageousness of the idea and the passion building in his eyes, she nodded. "Why not? I've got a blanket in the sofa bed in my office from when I used to sleep here in the early days."

While Randy went for the blanket, Matt opened the tailgate of the wagon and knelt into the car to lower the top of the back seat to form a flat surface. As he jumped out again, Randy opened the blanket out over the scratchy carpeting. In a moment Matt had divested Randy of her stockings, blouse and undies and removed his own clothes. As he lifted her up onto the blanket, he noted the goose bumps on her arms.

"Here," he said, snatching up the sweater that he'd been wearing. "Put this on." He held it out for her, then pulled it down as her head and arms emerged from the neck and sleeves. Randy wrapped her arms around herself, relishing the traces of Matt's body heat. Then he climbed in beside her and closed the tailgate, enclosing them in the small, shallow space. But it lacked nothing in romance, she decided, as he took her in his arms and began to ply his magic.

Concentrating on pleasing and being pleased, Randy forgot where she was, the argument of last night and the uncertainty that still lay ahead. This moment was infinitely precious, and she lost herself in it, abandoning mind and body to the magic of Matt's touch.

Randy finally pulled the sweater off, raising her arms to Matt. But instead of kneeling astride her, he pulled her over him, reaching a hand up to the crown of her hair reminding her absently to watch her head before he took her mouth again.

"I love you," he repeated, writhing under her until she thought she would go mad waiting for the apex of the storm, the climax of this wild adventure.

And then it came, the hovering storm that always tortured her with its reluctance to appear, finally striking with the suddenness of ambush and flooding over her again and again, each wave crashing before she had recovered from the last.

Matt held her hands as she arched backward, crying softly in the final ebbing of her body. Collapsing on top of him, she resisted his efforts to push her up and put the sweater back on her.

"No," she said firmly, enjoying the feel of his hair-covered chest beneath her breasts. "I haven't touched you in so long."

He laughed softly and spread the sweater across her back, folding the other half of the blanket over her.

They lay in silence for a long time, enjoying the restoring balm of their closeness, the simple warm pleasure of each other's arms.

Randy finally propped herself up on her forearms, leaning on Matt's chest to reach up and kiss his chin. As he stroked her hair, she saw the same change in his eyes that came stealing over her. Their lovemaking, as always, had been beautiful, but it did not erase the problem that stood between them like a locked gate. Then she remembered that in the night she had thought she'd found a key.

She looked at him uncertainly. He pulled the sweater from around her and slipped it over her head.

"Put it on," he said. "I'll get your clothes."

Randy pulled the sweater down, hugging the still-warm, scratchy wool to her, and trying to quiet the racing of her heart. As she rose out of the euphoria of their back-seat adventure, the enormity of their problem seemed insurmountable and the possible solution she had held closely all day, very fragile.

Yet he had just made love to her as though he would die without her. It will work, she told herself bracingly. Of course it will work.

When Matt reappeared at the tailgate, he was wearing his slacks and T-shirt and carrying his shoes, her undies and skirt held in his other hand.

Self-conscious now, Randy slipped into her panties and skirt, wondering what had happened to her slip as Matt pulled on his socks and shoes.

Finally, they sat side by side on the tailgate. It was a moment before Matt finally asked, staring ahead of him, "So what do we do, Randy?"

She drew a deep breath. "I had a thought last night."

Another moment's pause. "Oh?"

"How long do you think it would be before you had things under control in Connecticut? I mean, say before your cousin Jeremy could take over?"

He frowned. "A year at least."

She, too, frowned. That was hard news, but the alternative to her solution was worse.

"What if . . . what if I went back with you on a sort of . . . conditional basis. If I can handle it, I'll stay the duration. If I find I can't . . . maybe we could live apart until your cousin can take over." There was a deep silence, and when Matt said nothing, Randy asked weakly, "Do you think that would work?"

He studied the bumper of the Morrison truck and shook his head, expelling a sigh. "Frankly, I don't see how it can," he said. Randy's small bubble of hope shattered. "I don't see how you can hope to adjust to life there without being committed to it. And I don't know how I'm going to function with the possibility hanging over me that you might walk away from me at any moment. No, it doesn't sound like it'll work." He turned to look at her, an expression of self-deprecation in his tired eyes. "But I'm desperate enough to give it a try. As long as I can count on you doing the same."

She nodded, a thin shadow of hope rising again. "And can I ask one more thing?"

He shrugged, looking already as though he had bargained away everything he valued. "Of course."

"Can we fly back here for the opening of Scannon Square in February?"

"If I can get away," he agreed cautiously, "sure."

Randy looked around herself at the garage in which she had often helped a frustrated mechanic find a problem, where she had sometimes slept after staying up half the night to meet a promised deadline, where she and Matt had made love amid the paradoxes that beset their lives. She already felt a terrible stab of loneliness.

"I'll need four or five days to get the office in order."

Matt nodded. "Fine. Are you finished here?"

She leaped off the tailgate. "Yes. I don't have to fix the headlight if I won't be here to use the car."

"Then we'd better get home. There's a lot to do."

Chapter Eleven

Will and Vivian drove Matt and Randy to the airport in Portland. Randy waved toward the large windows of the waiting area where her brother-in-law and her friend promised to watch the departure. She couldn't see them, but she knew that they were there, and she fought against the loss she felt at leaving them.

The DC-10 revved its jets and started down the runway, gathering speed. As the airport buildings flew past, Randy clutched the arms of her seat. She had never flown before and frankly felt that the laws of lift and thrust warranted closer scrutiny. She was suddenly tilted backward as the plane rose into the air like a foraging hawk. She drew in a breath and closed her eyes.

Then she felt Matt's hand on hers. "You're safe," he said with a smile in his voice. "Trust me."

She gave him a dark look out of one eye. "Are you going to come to my rescue like Superman if something happens to this darn thing?"

"Don't you doubt it for a minute. As soon as the 'Fasten Seat Belts' sign goes off, we can get you a drink. That'll help you relax. How did Bob McGraw feel about his new position as interim manager of Stanton Motors?"

Randy was forced to smile at the memory. "You'd have thought that I'd made him president of General Motors. I hope Eldon doesn't give him too hard a time."

"I'm sure Will would be glad to look in on the shop for you and check things out. You can always fire Phillips long distance if you have to."

When the seat-belt sign went off and Matt hailed a stewardess to order champagne, it was on the tip of Randy's tongue to tell him there was nothing really to celebrate, but she bit back the remark.

For the past five days Randy had made a Herculean effort to behave normally, not to pout or drop bitter innuendos regarding the move to Connecticut. But she was trying to suppress resentment so strong that cruel words seemed always just a breath away. She wasn't even sure whom she resented. Matt had no choice but to do his job; his parents couldn't help the circumstances in which they found themselves. And it wasn't her own fault that she had grown to love Scannon Cove with such intensity.

In her mind's eye she saw the wide Columbia River with its steady, exciting traffic, the green hills that nestled the town in the curve of the harbor and the city lights that made it all look like a mound of treasure at night. She felt a little like the spider that builds its web so carefully, so intricately, with a design no other spider could ever duplicate, and suddenly finds itself on the cold, dangerous pavement because of some intrusion that destroys the fragile framework of its construction. The only thought that comforted her was that she would come back to Scannon Cove for the opening of the square.

"Here you go." Matt held out her champagne, and she accepted it with a small smile.

His blue eyes took in the smile, then raised to her eyes, eyes whose expression he knew she kept carefully neutral every time he looked at her. She sent him no daggers or dirty looks, but she had forgotten herself with that little smile, and he found himself wanting to force her to hold the pose.

"Thank you," he said.

She frowned at him, looking from his face to the glass he had handed her. "I think that you've got that wrong. I say thank you, and you say you're welcome."

"I'm not talking about the champagne," he explained. "I'm talking about the fact that you've come with me and that you're not grumbling at me."

"Oh." She nodded, concentrating on the glass. "I'm saving that for a time when I need it. I can blackmail you later with this noble, stoic behavior."

"I appreciate the warning," he said with a grin. "Want to lean on me and try to nap? I know you didn't get much sleep last night."

That was true. She had been busy committing to memory all her mental images of Scannon Cove—sea gulls calling and following the fishing boats, the lunch-hour congestion she had always hated but now seemed so much a part of the town she wanted to remember, the smell of the garage, the intimate warmth of the bedroom in Matt's suite at the Cove Mallory where she had lain, curled against her husband's side.

Matt folded up the arm that separated their two seats and invited her to lean her head against his shoulder. Within minutes she was drifting off with images floating in her mind of scudding clouds over a sun-shot blue river. Matt and Randy changed planes in Denver. They were served dinner and more champagne, and Randy dozed off again, refusing to think about where they had come from and where they were going.

She awoke with a start, suddenly aware of people rushing noisily past her toward the rear exit. She turned to Matt in wide-eyed alarm, her heart lurching. "Have we crashed?" she demanded.

"No, sweetheart," he reassured her, giving her a grinning glance as he stood to reach into the overhead storage. "We've landed. Here." He handed Randy her tote and then her jacket.

When she tossed the jacket over her arm, he suggested that she put it on. "It'll be cooler in Connecticut than the Oregon coast."

So what am I doing here? she grumbled to herself, following him down the narrow aisle to the exit.

It was late and therefore dark, and Randy was tired despite having slept most of the day. After the interminable process of retrieving their luggage, Matt took her arm and started toward a car-rental booth. They were intercepted by a short, dark-featured man in jeans and a green down jacket.

Matt stopped in surprise. "George!" he said, reaching out to shake the man's hand. "I told Mother not to send anyone, that we'd be in too late."

George gave Matt and Randy a smile, and Randy gauged it at one thousand watts. "Your mother didn't send me, sir," George replied, relieving Matt of Randy's case. "I chose to come. And Ellen has soup and biscuits ready to eat. She insisted you couldn't go to bed without some home cooking on your stomachs."

Matt put an arm around the man's ample shoulders and pulled Randy forward. "Randy, I'd like you to meet George Thompson, the Mallorys' indispensable butler, chauffeur and moral support. George, this is my wife, Miranda."

The man removed a blue baseball cap, revealing a head that was bald except for a crescent of dark curls over each ear.

"Welcome to Connecticut, Mrs. Mallory," George said, shaking her hand. "My wife, Ellen, is looking forward to meeting the woman who caught Mr. Mallory."

Tired as Randy was, the prospect of hot soup was a bright spot on the horizon. And George's warmth went a long way toward relieving the homesickness she was fighting.

"I'm looking forward to meeting her," Randy assured him, "and her soup."

"Well, come along," George said briskly, moving out with bandy-legged efficiency. "The car's right outside the door."

As they headed home, Randy saw a very urbanized environment through the neon-lit darkness.

"Lots of factories and tall buildings," she said absently, her tone a little disapproving.

Matt turned to her in the dark interior of the car. "Yes," he said. "Yet sixty percent of Connecticut is still forested."

"Oh?" She sounded doubtful.

"And we've got twenty-eight state forests," George contributed proudly. "You're going to like it here, Mrs. Mallory."

Randy gave a silent harumph and settled back into the soft leather seat. So far there was no water, no sea gulls and no fishing boats. How would she ever be able to like it here?

When George pulled into the poplar-lined drive that led to a well-lit two-story house with a gambrel roof and dormer windows, Randy couldn't hold back the gasp. The house was enormous, and the driveway that circled to the front of it brought to mind parties from another century when drivers and carriages lined up along such a path, waiting to take the gentry home.

"It's so—" she swallowed as Matt turned to her "—big!"

"Has to be," he said. "My aunt and uncle are always coming and going, Dad has staff meetings here and Mom's always got some project under way that involves half the county passing through our living room. Oh, Lord!" Matt exclaimed as the front door opened, pouring more light onto the front porch. "They're still up."

"We tried to remind Mr. Duncan that the doctor said he was to be in bed early and not get excited," George said with a shake of his head. "But you know how he is. Even your mother can't do anything with him."

"He promised me he was going to cooperate with her when I left."

"I think he means to," George explained, turning in his seat after pulling up to the front door. "It's just that he's used to taking charge and doing things and he's frustrated because he can't. It's only logical that he worries about the business and the family. Your mother's afraid to leave his side, so she sits up with him and worries, too."

"Terrific," Matt said with a sigh.

"Shh," Randy cautioned, "here comes your mom." She opened her door as Julia Mallory ran down the steps, hugging her arms against the chilly autumn night. Randy stepped out and was surprised to find herself in a strong, tearful embrace.

"Oh, Randy!" Julia said, hugging her fiercely. Even in the light from the porch Randy could see that the beautiful, witty and supremely confident person she had met at the Cove Mallory had been transformed by her husband's heart attack into a tired, frightened woman who felt herself in danger of losing everything she held dear. No stranger to that feeling, Randy's heart went out to her. Julia finally pulled away and gestured helplessly, sniffing back tears. "Thanks for coming, Randy. I can't tell you how much Duncan needs Matt."

Matt came around the car and leaned down to hold his mother. "I thought I told you to be tough with Dad!" he scolded her.

"Here you are both up at midnight, and he's not supposed to even be downstairs."

"Well, now that you're here," Julia shouted, "you can handle him your way!" Her hands covered her mouth immediately in regret. Large tears spilled over her hands, and Matt could only look at her in surprise. Randy judged by his expression that Julia had never shouted at him in his life and that he'd never seen her cry.

With a sudden stiffening of her shoulders and dismissal of her personal concerns, at least temporarily, Randy put her arms around Julia and looked at her husband sharply over Julia's head. "Don't yell at her," she said. "If you were her size, could you push your father around?"

Still surprised, Matt shook his head. "She always has in the past."

"Well, she probably wasn't concerned about upsetting him then and maybe causing him to become more ill. Now..." She drew a deep breath, suddenly taking hold of her role as daughter-in-law. "I'd guess your father won't want to hear shouting or orders of any kind, however well-intentioned. Please promise me you won't yell at him."

Now Matt was looking at Randy as though he'd never seen her before. "I promise," he said at last.

"Then let's get your mom inside. It's cold out here." They started up the steps as George drove the car into the garage.

If anything could have reinforced Randy's cautioning, it was the sight of Duncan's pale face and the hand that trembled slightly on the doorknob as he held the front door open. Matt's father looked thinner to Randy and had the same frightened look in his eyes as Julia. His deep blue gaze passed over his wife and son and focused on Randy. His expression was a curious combination of belligerence and conciliation.

"He made you come," Duncan said, the same expression bouncing off his son, before returning to her.

Randy heard Julia's quiet, scolding "Duncan!" She squared her shoulders and moved into the room to give the man a brief hug. "No one makes me do anything," she said lightly. "I'm here because I want to be."

"And you?" he barked at Matt.

Matt followed Randy's lead and put an arm around his father's shoulders, guiding him to a chair. "Have you ever known me to do anything I didn't want to do?"

Duncan accepted the support of Matt's arm as he eased him down into the deep cushions. "I've known you to turn yourself inside out," he said irascibly, "to do what you felt morally bound to do. The fact is—" the older man paused and leaned his cane down against the chair, then fixed his son with a steely look "—I don't think saving your father's hide should be one of those things. You've got your own life to live."

"Right," Matt agreed, pulling off his jacket. "And right now my own life involves being a major stockholder in Mallory Inns. I'm working for myself as well as for you. Anyway, I've been itching to make some changes for a long time," Matt said, turning away from Duncan to lead Randy to a love seat. He winked at her as he did so. "Now that you'll be home and unable to interfere," Matt continued, pulling at his tie as he sat beside her, "I can implement them."

"What?" Duncan demanded, reaching for his cane as though he would wield it at his son.

Randy stiffened in alarm, thinking that Matt shouldn't be saying such things to a sick man. But she noticed that Julia appeared to relax and offered her son a covert smile as she excused herself to check on the soup.

Matt looked at his father innocently. "You know what I'm talking about. We've argued about them enough times in the past."

Duncan's gaze narrowed. "So, you decide to come back when I'm on my knees and make things run your way."

Matt nodded calmly. "That's about right."

The two men shared a long, even look, measuring each other as Randy guessed they must have done often in their relationship. Duncan finally leaned back with a ghost of the smile she remembered from the family party at the Cove Mallory.

"Good try, Son," he acknowledged. "You might have had me believing it if I didn't know you better. The whole board's in a panic. You've got one hell of a job ahead of you." He frowned at Randy. "And here your wife's been uprooted...."

Randy looped her arm easily in Matt's. "I'm not uprooted," she assured Duncan with believable sincerity. "Matt's here, so I'm here. It's as simple as that."

"And what are you going to do," he challenged her, "with a sick man, a hovering old woman—" he gave his wife what Randy could only label an affectionate glare as she returned to the room with a tray of soup mugs "—and household help that want to know your comings and goings at all times?"

"How many cars do you own?" she asked.

Surprised by the non sequitur, Duncan frowned at her. "Among us about five."

"I'll get them in the best running shape that they've ever been in." At his look of suspicion, she added, "I'm good, Mr. Mallory." Then she elbowed Matt. "Tell him I'm good."

Matt nodded. "She's good, Dad." He gave her a dry grin and elaborated further. "You have to put up with a lot of mouth, of course, but she's good."

"Did you ship your Berlinetta?" Duncan asked.

"No. Will's using it."

A short, plump woman Randy decided must be Ellen Thompson followed Julia into the room with biscuits and crackers. After Julia made the introductions, Ellen, about the same round proportions as her husband but with fair skin and blond hair in a bun, slapped Matt on the shoulder.

"Got snagged at last, eh? Pretty thing," she said of Randy. "Bet you didn't fight too hard."

Matt accepted the woman's familiarity as something he expected. "Now you can stop nagging at me."

"Not till I know," Ellen said, "when the first baby's coming."

Matt rolled his eyes in supplication. "About nine months after Randy becomes pregnant."

Ellen's gray eyes ran over Randy's trim waist and flat stomach. "Well, what are you waiting for, young Mr. Matt?"

Matt frowned at her. "I'd like to eat my soup first, if that's all right."

Ellen shook her head and turned back to the kitchen. "Some of us sure have our priorities confused."

Randy watched Ellen leave the room, both alarmed and amused by her teasing.

"Ellen loves Matt," Julia assured her, handing Duncan a cup of coffee. "She loves all of us. She's just not shy about it."

"I thought I wasn't supposed to have coffee," Duncan groused at Julia.

"It's decaffeinated."

Duncan put it on the lamp table beside him as though he planned to ignore it. "Have you ever had decaffeinated coffee?" he asked Matt. "Artificial bacon, vegetables that aren't salted, nothing but chicken and fish? It's not worth eating."

Matt laughed. "It'll be good for your waistline. Now you won't have to hold your stomach in at board meetings."

"I won't be going to board meetings."

"You might get to use the pool more often. You were starting to look like you'd swallowed Joshua's life ring."

Duncan smiled reluctantly. "Someday you'll get old and suddenly discover that your waist is wider than your chest. I hope that you'll have a son around to remind you of your weakness."

Matt toasted Duncan with his coffee cup. "So do I." Then he turned to Randy and toasted her, a challenge in his eyes. Giving him look for look, she raised her cup. "I'd love to see someone remind you of your weaknesses," she said. "If you had any. Who's Joshua?"

"George and Ellen's boy," Julia replied. "He's seven years old and just the dearest thing." Then, suddenly noticing her husband leaning back wearily in his chair, Julia sprang to her feet. "Duncan, I told you you'd be overdoing it if you stayed up."

"Get George," Matt told her quietly, "and we'll get him upstairs."

"I am not going to be carried," Duncan insisted, trying to sit forward. Obviously the effort was too much.

"You're not supposed to climb the stairs," Matt reminded him. "Unless you've bought a catapult, I see no other solution—except staying where you're supposed to be in the first place."

Duncan glared at his son with impatience but was apparently too tired to fight back verbally. George appeared instantly, and he and Matt made a seat of their hands and took Duncan upstairs, Julia hovering in their wake.

"Enough to eat, Mrs. Mallory?" Ellen asked, suddenly appearing to clear away the trays.

"Yes, that was perfect," Randy assured her. She stood to help gather cups and soup mugs. "It was thoughtful of you to stay up for us."

"Our pleasure. The folks really need you, you know." Ellen picked up the full tray and faced Randy with a frown. "They're both frightened, and it's making it hard for anyone to relax. I think you two being here will relieve that. There's nothing like young blood around to make a person feel alive." Ellen smiled warmly. "I was forty when I met George and was feeling and acting middle-aged. Then he made me feel all woman and more alive than I've been in my whole life. Then he gave me our baby and . . ." She shook her head, laughing. "I tell you. That boy has made me younger than I was at seventeen. I think everything's going to be fine for the Mallorys, but you've got to help them see that. Well, I turned down your bed. Sleep well and I'll bring breakfast up to you in the morning, it being your first day and all.''

Randy watched Ellen walk away, feeling as though the eye of a hurricane had just passed. *I'm only here temporarily,* she said to no one in particular as she started for the stairs. *I'm not likely to get that involved.* Then she remembered the way instinct had made her hold Julia and tell Matt off on the driveway and how she had told Duncan that she was here because she wanted to be and that she belonged wherever Matt was. It had been a fib of sorts, because she had sensed the older man's need to know that she had come willingly and that his son wasn't suffering the consequences of her displeasure with the situation.

When she cleared the top of the stairs, Matt and George emerged from what must have been Duncan and Julia's bedroom.

''Good night, Mrs. Mallory,'' George said, hurrying past her down the steps.

''Good night, George,'' she replied.

Matt put an arm around her shoulders and led her down a dark corridor to a door from which soft light poured. He led Randy gently into a room that was teal blue, yellow and beige, with wicker and quilted pillows that matched the quilt on the double brass bed. The off-white walls were decorated with soft watercolors and wildlife prints.

''This is a beautiful room,'' Randy said breathlessly, absorbing the warm mood of it while fighting a sudden confusion in her husband's presence. There was desire in his eyes, and she couldn't deal with that tonight. It wasn't that she was angry or that she would not welcome Matt's tender touch. But this was his territory, and she felt strange in it, as though it were already reforming her into someone different.

"Thank you for convincing my parents that you want to be here," he said, throwing open a deep wardrobe to show her that George had brought her bags up. "My father is frightened, and my mother is a wreck. It'll help them to know that you've come willingly—" he turned to her and took her face in his hands, his eyes searching the depths of hers "—even if you haven't."

For one swift moment, Randy saw pain in the bottomless blue of his gaze; then he leaned down to plant a chaste kiss on her lips and it was gone.

"I vote we shower in the morning. I can't wait to hit the pillow." He turned away from her as he pulled his wallet and keys out of his pockets, sat down on the bed and pulled off his shoes.

Within minutes Matt was in bed and Randy was in the bathroom, removing her makeup and slipping into her red-and-white striped sleepers. She had abandoned them while living at the Cove Mallory because fall had begun mildly and the hotel suite was much warmer than her drafty cottage. But October was brisk here, and the room was chilly.

Before getting into bed, Randy crossed the room to investigate a framed print that had caught her attention earlier.

"If this house catches fire tonight," Matt said lazily from the shadows across the room, "you're taking those off before we evacuate or you can just save yourself. I'm not going to be seen with you."

"You once told me I looked like a delectable candy cane in these," she reminded him over her shoulder. "Does this mean the honeymoon's over?"

He was silent a moment. There was not a sound inside the house or out. "No," he replied finally, "but it might be if you run around in those things in front of the Carversbury Volunteer Fire Department."

"You'd rather I took them off?"

He was silent another moment. Randy strained her eyes, unable to find his shape in the bed in the room's shadows. His voice came out of nowhere, like that of a ghost.

"Now," he asked, "or in the case of a fire?"

The remark was as suggestive as she was sure he intended, but she chose to ignore it.

"Is this the state flag of Connecticut?" she asked, again turning back to the print of the white shield on a blue background with its streamer bearing a message in Latin. The print was lit by the lamp on the wicker table in the corner; before she reached out to turn the light off, she read the Latin phrase hesitantly.

"*Qui . . . trans . . . lutit . . .*"

"*Qui . . . transtulit sustinet,*" Matt finished helpfully.

She turned the light out and started toward the sound of his voice. "What does that mean?"

He laughed softly and held the blankets up for her.

"What?" she questioned, trying to study his face in the dark. But he pulled her down into his arms and settled her comfortably against his shoulder.

"It means, 'He who is transplanted still sustains.'"

"You set me up," she accused drowsily, having no trouble relaxing against his chest.

"No," he said, laughing again. "The state of Connecticut did."

Chapter Twelve

Randy discovered in the week that followed that the state of Connecticut had set her up in other ways, as well. She liked it. Despite several days of trying hard not to notice the rolling hills of her surroundings ablaze with fall color, ignoring the fragrance of pungent evergreens and mountain laurel and attempting to remain apart from the comfortable warmth of the Mallory home, she liked it. It wasn't Scannon Cove, but if she had to be away, the Mallory estate in rural Carversbury, Connecticut, was not a bad place to be.

Matt was up early and off to Hartford every morning before the rest of the household had breakfast. Randy fended for herself before lunch, while Julia had her daily argument with Duncan, denying him the privilege of going downstairs and "getting something accomplished." Randy considered trying to help in the kitchen for something to do, but Ellen had that under control. George, with his customary efficiency, cared for the grounds and helped Julia with moving and bathing Duncan.

Unused to so much time on her hands, Randy took long walks, chatted with her in-laws in the afternoons and played with Joshua. She began to appreciate her surroundings and the warm people around her, but she longed for her full, hectic days at the office. She adapted to life in Carversbury secure in the knowledge that she and Matt would return to Scannon Cove in February for the opening of the square.

So far Duncan had not taken Randy up on her offer to service the Mallory cars, and she was reluctant to mention it again, afraid of annoying him. By her third week in Carversbury, she was seriously considering going to Hartford with Matt to look for a job. It would have to be in a garage, of course, and she wondered if staid old New England was any more tolerant of females in coveralls than conservative Oregon was. But relief from inactivity came in the rambunctious form of Joshua Thompson.

Randy had been drafted by Ellen to frost pumpkin-shaped sugar cookies. She was perched on a stool at the breakfast bar with a pan of cookies, a bowl of frosting and an already messy spatula. More at home with a wrench in her hand, Randy labored over her task.

"Mom!" Joshua burst into the kitchen, and Randy gasped, startled, frosting the first three fingers of her left hand. "I want to be a robot for Halloween!"

Ellen, cutting cookies, paused to reach down, floury hands held away from her, to kiss her son. "Oh, Josh," she said, frowning. "Why not something simple like a pirate or a clown?"

Joshua dipped his index finger in Randy's bowl of frosting. Plump and fair-haired, he had the bright warmth of both his parents, and their adoration had given him a charming confidence rather than spoiling him. He smiled at Randy with an irregular row of teeth, one front tooth just a jagged little bud and the other a still-rippled but almost fully developed second tooth. He put both arms stiffly at his sides and walked robotlike across the kitchen floor.

"See! Wouldn't I look good as a robot?"

"But, honey, I wouldn't know how to make a robot costume." Ellen went back to her cookies and rolled her eyes at Randy over her shoulder.

"It would only take a few boxes," Randy said, stabbing her spatula into the frosting. "A little tinfoil..."

"And could I have a light on my head that blinks and turns around?" Joshua asked excitedly, thrilled to have someone interested in his idea. "I can talk like a robot already."

He launched into a monotoned imitation of R2D2 of *Star Wars* fame.

"Honey," Ellen protested, "your mother's no mechanic."

Randy jumped off the stool and carried the finished cookies to Ellen. "These are finished, such as they are. I'm a better mechanic than I am a kitchen helper. Would you mind if I try to put together a costume for Josh?"

"Not at all. But don't let him run you ragged, you hear me?"

But run her ragged Joshua did, and Randy hadn't had so much fun in ages. Rummaging in the storage shed, they found boxes in graduated sizes and cut holes in them, testing them on Joshua for the right fit amid giggles and more robot talk, then covered them in tinfoil, depleting Ellen's kitchen supply. Randy found a pair of shimmery tights that could be made to fit Joshua with a few adjustments. And he had a white hooded sweatshirt that would keep him warm while trick-or-treating. He reminded Randy about the blinking, rotating light on his head.

"We'll have to get some things from town for that," Randy told him. "Saturday we'll go shopping, okay?"

Carversbury's architecture was typical of most New England towns that dated back to colonial days. There was a cannon on the courthouse lawn and a Main Street where cobbles were visible beneath the worn-down asphalt. Main Street shops had gables and small-paned windows and an occasional weather vane. Though very different from Scannon Cove, the town's age and charming nostalgia touched something familiar in Randy and made her homesick.

The few things that Randy needed to complete Joshua's costume were easily found, and they spent the rest of the morning filling a shopping list for Ellen.

Once home, Joshua gave Randy no peace until the two of them stood over the workbench in Will's garage, Joshua on a chair, wiring, soldering and gluing until Randy finally held up the box that would serve as the headpiece of the costume. Two eyes, a nose and a mouth were cut out of it. A red light bulb affixed to the top stood dark and still, a challenge to their ingenuity.

"Okay, Josh." Randy lifted the boy off the stool to the floor and placed the contraption gently on his head. "Let's see if it works." She handed him the remote-control device that she had rigged and stepped back, leaning down with her hands braced on her knees to carefully evaluate the results.

"Turn it on," she directed.

Joshua pressed the button on the control, and the light turned, flashing on and off as it rotated, casting eerie patterns on the walls of the dimly lit garage. Joshua hooted and jumped up and down, and Randy shouted, applauding their success.

A familiar male voice at Randy's ear said softly, "I hope this means that I've found the red-light district."

Randy looked up into Matt's grin. "Hi! What are you doing home? We haven't seen you before ten p.m. all week."

He shrugged, already changed from his suit into jeans and a red sweater. "Finished early. I thought that we'd take Mom and Dad out to dinner so they can have a change of scenery. Then you and I can go to bed early." He waggled his eyebrows wickedly. "What do you think?"

"You have to admire our creation one more time," Randy bargained.

"By all means."

Joshua obligingly pushed the button and squealed and jumped up and down again when the light flashed and rotated. Matt laughed and hugged Randy to him.

"What a woman. Josh, you make the best robot I ever saw. How about leading the way back to the house so we can show Mr. Duncan and your mom and dad how great you look."

Joshua was thrilled to oblige, and he reveled in the attention that he earned as everyone gathered to admire his costume.

"Let me see that," Duncan commanded, laughing. Joshua handed the older man the remote control and stood at the opposite end of the room. As the red light turned and blinked, everyone applauded Joshua's robot walk. Duncan looked up at Randy from his chair. His cheeks had a little color tonight, she noted.

"Told you I was good," she teased. He had been kind to her since her arrival, but he was neither an easy man to know nor someone to tease with. When he said nothing but continued to watch her, Randy said in embarrassment, "Well . . . it's a simple principle, actually."

"You know what I've got locked in the garage?" Duncan interrupted her. "Not the one where Will stores his stuff and not where we keep the family cars, but the other one, near the storage shed."

Randy shook her head.

"A Model-T touring car," Duncan announced.

Randy's eyes grew enormous. "Honestly?"

Duncan nodded. "Doorless. 1909."

"Can I see it?"

Duncan took hold of his cane and got to his feet.

"Dad, please." Matt gave his father a look of pained forbearance. "Can this wait until after dinner? If you let her in there now, before you know it, she'll be under the hood or on Will's rolling thing."

"Creeper," Randy corrected.

"Creeper—and we'll never get her out from under it or in it or whatever. Please, sweetheart. I've had my heart set on the Carversbury Café's chicken pot pie all day long."

"When we come back, I can look at it as long as I want to?" she wheedled.

"It's Dad's. It's up to him."

"Sure," Duncan agreed, smiling at her. "As long as you want." Then he turned to Julia, who was already shrugging into her coat. "I don't suppose that I'll be able to have the pot pie?"

"You can have the fillet of sole, a plain baked potato and a mild vegetable. Ellen, I want you to fix your family those steaks in the refrigerator and just go on home when you're finished. Well—" she turned to her family "—are we all ready?"

"I'm driving," Duncan said, heading slowly toward the door with his cane.

"No, you're not," Julia dictated.

"Then I'm having the pot pie."

"Duncan, I'm going to find another use for that cane!"

Dinner was delicious, and Duncan and Julia's gentle bickering didn't abate for a moment. Matt seemed more relaxed than she'd seen him since he'd taken over for his father. She looked up from her pot pie several times to find him watching her, lust undisguised in his eyes. Her cheeks flushed, and her heart began to race. They hadn't made love for a week because of his schedule, and she had missed him terribly. It was obvious that he had missed her, too.

When they returned home shortly after eight o'clock, Julia vetoed Duncan's wish to show Randy the Model-T himself.

"It's cold in that garage, and you've had a big evening," Julia said.

Duncan sighed and leaned on Matt's arm as they all trooped into the house. "I thought General Patton had gone to his reward," he whispered loudly to his son.

Matt nodded, biting back a grin. "But he lives on in his troops."

"Yes, well, I should get combat pay for what I put up with." Julia pulled her coat off and marched off to the kitchen, impervious to the teasing of her husband and her son.

The kitchen door swung closed behind her, and Duncan gave a sound that was half laughter, half emotion. "Got to keep after her," he said, "or she starts to worry. I suppose there's no point in telling you that I can walk up the stairs by myself."

"No, there isn't!" was shouted from the kitchen.

Matt and Randy burst into laughter, and even Duncan conceded a smile. "All right. But you'll just help me. George isn't here, and I won't have you getting a hernia by trying to carry me yourself."

"You're just afraid that I might be able to do it," Matt said, helping his father across the room.

"Damn right. Good night, Randy. You admire that car all you want, but don't mess under the hood until I can stand over you."

"I promise. Good night."

In a few minutes Matt was running down the stairs, dangling the garage keys in his fingers.

"You've got three minutes to look that baby over, then we're going to bed," Matt said, pulling her along toward the kitchen.

"Your father said..." Randy began to protest, running to keep up with him.

"My father is temporarily out of condition," Matt whispered, before pushing her through the kitchen door. "I, however, am in prime condition and frustrated beyond all endurance. Three minutes. No more."

"Three minutes for what?" Julia asked as they hurried through the kitchen to the back door. She was fixing a cup of coffee.

Matt and Randy looked at each other, both at a loss for an answer.

"An egg!" Matt blurted out. Randy guffawed as he yanked open the back door and pulled her through it into the fragrant night.

"An egg?" Randy giggled, following him blindly across the yard.

"I was desperate," he said, laughing. "I couldn't tell her what I really wanted in three minutes."

Matt finally pulled Randy to a stop, and she heard the keys working in a lock, though she could see nothing. Then he directed her to stay where she was while he turned on the light.

"Okay. Here it is." A fluorescent light suddenly blinded Randy, and she squinted a moment as her eyes adjusted.

Matt pulled a tarpaulin off an indistinguishable lump, and Randy found herself staring at a Model-T touring car, circa 1909. She put a reverent hand out to it, her eyes shining, a warm feeling filling her. This beautiful old vehicle did for her what flowers and paintings did for other women; it was art and beauty, crafted by careful, caring hands.

"Oh, Matt!" she breathed. The body was in perfect condition, though in need of a paint job, a new door handle and carriage lights. The upholstery was cracked with age and torn on the driver's side.

"It's magnificent!"

"It came with the house," Matt explained. "We bought it from a pair of spinster ladies whose great-great-grandfather fought in the Civil War. Ah, pardon me for being ignorant, but why are you so impressed? I mean it's a garden-variety Model-T, not a Daimler or a Humber or anything exotic."

Randy shook her head at his sad lack of understanding. "Darling, if you were an antique car collector, you'd be the kind who was after trophies and not a functional automobile that you could love." She walked around the car, touching the finely arched fenders, the high windshield, running her fingers along the rolled upholstery. "This 'garden-variety Model-T,'" she said, quoting his disparaging remark scornfully, "has an overall sales record over an eighteen-year run that's been beaten only by the Volkswagen Beetle. It popularized left-handed steering in America, and the demand for it led to the introduction of the moving assembly line.'' Randy stepped back and shook her head in admiration. ''She could do forty miles an hour, and she cost under a thousand dollars.'' She smiled at Matt. ''This is no garden-variety car, Mallory. This is a classic, a star.''

He hung his head down in shame. ''I stand corrected. However...'' He looked up at her and grinned wickedly. ''This car will be here every day in the foreseeable future, while I will be at work. Could we pay a little attention to my chassis? Run your fingers along my upholstery?''

''Turn your lights on?'' she suggested with a grin.

He nodded, throwing the tarpaulin back over the antique car. ''That would be a start. Come on.'' They turned off the fluorescents, locked the door and returned to the house arm in arm. Julia had thoughtfully disappeared, and they were able to stare dreamily into each other's eyes as they climbed the stairs without an audience.

The following week, Duncan was cleared by his doctor to go up and down the stairs if he took them slowly. Though his diet was still restricted, he took this new freedom as though it were a gift from heaven. And feeling magnanimous, he appointed Randy to restore his Model-T. She studied him, her green eyes wide with shock.

''Me?'' she asked.

He smiled at her. They were standing in the garage, the tarpaulin in a heap on the floor, the beautiful car in its neglected state looking like a woman with good bone structure in her face but no makeup.

''You claim to be good, don't you?''

"Yes, but my tools . . ."

"We'll send for them. Today. Now. Call your shop."

The tools arrived within a week. By the following week, Randy had the car completely disassembled to permit inspection and restoration of every part.

George built a crude engine stand for her, and Duncan called the local wrecker to lift the engine from frame to stand. Pieces and parts were scattered on newspaper all over the garage. Duncan observed the entire operation from an easy chair that Julia had insisted be moved from the house to the garage for his comfort. In a parka and a woolen cap he offered encouragement and criticism and general gossip while she worked.

Randy was careful to document everything, making sketches of all the assemblies she was afraid she wouldn't remember.

"Interesting lubricant in the transmission and rear axle," Randy said, wiping her hands on a rag as she came around the car and sank down on a blanket on the garage floor to lean against the car's frame.

"What's that?" Duncan asked. He poured her a cup of tea from a thermos Ellen had provided.

"Mud," she said, accepting the cup gratefully. "I wonder how long it's been since this car has run?"

"It's been sitting here for twenty years," Duncan admitted almost sheepishly, as though afraid Randy would scold him, "and the ladies who sold us the house and the car probably hadn't driven it in at least that long."

"If you didn't want it," Randy asked, "why didn't you sell it?"

"Oh, I wanted it," Duncan assured her, pouring coffee from his own thermos. "I just never had a minute to give to it." He frowned a little as he sipped from his cup. "Until now."

"Now you can enjoy life a little," Randy said gently, afraid that mood of frustration would overtake him again. "I'm sure that business and power are exciting, but aren't you anxious to catch up with everything else that you've missed? To have time to be with Julia and to spend wandering around this beautiful place?"

"I am, of course. It's just hard to see things move along without you when you've been their driving force for so long." Duncan sighed and smiled grimly at Randy. "Oh, I knew the day was coming. Matt's just too good at what he does. Already, a couple of years ago, my men were asking him what he thought, reciting to me *his* ideas and suggestions. And he takes care of his people every damn bit as well as he takes care of his job. That's an unbeatable combination."

Randy put her cup down, a little horrified at what Duncan was saying. "But the plan is that as soon as his cousin is able to step in, to take over, we're going back to Scannon Cove."

Duncan responded to Randy's apprehensive tone with a level look. "I know. I just can't think of one man in the organization, Matt's brother and his cousin included, who will ever be 'ready' to take over from Matt."

But Matt was grooming his cousin for the job, Randy told herself as she spent the next few weeks meticulously cleaning, brushing and filing. Then Will flew home for Thanksgiving and Jeremy, Matt's cousin, arrived for dinner with his parents, and Randy understood Duncan's comment.

Though Duncan's brother, Andrew, was older than he by six years, he was still a tall, strong-looking man. His wife, Anne, was small and fragile looking, and Jeremy favored her side of the family. Not much taller than Randy, he was warm and kind and could recite verbatim from the Mallory Inn's annual report without having it in front of him. He was extremely knowledgeable about the company, and he was sweet. But he had none of the dynamism, the energy, that characterized both Matt and his father. She couldn't imagine him staring down two angry employees and insisting they settle their problems peacefully.

Randy was quiet over the Thanksgiving weekend, her mind occupied with thoughts she was afraid to consider too closely but which refused to go away. She was beginning to suspect that now entrenched in the Mallory machine, Matt was never going to be able to leave here.

And as much as she had grown to like Connecticut, to love the Mallorys and the Thompsons, she longed for a glimpse of the Columbia River, to see sea gulls and tugboats and Concomolly Boulevard at noontime. She longed for her smelly garage and the sound of an intercom system calling her name.

Andrew and his family went home on Saturday. When Matt sank down on the sofa in front of the television with his father instead of turning to her, Randy changed her clothes and went into the garage to work on the Model-T. Torn between tears and temper, she settled on grumbling to herself as she fumbled with the transmission.

"I've seen more of this damn car's private parts than I have my husband's," she muttered angrily to herself as she scooted sideways on the creeper. She dropped a wrench with a clatter and picked up another.

"I'd like to overhaul his..." That interesting innovation in automotive science remained unspoken as Randy felt a light kick at her ankles. She craned her neck to see Matt's blue-and-white Air Jordans and the lower third of his faded blue jeans.

"Overhaul my what?" he asked.

"I'm busy," she replied unsociably.

She saw his weight shift to one foot. "Would you come out, please? I'd like to invite you to dinner."

"Somebody unplug the television?" she asked sulkily, dropping the wrench with a clatter again and wondering what she would do now that she was finished.

He kicked the sole of her shoe lightly. "Will you come out of there."

"No."

"Then tuck in your nose and your pretty bosom, because I'm pulling you out." And he did. Then he was standing astride her at her waist as she, still supine on the creeper, looked up at him. She was in a pair of Will's old coveralls that Ellen had laundered for her, with an old blue ski cap on her head to protect her hair from grease and her ears from the cold.

"What's the problem?" he asked.

Her eyes filled, and she seriously considered pushing off with her feet and rolling out from under him. But the driveway was at a downward angle all the way to the lake, and she suspected that the creeper had no hydroplaning abilities.

"Playing second fiddle to a football game for starters," she said, her voice breaking just a little.

"Oh, Randy!" Matt said in exasperation, reaching down to grab her hands and pull her to her feet. He gave the creeper a kick, and it rolled to the wall, settling there. "I wanted to tell Dad how things had gone this week. There's been a labor dispute in Dallas. I knew he was concerned about it." He put his arms around her. "Have you missed me?"

He tried to pull her closer, but she resisted, her hands spread flat against his chest.

"Don't," she said peevishly. "You'll get grease all over your white sweater."

He pulled harder. "I'm willing to risk it."

She pushed him away. "I'm not finished with the—"

Finally impatient, he took her firmly by the arm. "Yes, you are." He unbuttoned the top button of her coveralls. "What are you wearing under this?"

"Sweatshirt and jeans," she replied.

"Then get out of this," he ordered quietly, completing the unbuttoning process. "You've been pushing me away for two weeks now, and I've about had it."

"It's cold in here," she objected as he helped her step out of the coveralls.

"Fine. Then we'll continue this conversation in our room."

"Matt . . ."

But he wasn't listening. He locked the garage door and pulled her across the yard to the kitchen door. He led her up the back stairs to their room and pushed her inside.

She turned in the middle of the room to glare at him.

"I want you to tell me what's bothering you," Matt said, leaning against the door, folding his arms. "Something's been wrong since you started working on the Model-T. Are you homesick?"

"I'm always homesick!" Randy sat on the edge of the bed and pulled off her shoes. She tore off the knit cap and sat Indian-style in the middle of the bed. Her hair fell around her face in silky, brilliant disarray. "Matt?" She looked up at him with a frown between her eyebrows, the anger in her eyes now mingling with fear. "Are you ever going to be able to leave here?"

The anguish in her eyes was so at odds with the strength of her beauty, Matt thought as he moved to sit on the edge of the bed. "You know what the plan is," he reminded her gently.

"Sure I do, but will it work? Or are you so damned good at what you do that no one will be able to replace you?"

"No one is that good."

She sighed heavily, flinging the hat across the room. "Your father thinks you are."

Matt frowned. "I thought you two were getting along famously."

"We are. I know he wouldn't keep you here against your will, but it's as though he feels sure everything will sink without you."

"Jeremy is bright and hardworking and—"

"I know," Randy interrupted, "but he hasn't got it, Matt. Even I can see that. That's why you work eighteen hours a day, six days a week and get calls at home all day Sunday. I never see you anymore unless there's a telephone at your ear or I wake up in the middle of the night and watch you sleep." She shook her head in frustration. "The square opens in ten weeks. How are you ever going to get away for that?"

"I told you I'd try," he said simply. "Isn't that enough?"

She knew he meant what he said, but she'd observed the entire company's dependence on him long enough to know that any emergency could arise at any moment and that he would be the only one able to handle it. She could not dispel the feeling that something would prevent their trip to Scannon Cove.

"I love you," he said, gently stroking her knee. "I will do everything in my power to make you happy." As her expression softened, he reached out to snake a hand behind her neck and bring her with him as he fell backward on the mattress.

"Oh, Matthew," she said wearily, settling into his embrace as he wrapped his arms around her. His eyes were warm and loving, and she lost her concerns in their sparkling depths. "What's going to happen to us?"

"We're going to die in our nineties in the throes of passionate lovemaking."

The image of the two of them white-haired and pink-gummed made her laugh. "I suppose that if we're going to last that long we should keep in practice."

"Are you hustling me?"

She pulled his sweater up and ran her finger inside the waistband of his jeans. "Yes."

He breathed a weary sigh. "You know how reluctant I am about this sort of thing."

She planted a kiss at his waist. "Sure I do. I'm the one who paid off Joshua so he wouldn't tell anyone what he saw going on on the creeper in the garage last week."

He laughed throatily. "How did I know that the creeper was going to roll all the way to the door?"

"I warned you, but you didn't care to listen." She was nibbling on his ribs when he'd finally had enough. He gently clutched a handful of her hair, pulling her off him and placing her lightly back onto the mattress. Her jeans and sweatshirt were gone in a minute, and he found himself faced with—"Long underwear?"

"The garage floor is cold," she defended, giggling. "Besides, my long johns have rosebuds on them. Aren't they cute?"

He gave her a dubious grimace and removed them. He knelt over her with a frown.

"What's the matter?" She tried to sit up, but he pushed her back.

"You have a curious waffle pattern all over you from those things," he said, indicating the thermal underwear he had just thrown aside. "It makes you look a little reptilian."

She shrugged. "Some men might consider that a turn-on."

"That's leather, sweetie, not snakeskin."

"Oh, well, if you want to change your mind, I've got a car to work on, parts to—" As she tried to scramble away from him, he pulled her back and grinned, the grin becoming an indulgent smile as his eyes went over her face.

"The grim truth is that you could wear an all-over mud pack and I'd still fall victim to your charms." His clothes were dispensed with, and his mouth and hands wandered over her hungrily, tauntingly. She was lost in his swift role change from teaser to lover. Every cell in her body came to life, from the roots of her hair to the tips of her toes, and each part clamored for his touch. He satisfied each and every inch of her but failed to still the tumult building inside.

Coping with the need to feel his body under her hands as well as to be touched by his, Randy stroked, caressed and kissed him. She explored the hot wall of his chest, the ripply trunk of his body, the sinewy legs until he gasped, catching her by her shoulders and shifting her under him.

"You *do* do the best body work for miles," he groaned, entering her, filling her with the magic and wonder of his body and his soul.

Chapter Thirteen

To everyone's surprise Will brought Vivian home for Christmas to announce their engagement. At first, Julia and Duncan were taken aback by Viv's flamboyance and her frequently outrageous remarks. Soon, however, they were caught up in her excitement as she planned the wedding and the honeymoon in New Mexico, where Will would be working in the spring. They were completely won over by the way Viv glowed in Will's presence and hung on every word he spoke.

Matt managed to get a few days off the week before Christmas, and the two couples went Christmas shopping together, put up the tree, strung popcorn and wrapped presents.

"We've got to get serious about Dad's gift," Will said. He was lying on the sofa, his head in Vivian's lap. "What about one of those chair things that'll take him up and down the stairs?"

"He'd kill us!" Matt vetoed the suggestion with a laugh. He sat on the floor, leaning against the foot of the sofa, Randy sitting between his raised knees. He took a sip from a cup of eggnog and offered it to Randy. "It has to be something that'll cheer him up rather than remind him of his limitations."

"I know what!" Randy said, slapping Matt's knee in her enthusiasm and splashing eggnog on him as she turned.

"Go ahead," Matt groaned. "Beat me, drown me. See what you have to look forward to, Will? Constant abuse, continual—"

"Will you listen!" Randy laughed, dabbing at the spot on his jeans with her napkin. "We'll give the Model-T a paint job and new upholstery as a gift."

"That's brilliant," Matt said, hugging her to him. He turned to look at Will, who was grinning approval. "Okay with you?"

"Sounds perfect."

"You've got the car all back together?" Matt asked Randy. "No pieces left over?"

She looked indignant. "Of course not."

"How do we wrap a paint job in two days?" Will wanted to know.

"Your artsy fiancée whips out her calligraphy pen," Randy explained, "and we make him a gift certificate. I'm sure that there's somewhere in Hartford where we can buy authentic paint colors and find the right uphol stery fabric."

"We should buy him wooden wheels," Will added, "and varnish them like—"

"No," Randy interrupted. "They didn't do that until a few years later than this model."

"I didn't realize that you were such a pro on restora- tions," Will said, sitting up. The room was darkening, and dinnertime activity could be heard coming from the kitchen.

"I'm not," she admitted. "But I've been studying as I go. Pre-World War One wooden wheels weren't varnished. But wooden wheels might be something that he'll want, anyway."

"Okay. The certificate will include optional wooden wheels." Will turned to Vivian. "Have you got that, madame calligrapher?"

"Right. We'd better get cleaned up for dinner. My hands are full of pitch from the garlands we hung on the banister."

As Will and Vivian disappeared up the stairs, Matt held Randy closer. "You're really enjoying the restoration, aren't you?" he asked.

She nodded. "A great deal. I've learned a lot."

He rubbed her shoulders gently. "Think there's a future in it for you?"

She turned to smile into his eyes, her own pleading for understanding. "You know where my future lies."

"Yes." His voice was solemn, his grip on her arm firm. "With me."

To RANDY, for whom the holidays had always been painful and lonely, Christmas in Connecticut was filled with warmth and laughter and all the things she knew she'd been missing all those years. In her short two months in Carversbury, she had indeed become a Mallory. Julia and Duncan were Mom and Dad to her, and her thoughts and opinions held as much weight with them as Matt's and Will's. Duncan was more likely to listen to her admonitions about what he should and shouldn't do than anyone else's, and Julia was constantly showing her off to her friends and boasting about her to anyone who would listen.

George and Ellen thought as much of her as they did the rest of the Mallorys, and Joshua, disregarding convention and Randy's advanced age, asked her to marry him when Matt was out of the picture.

"What did you tell him?" Matt asked. It was a cold January night; Julia and Duncan had gone to bed, and Matt and Randy were sitting back to back on the hearth rug in front of the fire as she related the story.

"That I'd have to be a bigamist and have two husbands, because by the time he was old enough to marry me, you'd only be in your late forties."

"Sounds fair. He should be head of NASA or the Mafia by then. He could support us both."

They laughed together, and then silence fell between them, not the comfortable silence of accord but the unsettling silence of problems unresolved.

"Have you made plans for going back to Scannon Cove in February?" Randy asked casually.

"My secretary can make reservations for me a day in advance if need be," he said.

She heaved a small sigh. "Meaning you're leaving your options open in case things change?"

"Meaning the dispute in Dallas is still unsettled and anything can happen," he replied patiently. "If it comes to a strike, you can always go without me, can't you?"

Randy turned toward the fireplace, and Matt moved beside her. "You could have come here without me," she said, turning to face him, the fire burnishing the side of her face, flaming her hair. "But you didn't want to."

"Isn't that a little different?"

"I don't see why," she replied, trying hard to keep her voice even. "You know how badly I want to visit, how much I put into that project and what it'll mean to me to see it finished."

He nodded. "I do. But if Dallas becomes a serious problem, I won't have a choice."

Her shoulders sagged, and she looked into the fire. "Interesting how I'm always the one with the choice. Do what I want or do what you want. Only it's no choice, is it, if I want to keep you?"

"Maybe it hasn't occurred to you," Matt said heavily, "but it's exactly the same choice I have—or don't have. I can do my job, or I can go with you to Scannon Cove. Either way somebody loses because of me. Does that seem like a choice to you?"

They were silent for a long moment; then Randy said quietly, "Maybe it's just not going to work out, Matt. We . . . we had considered that it might not."

"Yes," he said, "I know."

Something about the fatalistic way he said that stabbed at Randy, and when he stood and helped her to her feet, she looked at him with eyes that were filled with pain.

When they had considered their problem the night she decided to come with him, it was on the basis that if she wasn't able to stay, she would go back to Scannon Cove and wait until he could come to her. But the way the situation stood now, if she went back to Scannon Cove, Matt would never join her. He was needed here. He had to stay here.

"Don't look like that," he said gently, turning her toward the stairs. "The square isn't opening for another month. Everything in Dallas could be settled by then."

Randy followed him upstairs, settled into his arms, as she always did, and lay awake as he slept, knowing that more than Dallas and Scannon Cove were at issue here. They were simply representative of the unresolved conflict between her undiminished longing for home and Matt's important position at the helm of the Mallory Inns. Both she and Matt would be forced into choices they'd been avoiding, and she feared for their marriage.

Two days before Matt and Randy were to take the plane to Portland, the Dallas dispute did blow up in their faces with a strike and angry demands. Randy sat in complete dejection in the middle of the bed and watched Matt pack.

"You never planned to come back with me," she accused. She realized that wasn't fair, but she was beyond caring.

"That's not true, and you know it," he said, walking from the dresser to his suitcase at the foot of the bed with a stack of underwear.

"Then why can't someone else go in your place?"

"Because the Dallas house's major complaint is that management doesn't care about their problems. I could prove that they're right by sending someone else in my place."

"Slick," she said. "You've always got a good answer."

"The truth is always a good answer."

"The truth is," she said angrily, "that this company means more to you than I ever did. You eat and sleep the Mallory Inns! Do you even remember the last time we made love?"

"Yes," he said without even pausing to consider. He turned his back on her and went to his wardrobe. "The night before we had that conversation on the hearth rug in front of the fireplace."

She arched an eyebrow in surprise. "So you do remember?" Her face flushed, and her eyes filled with hurt. "And that was the last time, because you've been too tired."

He folded his shirts carefully inside and closed the lid of his suitcase. He looked at her, his eyes penetrating. "No, not because I was tired but because you've spent the last month waiting for just this very thing to happen. You wanted me to have to make a choice so I could make the wrong one. Then you could run home on the pretext of seeing the grand opening of the square." He leaned his hands on the closed case. "And you're not coming back. Do you think I can't see that in your eyes?"

"You could come..." she began weakly.

He shook his head wearily. "No, I can't. Do you remember the night you brought me the car keys to the Impala and we had dinner in the dining room?"

She nodded, a pointed lump of pain in her throat.

"You told me that for the first time in your life you were in charge of your own destiny."

"Yes."

"Well, that's a hell of a way to live," he said gravely. "Nobody is 'in charge' of destiny. It lives in the palm of God's hand, and if you try to take it in your own, all the living, all the learning and all—" he shook his head and his voice became urgent "—the loving is lost. You've got to step out in faith, sweetheart. You've got to let it lead you where it will, or you're just not letting the process work. Then you're just a piece of the scenery, beautiful but inanimate."

Tears streamed freely down Randy's face. "So you're telling me goodbye?"

Matt sat on the edge of the bed and pulled her into his arms. "You've been telling me goodbye since you met me, Randy. I'm telling you that I love you, that the time I've had with you will live with me until the day I die. But I'm not rooted like you are, and I can't watch you die in my arms because I've pulled you up from where you want to be." He kissed her gently. "I'm sorry. I wish I were different, but I'm not."

"You said...that as long as I was...with you..."

"But you're not with me," he said. "That's the point. You've seemed happy here—everyone loves you—yet you've always been three thousand miles away from us in Scannon Cove. There's no future for us that way. I've got to go, Randy. Look at me." She raised tear-filled eyes from his shoulder, and the agony in them was almost more than he could bear. "Kiss me goodbye," he whispered. "I love you more than you can ever imagine."

She tightened her arms around his neck and met his lips, pouring out her love for him, concentrating on all that she felt for him. Then he tore away from her, grabbed his suitcase and jacket and left the room. The door closed behind him, shutting out all she had ever known of love.

George took her to the airport two days later, reminding her several times to be sure and let him know when she had confirmed her return flight so that he could pick her up. Though Randy had said nothing to Julia or Duncan, she knew by the way they were careful not to mention Matt that he must have told them what was decided. Julia cried when Randy said goodbye, and Duncan ordered her gruffly to get back as soon as possible, reminding her that he hadn't used his gift certificate yet for paint and upholstery and that he was counting on her to help him make the selection.

"Sure," she said, her voice breaking, betraying the lack of conviction behind it.

"You don't disappoint someone in my condition," he said with a manipulative whine. "It isn't safe."

She had hugged him fiercely and followed George out to the car.

"I'll be waiting for your call, Mrs. Mallory," George shouted after her as she went through the boarding gate.

Randy gave him a final wave, and the doors closed be hind her.

Will and Vivian met her in Portland. She knew instantly by their faces that her big smile and cheerful wave didn't fool either of them. Either Matt had gotten to them first, or she wasn't as good an actress as she thought she was.

Scannon Cove was so dearly familiar, so faithfully what she had longed for all those months, that her spirit was soothed the moment the state highway merged into Riverfront Drive. Randy had a bad moment when they passed the cannery that sat out on the rickety dock where she and Matt had had a beautiful picnic lunch. She turned resolutely away, admiring a new fence built around the house across the street. She moved into her old cottage, and except for a slight musty smell that first day, it was almost as though the past eight months had never existed.

Randy spent her first full day in Scannon Cove just walking, breathing in the familiar smells of winter on the river. The air was cold and fresh, and she felt intoxicated by being back.

The opening of Scannon Square was a media event. Television cameras were there, and the radio station was broadcasting live. She spent an hour showing newsmen through the busy complex. Later, standing in the middle of the bustling crowd, she felt a sense of pride surpassing anything that she had ever known before. But the pride was less satisfying than she expected. She blamed it on jet lag and continued to smile.

Randy and Will and Vivian partied into the night at the Cove Mallory, and she learned that they were leaving for Connecticut next week and would be married there before the New Mexico project began. She took the news with another glass of champagne and admirable aplomb.

"How are things going at the dealership?" Randy asked Viv. She hadn't visited yet, not wanting to just drop in on Bob McGraw without calling first. Up to this point, she'd been too involved in the opening of the square.

"Very well. Bob seems to be a born manager," Viv responded. "Even Eldon is being cooperative."

"Good," Randy said, toasting Stanton Motors. "Glad to hear it."

When she went to the shop the next day, she found what Vivian had said was true. From the parts department to the garage, everything was clean and orderly, and there wasn't a cause for complaint anywhere. Everyone greeted her warmly. Gordie took her to lunch. Jake told her he hadn't lost, broken or destroyed anything in two whole months and that Gordie had told him if that pattern continued he'd put him in the apprenticeship program and start training him to be a mechanic. Bob looked as though he belonged behind her desk but was willing to vacate it the moment she walked into his office.

"No, no!" she said, pushing him back into the chair. "I'm not ready to come back yet. I was just wondering if you needed anything or if there was anything I could do."

Bob shook his head. "We seem to be doing fine. But I won't take it amiss if you want to check for yourself."

"I've done that, and you're right. Everything's fine."

"When are you and Mr. Mallory planning to come back?"

She shrugged. "Not sure yet. We'll just leave things as they are for now."

"Whatever you say." Bob looked a little relieved as she reached out to shake his hand.

Prowling restlessly from room to room in the cottage, Randy finally changed out of the suit in which she had visited the agency. She put on jeans, a sweater, a heavy jacket and a ski cap and walked down to the old cannery. The day was overcast and drizzly and so generally gray that it was hard to find the horizon. Water and sky met in an indistinguishable smudge of bleak cloud and wave. She walked slowly out on the dock, dodging holes in the rickety boards, looking up when she reached the end and closing her eyes to the light rain, hoping that it would cleanse her of her deep and abiding heartache.

She could not remember ever being so miserable. She had seen some hard times in her life, but being without Matt had to be the worst for her.

Randy had spent the last four days coming to the painful conclusion that Scannon Cove was a warm community, a beautiful place, dearly familiar and a very important part of her past. But it was no longer home. Not simply because the new manager of the Cove Mallory now lived in the suite she had shared with Matt and not because Bob McGraw was doing fine at Stanton Motors without her. It was because Randy was no longer the young woman who had once lived here. She was no longer the frightened fourteen-year-old who had arrived in a state car, prepared for yet another failure, but who found herself understood and loved for the first time and had taken root here to become a successful woman. That woman had found a loving, caring man and metamorphosed into someone else again because of his love. She was no longer the Randy Stanton who absorbed her happiness from a town where she had first felt wanted. She was Randy Stanton Mallory, who stood beside Matthew Mallory and made cellos rise, violins cry, and filled the air with music. The Connecticut air. Or whatever air they happened to be breathing at the time. Randy paced at the end of the dock as realization washed over her. She was no longer the Randy who stood in one place like a piece of the scenery. She was finally a woman who could be content to trust her destiny to the hands of divine providence and step out bravely to follow wherever it led—because Matthew Mallory was walking beside her. But following the impact of that simple truth came the chilling fear that this realization had come too late.

Randy turned to run back to the cottage, intent on telephoning Dallas and leaving a message for Matt. But a figure was walking toward her out of the bleak landscape, and she stopped, narrowing her eyes. Still at the opposite end of the dock, the figure, a solitary male in jeans and a tan parka, stopped also. A gull dived by him on patrol for lunch, but he didn't seem to notice it. He was staring at Randy, his blond hair ruffled by the wind.

"Matt!" she whispered, her throat closing, her heart beginning to pound.

She took a step toward him, and he picked up his pace, his stride eating up the distance between them until he stopped a few feet away from her. His handsome face was pinched from the cold, and he looked tired, though the blue eyes that roved her features were warm and bright. When his gaze finally settled on her wide eyes, it was filled with tenderness and a longing Randy identified as her own.

Matt and Randy stared at each other for a long moment, several feet still separating them. She fought the urge to throw herself into his arms, afraid to misinterpret his presence here. Her mouth opened to speak, but she had to try again before the tentative sound came out.

"Hi." When he said nothing but continued to stare at her, she asked, "How did you know...where to find me?"

He pulled his hands out of his pockets and reached out to take the ski cap off her head. He came a step closer and ran a handful of her hair through his fingers, appearing distracted by it for a long moment. Then he refocused on her pale face. "When you weren't at the cottage, I just followed a hunch. How've you been?"

How did one describe the pit of loneliness, she wondered. But still unsure of his intentions, she replied carefully. "Fine. You?"

His expression became wry, and he toyed with her hat, finally looking at her to admit, "I can't eat, I can't sleep and my insides are in a knot."

She frowned sympathetically. "Tough negotiations?"

"No." He shook his head. "I tied those up in thirty-six hours. Probably one of the fastest settlements on record."

Her heartbeat was about to choke her. "Then why...?"

And she had her answer the next instant when he pulled her into his arms, crushing her against his thick coat. For a long, delicious moment he simply held her; then he took her face in his hands and stared at her, devouring her with eyes filled with emotion. "Despite all my noble claims," he groaned, "about not being able to watch you fade away in my arms because I've transplanted you...I can't live without you, even for four days! I saw you and heard you everywhere I went, and when I closed my eyes, images of you haunted me, becoming nightmares because you would disappear. My world is a black hole without you, Randy. I don't even think I can convey in words how much I need you."

"Oh, Matt," she said, weeping, planting kisses in the warmth of his neck as he pulled her to him again. "I've been miserable. I missed you so much!"

"Well, that's good news!" Still crushing the breath from her, he rocked her gently, making the bleak, gray dock a warm and sunny place. "I'm sorry. I know what you gave up to come to Connecticut with me. And I think I know what it cost you." He walked her to the end of the dock where they could lean against the railing and look out at the river and the gray shape of Washington state looming in the distance. "But I spent the time on the plane trip here working on a solution for us."

"That won't be necessary," she said, smiling up at him. "I'm coming home."

He opened his mouth to speak, then stopped, frowning down at her in confusion. "What?"

"I'm coming back to Connecticut," she repeated.

She returned his thoughtful study of her eyes with a clear, green gaze.

"I see." He straightened away from the railing and cupped her face in his hands, pressing the silk of her hair against her cheek. "Did something go wrong?"

"No," she denied easily, resting her hands at the belt of his parka. "Everything's fine."

"No trouble at the shop?"

"No, they've got everything under control. I was thinking that I'd make Bob an offer he couldn't refuse."

Matt's look remained cautious. "How'd the opening of the square go?"

"Fine."

"Did everybody turn out?"

"Everybody. The press was here from Portland, and I was on the front page of the *Oregonian*, cutting the ribbon."

He leaned down to kiss her lightly on the lips, almost as though in apology for the next question. "Then why, Randy?"

She smiled at him, the freest smile he'd ever seen on her. With a mittened finger, she tapped the front of her jacket in the vicinity of her sternum. "That woman inside me is finally free," she said, her voice quivering a little at the admission. "Scannon Cove is no longer home to me. Home..." She paused to say the word again, giving it all the feeling it had come to hold for her. "Home is in your arms, Matthew. Please, take me home."

Emotion leaped in his eyes and tightened the muscle in his jaw as he pulled her to him. Words failed him, and all he could do was hold her. He thought with a sense of wonder that for all he had experienced in life, he had never known the meaning of it until this very moment. There were no more mysteries in the universe. Life, truth, heaven... was Randy.

"Come on," he said finally, his voice ragged. "Let's go back to the cottage."

"YOU'RE SURE that you can go back?" Matt and Randy were sitting side by side on the sofa in her cottage, facing each other, his arm resting along the back and his fingers toying absently with her hair. "Please, tell me the truth. Because there's another solution if we need it."

She smiled at him. "And what would that be?"

"I'll just move administration out here."

He said it so easily, as though it were a simple matter of one desk, one man and one file drawer instead of the entire top floor of the Hartford Mallory and over a hundred people.

"No." She tilted her head to rub her cheek against the fingers playing with her hair. "I'm not the same anymore. If you see something in my eyes that makes you doubt my sincerity, it's emotion and not regret.''

He kissed her forehead. "Mind reader."

She rested her arm along his, stroking the corded muscle in his upper arm. "You have to understand what a job it was to build Miranda Stanton. When you're a child with a past you'd rather forget and a present that's always changing, you have to do something to lend yourself a little permanence. A shell is a versatile defense. You can hide behind it so that you don't get hurt and lean against it when there's no one else around. Al and Donna made substantial dents in it, but . . .''

Tears rose in Randy's eyes, and she was surprised and touched to see them in Matt's, as well. She ran her hand along his shoulder, feeling warmth and durability. He closed his arms around her, holding her loosely in their circle, trying to shield her from what he thought for a moment was pain. And then she smiled.

"It wasn't until fifteen minutes ago that I became totally free of it. When you've hidden for so long, being vulnerable is scary."

His hands rose to frame her face, thumbs brushing away her tears. "Surely you know that anything meant to hurt you would have to go through me first."

She put her arms around him and hugged him fiercely, because she knew he meant every word. Then she pulled back, her lashes dark and wet, her eyes filled with life. "Thank you, darling. But I don't need a shield. I need a . . . a codriver. Somebody to help me read the map and the road signs." She winked at him, feeling suddenly so happy it hurt. "And to change a tire for me in bad weather. And I'd be honored to do the same for you."

"You're hired," he said instantly, "and I am yours to command."

"Oh, Matt." Randy clung to him as he shifted to recline on the sofa, tucking her in against the back of it beside him. "Do we have to go back tomorrow?"

He smiled, his fingers combing the hair back from her face. "No, I've got two weeks off."

Her eyes widened in surprise. "You're kidding!"

"No, I'm not. Jeremy is in charge, with my father ready to lend a hand if necessary. When I get back, my first order of business is going to be hiring an assistant. He's going to learn to be my shadow so that I can get away more often."

"I'll applaud that," she said, resting her chin on his chest to look at him. "I thought that maybe I could open a shop in Carversbury and do classic car restorations. If I spread the word and am good enough, I'll bet people would come from all over New England."

"I'm sure they would. Particularly with my father as your PR man."

Randy smiled. "How are your parents?"

"They'll be better when they know you're coming back. I was supposed to offer you a bribe, but since I didn't need it . . ."

"What was it?" she asked.

He shook his head. "Well, it's kind of irrelevant now. . . ."

"Matthew . . ." she warned, tickling the set of ribs closest to her hand.

Laughing, he caught her wrist. "All right. They're giving us a delayed wedding present."

"What's that?"

"Property on the other side of the lake. I think we should build a house there. We can still keep this place for trips to the West Coast."

Randy frowned. "Wouldn't they be hurt if we moved out?"

"I don't think so. Anyway, it's time we had some privacy," he said firmly. "And once we have kids, we'll need the room."

She scooted up, resting her forearms on his chest, smiling into his eyes. "Kids, huh?" The thought of a child of theirs sent a ripple of excitement along her spine. "I hope we have girls."

"Girls would be nice."

"But your father has such fun with Joshua. We should have one boy."

"Will and Vivian can have boys." Matt took a firm hold of her forearms and pulled her up close enough to kiss. "They should be prepared to do their share."

Randy laughed. "I'm sure they will. They're getting married next week, you know."

Matt nodded. "Yes. I talked to Will about it when I called to check on you."

Randy looked at him in surprise. "When was that?"

"Every morning for the past four days," he replied. "They want us to stand up for them. So I thought we could spend a few days here, then follow them home long enough to do our duty." He laughed wickedly. "Then we'll find one of those places in the Poconos that has heart-shaped bathtubs and vibrator beds and have a real honeymoon."

She smiled dreamily and leaned down to nibble at his bottom lip. "I enjoyed the other honeymoon."

"So did I." He shifted her so that he could get to his feet and lift her in his arms. "But I promise," he said, his eyes filled with tenderness and love, "that you'll enjoy this one even more."

Epilogue

Replete with crab salad, cheese bread and champagne, Matt sat in the warm grass, leaning against the trunk of a centuries-old oak. A bee droned around his head, and the midafternoon lakeside quiet was dispelled by the lyrical chatter of robins in the surrounding trees.

Raising a knee to support the hand from which dangled an empty champagne glass, Matt watched lazily as his wife and daughter played peekaboo with the red-and-white checked tablecloth on which they had spread their picnic.

Randy draped it over her head, and Julie, resplendent with her mother's red hair, her father's blue eyes and her own pink cheeks, studied Randy in fascinated silence. Sitting cross-legged on the grass in front of Julie, Randy lifted the front of the cloth and chanted, "Peekaboo!" The baby broke into delighted giggles and grabbed for the checkered cotton, indicating that it was her turn.

Randy draped the cloth over Julie, completely covering the baby's plump body in its denim rompers, then lifted the front and looked under, repeating the words of the silly game.

Delighted at being discovered, Julie clapped her hands and giggled, showing a perfect row of four teeth. Matt laughed aloud. Then, the smile still lingering on his lips, he studied his wife and daughter with the paralyzing awe that came over him every time he saw them together.

Julie would one day be a clone of Randy; that was already obvious even to strangers. And both of Matt's women loved him. When he thought about that, he, Matthew Mallory, chairman of the board of Mallory Inns, unflappable in a crisis, would find himself on the brink of tears.

As Matt watched, Julie, just learning to take a few careful steps, stood and toddled off away from Randy, her pudgy arms raised in balance. As her momentum increased, she squealed in delight.

Casual in jeans and a blue-and-white cotton shirt, Randy shook her head at Matt. Laughing, she stood to follow their daughter.

There had been so much laughter shared between him and Randy over Julie, so much pride and so many plans. Even without considering the baby, he had felt growth in his and Randy's relationship. They enjoyed the wonderful comfort of friendship coupled with a lively passion that would never quiet. They could communicate with a look and had plumbed the depths of each other in their lovemaking. If only he was able to hold back the passage of time.

Now, over two years since he'd taken charge of the company, Mallory Inns was at a crossroads. The company could simply fortify its position as a major chain of superb American hotels, or it could go abroad in search of a whole new world. The idea of expansion had intrigued Matt. He had felt himself develop this year, strengthened by Randy's enthusiastic and unfailing support and the exciting drive generated by the challenge of having a family.

But he would turn away from the idea today if he saw one cloud pass through Randy's eyes. Much as a European move intrigued him, he would keep the inns in America rather than jeopardize their marriage.

As Randy and Julie disappeared down the slope to the lake, Matt got to his feet and wandered after them, hands in his pockets, eyes on the gentle blue sky. Randy had seemed happy in the two years she'd been with him in Connecticut. He had felt nothing withheld by her, detected no resentments and no grudges. Her classic-car restorations shop was almost busier than the local garage, and all her clients had nothing but praise for her work.

The 1938 Chevrolet sedan she had restored for him as a birthday gift had made his contemporaries green with envy. His memory of her grin of delight when she had driven it up their driveway to present him with it still gave him pleasure. She had adjusted to life away from Scannon Cove, but how would she feel about a move to Europe?

As he started down the slope, Julie came toddling toward him, giggling shrilly, Randy running slowly in mock pursuit. Leaning down to scoop the baby up, Matt swung her onto his shoulders and grinned at his wife.

"Quit picking on my baby," he teased.

She laughed, falling into step beside him as he walked along the bank, Julie's little ankles grasped in his strong hands, her small fingers gripping his hair.

"She's a typical woman. She loves to be chased."

He looked at Randy over Julie's denim-clad knee. "Is that spelled s-e-d or s-t-e?"

Randy fluttered her eyelashes coyly. "She takes after her mother. Definitely s-e-d."

"Hmm," he muttered wickedly. "We'll go into that further tonight."

"Will and Vivian are coming up tonight, remember. And your mother and father and Jeremy tomorrow. You'd think the queen mother of England was having a birthday instead of our little munchkin."

He smiled down at her. "We still have the privacy of our room. We'll just have to be more quiet, that's all."

"Sounds good to me. I guess that I can control myself," she said, with a wicked gleam in her eyes.

As they continued to walk, Randy looked up at Matt's pensive profile, recognizing the frown that had marred his brow all morning.

"What's on your mind, Matthew?" she asked, her tone brisk.

"Sex," he replied.

She grabbed the back of his shirt and pulled him to a stop. Wearing that no-nonsense face he'd seen her use when dealing with a difficult customer, she reached her hands up for the baby.

He swung Julie down and put her in Randy's arms. She settled Julie on her hip, gave her a cracker out of her pocket and faced Matt squarely. Her hair was pulled back, a soft aureole of curls framing her face. She looked like a Victorian photograph. The set of her jaw, however, was more reminiscent of a Chicago Bears quarterback.

"It's the fact that the Mallory Inns is looking to expand to Europe, isn't it?" she asked without preamble.

He looked at her carefully, not sure what that determination meant. "Yes," he admitted. "How did you know?"

"I know that branching out to Europe is under consideration because your father and brother were talking about it on Mother's Day. And I suppose it's a logical step.'' Her jaw softened a little. "Are you afraid I won't want to travel around Europe with the baby?''

He looked straight into her eyes, startled for a moment by her perception. "Something like that. Actually, I thought you might not want to travel at all. I know you've been happy here, but Europe is...'' He paused, searching for the right words.

"Europe is where they have Mercedes SSKs and MG TCs and Rolls-Royce New Phantoms,'' she finished enthusiastically. "I'm sure I'd love it there.''

"You don't think that the move would be harmful to Julie?''

"She'll grow up with a very cosmopolitan education. I think it'd be wonderful.''

He smiled, and the love in his eyes made Randy's heart race. "And that from the woman who once wouldn't budge out of Scannon Cove.''

"You put music in my life,'' she said with an artless shrug. "You gave me love; you gave me Julie....'' She paused as she gave the baby a kiss. "You gave me wheels, Mallory. I'm an almighty four-hundred-cubic-inch V-8 engine with a four-barrel carburetor!''

Matt laughed, pulling her to him, cradling both her and Julie, who now lolled sleepily against her mother's shoulder.

"You know, I've loved you almost from the moment I met you,'' he said, the quiet tenor of his voice reflecting astonishment. "Yet your generosity continues to amaze me.''

"I love you and want to be with you,'' she said, shrugging off his praise. "I think that's more selfish than generous. When were you hoping to get plans under way?''

He began to lead her lazily back to the picnic site. ''I thought the three of us could take a long business/vacation trip at the end of the summer. Scout out locales, decide where we'd like to place our first house in Europe.''

''Oh!'' A vacation for just the three of them sounded delightful, even a working one. ''I'd love that!''

Julie's head popped up at Randy's excited exclamation, and she fussed sleepily, rubbing her eyes.

''I guess it's time for a nap,'' Randy said with a sigh, rubbing Julie's back. ''But I hate to go home. This has been such a wonderful day.''

''We can steal another few minutes,'' Matt said, taking Julie from her. ''Right under this tree where we can still keep an eye on our stuff.''

''But Julie . . .''

''She'll sleep on me,'' he predicted, and was blessed immediately with the baby's cooperation.

Watching her sleeping daughter, Randy sank to her knees with Matt and gave him a jealous look. ''I hate it when she fusses at me and falls asleep for you.''

''You just have to have the knack,'' he said, his tone teasingly superior.

She snickered. ''And a shoulder the same width as her crib.''

Matt leaned against the trunk of the oak and pulled Randy in between his knees to rest against his other shoulder. ''You've always liked it,'' he reminded her.

''Mmm.'' She settled comfortably against him, watching the sun-shot lake and absorbing the sweet stillness of the afternoon. She heaved a heartfelt sigh.

Matt kissed her forehead. "What did that mean?"

"That I love you," she said, securing her arm around his waist, "and that, in your arms, the whole world is home to me."

Harlequin American Romance

COMING NEXT MONTH

#177 BEWITCHING HOUR by Anne Stuart

Despite Sybil's position as secretary of the Society of Water Witches, her psychic skills were notoriously mediocre. When Nicholas Fitzsimmons entered her bookstore, her suspicions were confirmed: Nick was a skeptic who scoffed at premonitions and everything else that mattered to her. But, despite their great differences, there was an attraction that could not be denied.

#178 THIS DAY FORWARD by Elizabeth Morris

Business was brisk at Weddings Unlimited, and it was expanding in ways that Andrea Kirkland had never dreamed of. But none of this on-the-job experience helped her relationship with Matt Donaldson, who stubbornly insisted that he was not entitled to love. That is, until the citizens of Laurel Valley stepped in and said their piece about happy-ever-after.

#179 SILENT NIGHT by Beverly Sommers

Nancy didn't have a spare minute. She taught English to some of Manhattan's toughest kids. After school her time belonged to Joe. But keeping busy wasn't enough. For her own sake, and for Joe's, she had to find answers to the nightmarish enigma of her old life—before she was free to live her new one.

#180 INTIMATE STRANGERS by Saranne Dawson

Patrick had returned from the dead. Megan was terrified of seeing him again. They'd been newlyweds twelve long years ago when he'd been sent overseas. So much time had passed—and they had changed. Could Megan find anything in him that she'd loved and cherished a lifetime ago?

Janet Dailey
Americana

Don't miss a single title from this great collection. The first eight titles have already been published. Complete and mail this coupon today to order books you may have missed.

Harlequin Reader Service

In U.S.A.
901 Fuhrmann Blvd.
P.O. Box 1397
Buffalo, N.Y. 14140

In Canada
P.O. Box 2800
Postal Station A
5170 Yonge Street
Willowdale, Ont. M2N 6J3

Please send me the following titles from the Janet Dailey Americana Collection. I am enclosing a check or money order for $2.75 for each book ordered, plus 75¢ for postage and handling.

_____	ALABAMA	Dangerous Masquerade
_____	ALASKA	Northern Magic
_____	ARIZONA	Sonora Sundown
_____	ARKANSAS	Valley of the Vapours
_____	CALIFORNIA	Fire and Ice
_____	COLORADO	After the Storm
_____	CONNECTICUT	Difficult Decision
_____	DELAWARE	The Matchmakers

Number of titles checked @ $2.75 each = $_____ .

N.Y. RESIDENTS ADD
  APPROPRIATE SALES TAX $_____

Postage and Handling $___.75___

                      TOTAL $_____ .

I enclose _____

(Please send check or money order. We cannot be responsible for cash sent through the mail.)

PLEASE PRINT

NAME _____

ADDRESS _____

CITY _____

STATE/PROV. _____

BLJD-A-1

Take 4 books & a surprise gift FREE

SPECIAL LIMITED-TIME OFFER

Mail to **Harlequin Reader Service**®

In the U.S.
901 Fuhrmann Blvd.
P.O. Box 1394
Buffalo, N.Y. 14240-1394

In Canada
P.O. Box 609
Fort Erie, Ontario
L2A 9Z9

YES! Please send me 4 free Harlequin American Romance® novels and my free surprise gift. Then send me 4 brand-new novels as they come off the presses. Bill me at the low price of $2.25 each —a 11% saving off the retail price There are no shipping, handling or other hidden costs. There is no minimum number of books I must purchase. I can always return a shipment and cancel at any time. Even if I never buy another book from Harlequin, the 4 free novels and the surprise gift are mine to keep forever.

154-BPA-BP6F

Name _____ (PLEASE PRINT)

Address _____ Apt. No. _____

City _____ State/Prov. _____ Zip/Postal Code _____

This offer is limited to one order per household and not valid to present subscribers. Price is subject to change

DOAR-SUB-1RR

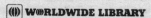